Life Models

A Novel

by D. H. Jonathan

Naturale Publishing
Fort Worth, TX

Cover art by M.H.Pasindu Lakshan

First Edition

ISBN: 1-7330908-0-0
ISBN-13: 978-1-7330908-0-3

For Jen.

1

The first time I ever laid eyes on Lydia Nelson, she was as naked as Lady Godiva on that legendary eleventh-century ride through Coventry. I didn't have any advantage over Lydia though; I was just as naked as she was. The other twenty-three people in the room were fully clothed.

I had been a model for figure drawing classes at the University of North Texas for a little more than a year. It was a Thursday in mid-November, the time of the semester when most of the advanced figure drawing classes, and a few of the beginning ones, used two models at a time, usually in one long pose. I had already done one such class earlier that week, with a young waif of a girl named Kelsey. I had been familiar with Kelsey before we shared the platform, as she and I had met several times in the little changing room that was shared by all the models. I'd call it a dressing room, but there were equal amounts of both undressing and dressing in it. If UNT's art program wasn't the biggest in the state, it had to be a close second. Mondays through Thursdays there were at least two classes using models at any one time. The models' changing room was a chaotic hub of activity just before 11:00 AM and 2:00 PM, when one set of classes ended and another began.

I always arrive early at every model booking, and that Thursday two o'clock class was no exception. Two other models were in the changing room when I got there, getting dressed from the previous session. One of them was Walter, who was a fixture in the art department. He had been a model at UNT for at least twenty years and was the only person on the department's model list older than I was. The other model was a curvy blonde twenty-something student named Rochelle. I gave the courtesy knock on the changing room door and entered. Rochelle was topless with a bra in her hand, her young large breasts seeming to defy gravity.

"Hey guys," I said as I slipped into the room, being careful to make sure that the door didn't swing too far open, not that Walter or Rochelle would have minded. Spending three hours in one's birthday suit in front of a classroom full of art students changes one's sense of modesty. Rochelle didn't even bother to try to cover herself during the second or two that I had the door open.

"How goes it?" Walter said from the corner of the room where a column of small lockers stood.

"Awesome!" Modeling always put me in a good mood. I didn't need the money, and I loved the job. "Rochelle, how are you?"

I set my bag on the counter next to Rochelle's stuff, zipped it open, and rummaged around for my robe.

"Ready to go home and soak in a hot bath," Rochelle said as she slipped into her bra and tried to fasten it in the back.

She continued to struggle as I pulled my shoes and socks off.

"Do you need some help with that?" Walter asked.

"No, I just about got it," Rochelle grunted as she managed to get the first hook threaded. "Just did a three-hour reclining pose with my left hand propping up my head, and now my arm just doesn't want to bend anymore."

"How many breaks did you get?" I asked as she finished with the bra.

"I only took two."

That meant that she was in pose for three periods of at least forty-five minutes each.

"You are an iron woman," Walter said. "Don't wear yourself out though."

Of all the art models on the school's list, Rochelle worked the most hours. She had a beautiful voluptuous body, could hold interesting poses for long periods of time, and, most importantly, was dependable.

Walter slung his backpack on and started for the door. "I gotta go to the boring regular job. Catch y'all later."

Rochelle and I both said bye as Walter slipped out. He delivered pizzas when he wasn't modeling. I looked at the schedule on the wall as I slipped out of my pants and saw David Michaels & Lydia Nelson printed in the Thursday 2 to 5 Room 324 column.

"Do you know this Lydia I'm supposed to be modeling with?" I asked Rochelle.

"Nope. I saw her name on the schedule last week, but I've never met her."

"You should hang around," I suggested. "If she doesn't show, you might get some extra hours." The thought of sharing a platform for three hours with a nude Rochelle was a very pleasant one.

"I would, but I'm beat. She should be here though."

The UNT model coordinator, a graduate art student named Chloe, was very unforgiving of models who didn't show up when they were scheduled. If Lydia had missed her assignment last time, Chloe wouldn't have scheduled her again this week. Rochelle pulled her t-shirt on as I whipped mine off.

"Good luck with 'Lydia,'" Rochelle said.

I was naked by then, shaking my robe out and trying to find my sleeve, which had been turned inside out after my last session. Rochelle backed out the door, looking at me and winking as she went.

"See ya," I said, and then I was alone.

I put my robe on and tied the sash. My house slippers were still in my bag. I pulled them out, dropped them on the floor, and slid my bare feet into them. I thought about staying in the changing room and waiting for Lydia, just so I could introduce myself to her before we had to spend three hours naked on a small platform together. According to the clock on the wall, I had four minutes until the scheduled start of class. I folded my clothes and set them on the top of my modeling bag.

The changing room door swung open, and a young Hispanic girl named Maria rushed in. I glanced at the schedule again and saw her name listed in the room next to mine, a beginning figure drawing class. Maria tended to be shy when changing, doing as much of her disrobing under her robe as she could. I decided to vacate the room and give her some privacy.

"Hey there," I said as I grabbed a couple of clean bed sheets from the stack in the corner.

"Hey. Sorry for barging in. I'm running late."

"That's OK. Have a good class."

I slipped out and headed toward Advanced Figure Drawing, room 324. The halls were crowded with students walking to and fro, either leaving or going to class. I've always felt a bit strange walking through all this activity in my slippers and bathrobe, but nobody ever pays me any mind. They are all art students, used to seeing models in the corridor.

The door to room 324 was propped open when I got there. Audrey, the figure drawing instructor, was pushing the model stand from the center of the room toward the far wall, the flat wooden legs making a loud grating sound as they scooted across the floor. I rushed over to help her, setting my sheets down on the platform as I pushed with her.

"Thank you, David," Audrey said once we had the model stand against the wall. "You didn't have to do that."

"It's OK. How have you been?"

"Good." She hopped up on the model stand and moved the cushioned bench from the center of the platform to the edge so that it was against the wall as well. "We're going to do one long pose today, after the warmups."

"OK," I said. I had expected as much this late in the semester. Most classes tended to try to get really finished drawings toward the end. And there would be two models to draw which meant that the students would need as much time as possible to get both figures.

"We're supposed to have another model too," Audrey said. "Someone named Lydia. Do you know her?"

"No, never met her," I replied.

"You don't mind, do you? Posing with someone you've never met."

I shrugged. "It's just part of the job. I'm happy I get to model as much as I do."

"Good. I hope she's OK with it too. I'm always a little nervous when Chloe schedules me a model I've never met."

I stepped out of my slippers and up onto the platform with my bare feet. The floors in the drawing studios were almost always covered in black dust from all the charcoal used for drawing. The soles of my feet had been jet black after my first two modeling gigs, so I bought the house shoes to wear when I'm not on the model stand.

I set my folded sheets down on the bench and sat on them. Students filed in and started setting up at their easels. I had modeled for this class five times before over the course of the semester, so I amused myself by guessing which easel a student was going to take when he or she first walked in. I was right every time. Most people are creatures of habit, and art students are no different.

"Everyone, start with newsprint," Audrey told them while they were setting up. "We're going to do just a few gestures at the beginning."

Audrey usually had me do about five to ten quick poses, only about a minute each. I would take a lot of athletic positions, poses I couldn't have held for much longer than that minute.

"We're going to go ahead and start," she said after checking the time on her phone.

I took that as my cue, and I stood and started untying the sash of my robe. Audrey noticed and bounded toward the hall to close the door. I wasn't even thinking about the door being open. I was thinking about what to do for the first pose. Chances were, anyone walking by in the corridor here in the Fine Arts Building had already drawn me in other classes.

Audrey got the door closed and had her phone in her hand. Some drawing teachers like to keep time during the gesture poses; others just have me count the seconds in my head. Audrey liked to keep time herself. I slipped the robe off, savoring the feeling of the cool air on my bare skin, stirred from whipping my robe around as I tossed it aside. I took a quick glance around the room and wondered if any of the students, most of whom were hidden behind their easels, felt envious that I could be so primal, purely human, while they had to keep conforming to societal custom. And then I realized that most of them would probably be mortified if they had to be the only naked person in a room full of people.

"First pose," Audrey snapped.

I looked up toward the ceiling, spread my feet apart, and drew my right arm back, imitating a javelin thrower's stance.

"Go," Audrey said to her students.

The room was quiet except for the furious scratching sounds of charcoal on paper as the students tried to capture my form. I spent the entire minute trying to come up with an idea for the next pose.

"Change," Audrey called.

I took a twisting position with my arms pushing away from me. My feet were pointed toward the door, but with the turn of my body, I wound up looking away from it.

"Go," Audrey said again.

About fifteen seconds into the pose, I heard the door open and close.

"Hi, I'm Audrey."

"Lydia. Sorry I'm late."

"That's OK. We're doing warm up gestures right now," I heard Audrey tell the newcomer. "If you're ready, you can jump in on the next one."

"I can do that."

I heard Lydia at the edge of the platform behind me and felt the rush of air of her robe coming off and being set down close to where I had set mine. Even though Audrey was keeping time, I had begun counting in my head when I had heard the door open. I wanted to see this Lydia, so I was more than ready to break this pose.

"Change," Audrey finally called.

I turned and saw Lydia Nelson. The first thing I noticed was her eyes, as dark a green as the leaves around the poinsettias that I always saw around Christmas. She was short, around five foot-two, with brown hair and freckles on her shoulders. Her breasts were small, with large nipples that made the breasts seem even smaller. She was just a little soft around the waist, enough that some might have called her a bit chubby. Her thighs were thick but muscular. As I took that quick glance at her, I couldn't help but notice that her pubic area was completely hairless which, along with her small breasts, gave her an almost childlike appearance. I had seen most of the female models at UNT in the nude, either in the changing room or while sharing a platform in class, and all of them had some form of pubic hair. I could imagine that they felt that the hair gave them some form of covering over their most private areas. But Lydia was apparently different. I could see every fold of skin as well as a hint of labia peeking out even though she was standing with her legs more or less together.

My gaze had only strayed from those striking green eyes for less than a second before returning. I smiled and mouthed the word, "Hi" before taking a tug of war pose. She returned my smile and whispered, "Hey."

"These will be two-minute poses now, since you have two figures to draw," Audrey told her students. To Lydia and me, she said, "That OK?"

"Sure," Lydia said, and I nodded.

"All right, go," Audrey said both to us models and to her students.

Lydia immediately took an opposing tug of war pose as if we were on opposite ends of the same short rope, the edges of our feet almost touching. I smiled, and she smiled back. Her green eyes seemed to sparkle. I looked at my arms, my hands holding the invisible rope, my gold wedding band on the ring finger of my left hand. Seeing the ring made me think of Glenda. What would she have thought of me making eyes at a girl who was probably young enough to be my daughter?

We did two more short poses, and both of them were interactive.

6

When we broke from the tug of war pose, Lydia took a position as if she were throwing a ball. I pantomimed a wide receiver trying to catch a pass. For the final gesture, I put my hands over my head and bent forward slightly, as if I were crying in anguish. Lydia did a standing pose with an arm outstretched, as if she were offering me a tissue.

"That's time," Audrey said to signal the end of the last pose. "Those were awesome poses guys."

"Thank you," I said.

"Now," Audrey addressed the class, "I want you to take out your good paper. We're going to do one long drawing…"

I turned to Lydia as Audrey continued her instructions and held out my hand. "I'm David. David Michaels."

She smiled and took my hand in hers. "Lydia."

There was a moment of awkward silence, made more awkward by the fact that we were both naked and kind of in limbo. Audrey hadn't told us to take a break, and we didn't know how long she would be talking to the students. To robe up or not, that was the question. Lydia, to her credit, apparently didn't feel the need to immediately cover up like many other female models with whom I had worked.

"So how long have you been modeling?" I asked in as low a voice as I could.

"Just started. I didn't have any idea I would model with a guy my second time out."

"They double us up sometimes at the end of a semester. You did great gestures though."

Lydia smiled. "Thanks."

"Are you OK with it?" I whispered as Audrey continued talking to her class about the upcoming drawing. "Modeling with a guy, that is."

"Oh yeah," she said, and she seemed to take a quick glance down at all of me. "I think of it as a perk."

I laughed, probably a little louder than I should, and Audrey stopped talking.

"OK," she said, "let's get you two into a pose."

She was near the light switches, and she turned off the overhead fluorescents and made sure all the rows of spotlights were on. I figured that Audrey wanted us sitting on the bench somehow since she had gone to all that effort to move both it and the model stand against the wall. I grabbed the sheet I had brought from the changing room and unfolded it so that it covered the entire bench.

"Damn it, I forgot to get a sheet," Lydia whispered.

"That's OK. This is big enough for both of us."

Lydia and I sat next to each other and started adjusting our positions as Audrey watched with a critical eye.

"After seeing your gestures, I'd like to get you into something interactive," Audrey said. "Like maybe you're having a conversation or an argument or something."

I turned and sat on my left hip with my lower leg on the bench and my right foot on the floor. Lydia put her left foot on the bench with her knee close to her shoulder. Her other foot was on the floor with the knee fallen toward me, and I couldn't help but notice how exposed that pose made her, to me more so than to the art students. I could see just about every gynecological feature, even the couple of hairs that her razor had missed. Lydia either didn't realize or was pretending not to notice how much she was revealing. Or perhaps it was a non-issue to her. Since I had started modeling, I had always tried to take the attitude that each body part was just something that made up the whole. For the art students studying the body, a penis or a vagina should be considered as present and as necessary as a knee or an arm. That's the ideal attitude anyway, but not all students, or models for that matter, adhere to it. I've heard more than my share of giggles at the beginning of a semester. I've seen students move to either get or avoid a more explicit view of my genitals.

"How's that?" Lydia asked Audrey.

"That's OK, but I was hoping to see a little more variation between the two of you."

If I hadn't been staring at Lydia's vulva for that brief moment, I might have realized sooner that not only was my pose similar to Lydia's, but my current position would have quickly constricted the circulation in my left leg. I would have lost all feeling in that foot just a few minutes into the pose.

"I could stand up," I offered.

"Are you sure?" Audrey said, echoing the typical response I got from art professors whenever I suggested doing a long standing pose. "This is going to be for the rest of class."

Most art teachers were hesitant to ask their models to do long standing poses, but I had always found those standing positions easier than seated ones. Blood circulation was much better, and I much preferred weary muscles to a loss of feeling.

"No problem," I said, jumping to my feet and almost immediately regretting it. My contemplation of Lydia's reproductive organs had had a stimulating effect on my own, and my enlarged, but thankfully not erect, penis swung and swayed a little too much when I had bounced to my feet. Audrey didn't seem to notice, but I saw a blonde girl in the corner smile and blush.

I stood beside the bench, trying not to block any students' view of Lydia. The trick to being able to do a longer standing pose is to try to get as close to an equal distribution of weight on each foot as possible while still making the pose at least look somewhat contrapposto. Letting the arms dangle was never a good idea for circulation, so I put both of my hands on my hips.

"I don't like both of your hands on your hips," Audrey said, almost immediately.

I let my left hand drop and then shook it around trying to figure out what I should do with it.

"He could put his hand on my shoulder," Lydia offered.

"You sure?" I asked.

Lydia nodded, and I placed my hand on her nearest shoulder. Her skin was soft and smooth and surprisingly warm. Audrey walked from one side of the room to the other, looking at the pose.

"That looks good. I like the dynamic of one standing figure and one seated. And it's got really great light from over here." Some of the students murmured in the affirmative. "OK, we'll go ahead and go with this. David, Lydia, are you both OK?"

"Good to go," I replied.

"Yes," Lydia said at the same time.

I was standing parallel to the long side of the platform, facing Lydia. I tried to fix my gaze straight ahead at the far corner, but shifting my eyes downward just a tiny bit gave me a view of Lydia. I did not make eye contact with Lydia at all while we were in pose; her designated stare point was straight in front of her, at an area of my body between my navel and my thighs.

"You OK?" Lydia whispered to me.

"What?"

"I don't mean to stare at you like this, but it's too late to move my head."

"It's OK," I whispered back to her.

I took a deep breath and settled into my pose, trying not to contemplate the fact that a young naked girl would be spending two and a half hours staring at my exposed genitals at extremely close quarters. She might as well be staring at my elbow I tried to tell myself. Wasn't that the attitude I always tried to have, that all parts were equal in making up the whole? Some ideals are difficult to put into practice. I wondered how many other jobs would put one in such an unusual situation, and I had to stifle a laugh. I wondered what my old church friends, most of whom I hadn't seen since Glenda's funeral, would have thought if they could have seen me then.

I had started modeling for art classes twenty or so years before, when I was a young college student away from home for the first time. My dorm roommate at the time couldn't understand why anyone would ever consider doing such a thing, and I still remember being unable to explain it to him. I had grown up in a conservative household. Nudity was confined to the bath and shower and, in the summer, the very quick transition to and from regular clothes and swimsuits. When I got off to college, modeling for art classes appealed to me from the very moment that I heard that figure drawing classes needed people to pose nude. I always figured that it was my form of rebellion. I never drank or smoked throughout high school and even away at college, my drinking was minimal. But I have always suspected that the thought of taking my clothes off in front of a roomful of fellow students would have scandalized my parents. As far as I know, they had never found out about it.

I guess I modeled because I liked being looked at. Public speaking never appealed to me. In fact, getting up to speak in front of a large group of people was as attractive to me as getting a root canal. But being a model allowed me to be the center of attention for three hours without having to say a word. That was why I started modeling again when I went back to school. In fact, the day I registered for my first semester back was also the day that I walked into the art department office and filled out the application to be a model.

There is a difference between being looked at by a group of students who are diligently working on an artwork and being stared at by a fellow model on the stand with nothing but her own thoughts to occupy her time. I took a peek down at Lydia; her gaze was still fixed firmly on my groin area. When I'm in a pose, I think about all kinds of things, and when I run out of things, I count in my head to mark time. What was Lydia thinking about? I wondered. Was she assessing my genitalia? Or was she imagining what it might be like to touch them and feel them?

I felt flush, my breath starting to quicken, and I knew that I had to push all thoughts of Lydia away. In a normal situation, a man can hide his attraction to a woman, but there is no hiding anything on the model stand. I glanced down again, without moving my head position, and saw that Lydia's eyes had grown a little wider, her mouth curled in a smirk. I looked back up at that far corner, trying to take slow, deep breaths, and thought about Game 6 of the 2011 World Series.

Growing up in North Texas had made me a fan of the Texas Rangers baseball club, and that game in St. Louis had been the most gut-wrenchingly awful experience Rangers fans had ever had to endure. I remembered the suspense, the anticipation of seeing the Rangers finally, after forty long years, winning their first World Series championship. They had been one strike away in the ninth inning, but David Freese had hit a long fly ball that Nelson Cruz just wasn't able to catch to secure that ultimate win. Two runs scored, and the game was tied. The Rangers scored two runs in the top of the tenth, and we all breathed a sigh of relief. Maybe we would win this after all. But no. A Lance Birkman single in the bottom of the tenth tied the score again. David Freese struck again in the eleventh, homering and giving the game to the Cardinals. After the devastation of Game Six, a Cardinal win in the seventh game seemed like a forgone conclusion, and it was.

As much as I hated to think about something so frustrating, it worked in halting my physical crisis. I took a nice easy breath, but I didn't dare glance down at Lydia. If she wanted a free study of the male anatomy, that was fine with me. But just that fleeting thought started me going again, and I again had to recall the Rangers blowing that World Series.

Audrey gave Lydia and me four breaks from the pose during the class, and one of those was the big fifteen-minute break for the students. Lydia donned her robe and disappeared while I was working the kinks out of my back. I assumed she went back to the changing room. Maybe she got dressed and ran down for a smoke break, although I didn't even know if she was a smoker. I put my robe on and sat down in the teacher's chair during the breaks. I wondered if Lydia was purposefully avoiding me, but when I thought longer about it, Lydia was in a seated pose and wanted to be up and around for her breaks while I was in a standing pose and wanted to sit and rest.

When the class ended, my left shoulder was throbbing. Why was it that standing poses were always harder on my shoulders than my legs? Audrey thanked us profusely for a wonderful pose, and the students even clapped in applause just a little bit. I noticed Lydia blushed as I took a playful bow. We put on our robes and walked together to the changing room.

"You did great," I told her, knowing that I had the most modeling experience and somehow felt it necessary to encourage the newcomer.

"No, you did awesome," Lydia said. "I don't know how you can do a standing pose for that long."

"Standing poses aren't that bad," I replied.

"Well, better you than me then."

I arrived at the changing room first, meaning to open the door for Lydia. I knocked twice on it first, and I heard Maria's voice say, "Just a sec."

I turned to Lydia and smiled. We were standing in the hall in bathrobes, waiting. The door opened about five seconds later, so we didn't have to wait long.

"Sorry," Maria said.

"It's OK," I said.

It takes all kinds to do this unconventional job, although I thought it was funny that someone could be completely naked in front of a room full of art students for three hours and then balk at letting her fellow models see just a little flash of flesh as she changed into her clothes.

Maria went back to packing her things as Lydia and I walked in and closed the door. I smiled at Lydia as I rolled my eyes at Maria. Lydia gave me a half smile and seemed to pick up on what I was thinking. Almost in unison, Lydia and I took off our robes and tossed them on the counter. Maria looked up from her bag and murmured something inaudible as her head pivoted away.

"How was your class?" Maria asked toward the wall but to us.

"Long, but good," I said as I kicked off my slippers.

"Not too bad though," Lydia added.

I looked at my feet and saw charcoal on the soles. There was no getting away from the stuff even with my slippers. Maria was still getting her things together and trying not to look at Lydia or me, me especially. I squeezed past her so that I could get to the sink and wet a couple of paper towels.

"I hate having dirty feet," I said.

Maria looked down and then quickly back up.

"Me too," she managed to say in a voice barely above a whisper.

I leaned against the wall and started wiping my right foot with the wet paper towel. Lydia, still naked, was folding up her robe, and I could tell that she was trying to hold in a laugh. Maria slung her bag over her shoulder and headed for the door. She paused at the door and took a quick glance at Lydia and me.

"I'm leaving," she said.

"Have a good one," Lydia said, still nude as she was just then taking her street clothes out of her gym bag.

"See you later," I offered.

Maria, finally seeing that we were unconcerned about the door opening on us, shrugged and slipped out of the changing room. Lydia waited about five seconds before bursting into laughter.

"Oh, my God," she said, "how can she bring herself to pose?"

"Hey, it pays better than any other campus job," I said as I dried off that first foot. "For students, I mean."

"How long has she been modeling?"

"Just this semester. Maybe we helped her lighten up."

"God, I hope so."

As I wet another paper towel for my other foot, I looked at Lydia as she unfolded her jeans. She certainly wasn't the traditional beauty queen type, but I could not deny that her wide hips, thick waist, and muscular thighs made her attractive. And she seemed totally at ease with her nudity.

"You seem pretty comfortable with this, and you just started," I said.

"I'd live in a nudist colony if I could. When I'm home, I'm naked, ever since I was a kid."

"Your parents were OK with that?"

Lydia shrugged. "It was never a big deal. Mom was a big hippie back in the day."

She slowly stepped into her jeans.

"Do you usually go commando?" Even as the words came out of my mouth, I thought it presumptuous to ask such a personal question.

"Always. Well, almost always."

I dried my other foot and threw all my used paper towels away. Lydia quickly turned her eyes away from me whenever I looked in her direction, so I could tell that she was watching me. I stopped looking toward her as I unpacked my bag while still trying to see her in my peripheral vision. Had she not had enough of looking at me during the class?

"It was nice working with you," she said as she grabbed a green t-shirt with a large black peace symbol on the front from her bag and pulled it on over her head. Her small breasts made wearing a bra unnecessary.

"I enjoyed it," I said. "It was fun."

I rummaged in my bag, moving the tighty-whitey Hanes briefs aside. Even though she had spent three hours staring at my naked body, letting her see me in my underwear didn't seem right. I pulled out my pants and started stepping into them. Lydia didn't say anything about my going commando. Once I had my pants fastened and zipped up, she concentrated on getting her shoes and jacket on.

"Do you get to do double model sessions a lot?" she asked.

"Just at the end of the semester. They used to do them all the time, but I guess their budget got cut or something."

"That sucks."

I shrugged. I normally liked being the only model in a class so that all the attention was on me. Modeling solo also cut down on any awkwardness, like having a female model stare at my genitals from less than two feet away for almost three hours.

"I know," I said. "I like getting as many hours in as I can."

Lydia was gathering two of the college text books that had been left at the far end of the counter and stuffing them into her gym bag.

"You a student here?" I asked.

"Yep."

"What's your major?"

Lydia shrugged. "Undecided right now. I'm just getting the basics out of the way."

"Well, believe it or not, I'm a student too. Political science pre-law."

"Really? How old are you?" She stopped and must have seen something in my expression. "I'm sorry. I didn't mean it to sound—"

"That's all right," I said, holding up my hand and shaking my head. "I'm 40. I finally decided to come back to school after ten years of talking about it."

"What made you finally decide to do it?"

I shrugged, not wanting to have to explain it. "I came into some money, and I was tired of my job."

Lydia seemed to take a quick glance at the wedding ring on my left hand. "Oh. That's cool."

I shrugged again and put my shirt on. Lydia grabbed her gym bag and stood near the door for a moment.

"Well David," she said, "see you around."

"Yes, I hope so. And if I don't see you before then, have a happy Thanksgiving."

"You too."

Lydia walked out of the room, and I sat down to put on my socks and shoes. I couldn't describe my frame of mind then after having spent almost three hours with her, both of us naked, the almost magical way our gesture poses had complemented each other's, the frankness of her gaze during our long pose, and her boldness in teasing Maria with me. Lydia was just a young girl, I told myself, and I tried to put her out of my mind.

2

Thanksgiving Day was the following Thursday, exactly one week after I met Lydia. The university was open the first half of that week, and I modeled for two back-to-back classes on Tuesday. Posing six consecutive hours is exhausting but satisfying. It feels like I'm putting in a full day's work. My own college classes were on Mondays and Wednesdays, so I modeled quite a bit for those Tuesday-Thursday sessions. I didn't see Lydia though, and her name was absent on that abbreviated week's schedule. Chloe, the model coordinator, tended to schedule new models sparingly until they had proven themselves both competent and reliable. I don't remember how much I thought about Lydia during that week. I'm sure she crossed my mind a few times, although I made a conscious effort to not think of her while I was nude on the stand in those Tuesday classes.

Thanksgiving had always been my favorite holiday growing up, but I hadn't had much use for it after my wife's wreck. Glenda's parents had issued an open invitation for me to have dinner with them each Thanksgiving and Christmas, but I had never taken them up on the offer. The hole of Glenda's absence was just too big for me to even think about going there. I had spent the last three Thanksgivings alone at home, watching football and eating TV dinners and frozen desserts. The Saturday after my modeling session with Lydia, my mom had called and practically begged me to make the trip to Wichita Falls to eat Thanksgiving dinner this year with her and my step-dad.

"Tammy will be here," Mom had said, referring to my sister who lived in Colorado Springs with her husband Carl and their two daughters.

"I'll think about it," I had told Mom.

I didn't want to go, being quite settled in my new misanthropic lifestyle. Mom had come to my house the evening of that first Thanksgiving without Glenda, bringing me leftover turkey and dressing. I ate it, but, still numb from recent events, I hadn't felt like talking much. Mom would ramble on about any subject that didn't have to do with Glenda, but I would just mumble "Mmmm-hmmm" whenever I thought that she wanted a response and giving short three or four word answers to any direct questions she asked me until she finally got frustrated and left.

"I worry about you," Mom said on the phone Saturday after I told her that I would think about going to her house.

"I know," I said. "But I'm fine. I'm getting out of the house. Going to school."

She had always bugged me about living like a recluse since quitting my job when the settlement money from the wrongful death lawsuit came in.

"And how is school going?" she asked. I made up some answer, but she kept asking more questions. It took me a half an hour to get her off the phone.

When I woke up on Thanksgiving morning, exactly one week after meeting Lydia, I didn't know what I was going to do. I took a shower. When I got out, my cell phone showed two missed calls, both from my mother. She was never going to leave me alone, so I gave up and decided to make the drive to her house. I hadn't seen Tammy or her family since Glenda's funeral, and I thought it would be good to visit with them. I wondered if I would even recognize the girls.

I managed to make it all the way onto Highway 287 before Mom called my cell phone again.

"Hello Mom," I said.

"Davey, you sound like you're driving."

"I am. I am on my way to your house."

"Wonderful! Everyone will be so excited to see you!"

"I hope so," I said. "I should be there in less than two hours."

"Now, we're not going to eat until about one o'clock."

"That's OK. It'll give me time to visit."

"Yes, it will. I love you honey."

"I love you too Mom."

"Now hang up and drive."

"Yes ma'am."

Mom always worried about something. She told me never to talk on my phone while I'm driving. Glenda had been on her phone with me when her accident happened, but her being on the phone had nothing to do with what had happened. An extremely large settlement check from the company that owned the truck that hit her was proof of that. Still, Mom used it as another thing to worry about, although she had always warned me against talking on the phone while driving long before Glenda's wreck ever happened.

I turned on the radio and listened to classic rock all the way to Wichita Falls, using the scan function to find another station whenever one would fade. Arlo Guthrie's "Alice's Restaurant" started as I drove into Mom's neighborhood. I drove around for twenty minutes just so I could listen to the entire thing, singing along to the chorus at the end. I pulled up at her curb just as an irritating commercial for some local heating and air conditioning company started playing. Mom must have been watching for me through her screen door because she was at the curb before I could even get out of my car.

"Davey!" she cried and put her arms around me as I stood with my car door still open.

"Hey, Mom."

"I'm so happy you came."

She finally let go of me and stepped back to look at me.

"You've lost so much weight," she said.

I knew I hadn't lost any weight, but I just shrugged rather than argue. A steady diet of fast food and Hamburger Helper was not conducive to losing weight, although I was prone to taking long walks through my neighborhood when the weather was nice.

"Not that much," I said just to say something.

"We'll fix that today. Come on in the house. Tammy and Carl can't wait to see you."

I locked the car and shut my door, and we started toward the front door. Mom still couldn't keep quiet.

"How are your classes?" she asked.

"They're good. I think I'll make a 4.0 grade point average for the semester."

"That's wonderful!" Her voice seemed too excited, to the point of being melodramatic, patronizing.

We reached the stoop, and I opened the screen door and held it open for Mom. "Thank you dear," she said. I could hear a football game on the living room TV. I followed Mom into the house. Everybody jumped up from where they had been and met me before I could get out of the foyer.

"David!" my sister Tammy cried as she got to me just ahead of her daughters and threw her arms around my neck. She held me for far too long. Her younger daughter, Lori, had grabbed my leg, and I wondered if they weren't both trying to tackle me. "I'm so glad you're here," Tammy said when she finally let go.

"Me too."

Carl was standing behind Tammy, and he reached out to shake my hand. No hug from him, thankfully. "Hi David," he said.

"Good to see you Carl," I said and shook his hand. "And who is this person on my leg?"

I reached down and picked the girl up.

"Believe it or not, that's Lori," Tammy said.

"Lori Little-bit?" Her name was Lori Elizabeth, but when her big sister said it, it had come out Lori Little-bit. The rest of the family adopted that name. "You're not so little-bit anymore," I told her. "How old are you now?"

"Seven," she said with a giggle. The way I was holding her was apparently tickling her armpits. So, I did what any decent uncle would do. I tickled more until she squealed and squirmed so much that I had to set her down before I dropped her.

"Do you remember me?" I asked, realizing that it had been four years since I had seen her.

"We have pictures of you. You're Uncle David."

I looked at the older girl standing next to her. She looked like a miniature version of my sister, with shoulder length blonde hair and blue eyes.

"You must be Jenny," I said. She nodded. "How old are you?"

"Ten," she said as she looked at the floor.

"You don't need to be shy around Uncle David," Tammy said.

"It's OK," I said to Tammy, and I kissed the top of Jenny's head.

"Come on in David," Robert, my step-father, a former Marine drill sergeant, called in his booming voice.

I walked past Tammy and Carl and into the living room. Robert was struggling to get out of his recliner. "Goddamn knee," he muttered as he finally got to his feet.

"Robert," Mom said in a threatening tone, warning him against his language.

"How are you, Robert?" I said. I had never been able to call him dad or any variation thereof even though he had been married to my mother for twenty-three years. He'd had his left knee replaced just after Glenda's accident, but the operation had apparently not been a complete success since it still gave him problems.

"I'm getting by," he grumbled. "Weather changes are a bitch." We shook hands, and he waved me toward the couch. "Take a seat."

"Here Davey," Mom said, "I'll take your coat."

I slipped it off and handed it to her. She took it away toward her bedroom, and I sat on the couch, preparing myself for a barrage of questions but only wanting to watch football.

"Who's winning?" I asked just before I found the little score box in the upper left corner of the screen.

"Lions are up 7-0," Robert said. He didn't say anything else as, on the television, the Lions' quarterback was sacked while trying to run out of the pocket. We had never talked much, and our relationship had always seemed strained, maybe because I had never taken to calling him anything but his first name. Not long after he had married Mom, Tammy had gone through a stage where she wanted everyone to call her by her actual name Tamara. I had called her Tammy one night at dinner, and Robert had jumped all over me about calling her Tamara. "Well excuse me," I had said, "but you haven't known her as Tammy for years and years. You just got here." I still remembered the hurt look on Robert's face and the admonishment of Mom. Looking back, it seemed like such a minor transgression by a teenage boy, but I really didn't have any other explanation for the strained relationship.

Tammy sat next to me on the couch, put her hand on my knee, and said, repeating what she had said when I arrived, "I'm glad you're here."

"Me too," I said with a smile that I hoped didn't look too forced.

We watched the game while Mom, and occasionally Tammy, worked in the kitchen. The conversation focused around the two quarterbacks, the play calling, the referee, and the commercials, and I slowly relaxed. It started to feel like home again even though Glenda's absence never left my thoughts. The photo of Glenda and me was still on the fireplace mantle, and I kept glancing over at it. The picture was taken at a Target portrait studio just before Glenda's last Christmas. She and I had been married eight years at the time. We were both smiling in the picture, but I remembered how we were feeling that day. Just two weeks before, we had agreed to stop all the fertility treatments that had been failing us for six years.

Just thinking about the feelings of disappointment month after month, the two in vitro procedures, the pills we took, the detailed calendar we kept of Glenda's monthly cycles, and those stupid boxer shorts I forced myself to wear to "keep the boys cool" to promote more sperm production still made my heart ache. July 2013 had been the rock bottom. The pregnancy test had finally turned up positive, and our doctor had confirmed that Glenda was pregnant. The ultrasound even showed a visible heartbeat. We were so ecstatic, with such feelings of relief and happiness. We joyously announced the pregnancy to everyone who had long been pestering us with "When are you going to have a baby?" questions, our family, people at church, and people at both of our jobs. We started talking about names and had even picked out a girl name, Nicole Grace. Before going to bed every night, I caressed Glenda's belly and whispered to my child that I loved her and couldn't wait to see her. For some reason, I always envisioned a daughter.

That joyful feeling lasted less than two weeks. Glenda called my office phone on a Monday afternoon. "I'm spotting," she had said and sobbed. I abandoned work and rushed to her OB/GYN's office, arriving just a few minutes before she did. The doctor explained that a little spotting was normal in the early stages of pregnancy, and after a quick look on ultrasound, he said that he thought the baby was OK. A week later, at our regularly scheduled appointment, the baby wasn't OK. The heartbeat was gone.

The doctor called it a blighted ovum. To Glenda and me, our long-awaited and much beloved child had died. Neither of us could bring ourselves to tell any of our friends or acquaintances. We could barely talk about it ourselves without breaking into tears. We just stopped talking to anyone. Whenever anyone asked me about the baby, I just didn't answer them. People soon got the message without us having to say anything.

After a week and a half, Glenda was still carrying our dead child, and our doctor had to do some horrible thing called a dilation and curettage. He called it a D & C. Glenda called it ripping her heart out. We both missed a week of work and spent most of that week in bed binge watching newly purchased DVD sets of all ten seasons of *Friends* but not laughing very much.

We went back to the fertility specialist that October, but it was more of the same disappointment. Finally, just before that Christmas season that was to be Glenda's last on earth, we came to the painful decision to just give up. We had looked at adoption, even international adoption, but the cost was prohibitive. We both worked, and our level of debt from all the crap we had bought, not to mention the fertility treatments, necessitated both of us continuing to work. And since we both worked, our house was a wreck most of the time. Because the house was such a wreck, we ate out a lot. And because we ate out so often, our debt never seemed to go down despite the large payments we made on our credit cards. We could never see a future where one of us could stop working to take care of house and baby. Knowing that we could never pass the home study in the adoption process, much less afford all the fees, we gave up. And a month after that, we posed for that family portrait knowing that that was as big as our family was ever going to get.

As much as I tried to watch the football game, I kept turning to look at that photo. I had other pictures of her up in our house, my house now, but I guess I was used to seeing those day after day. We had been in such a poor state of mind when we got that Christmas portrait done at Target that we gave every single print away. I felt as if Glenda was watching me now from the photo. Yes, she was smiling, but there was something more in her gaze, something knowing, piercing. She used to give me that look whenever I had done something I shouldn't have, like, for instance, spending a hundred dollars on an Alfred Hitchcock DVD set. This stare from the photo was much more serious than the one for the Hitchcock set.

I finally jumped up and went to the kitchen.

"You need any help Mom?" I asked.

"You could help me set the table," she said.

So I helped her. And we had a nice Thanksgiving dinner. I ate too much as usual. The Cowboys were about to start playing when we finished, but I really didn't want to sit in the living room under Glenda's stare again. I carried a stack of plates into the kitchen and helped Mom rinse them.

"I think I'm going to take off," I said.

"Really? The Cowboy game is about to start."

"I'd rather not drive back in the dark."

"Well..." I knew that excuse would appeal to my constantly worrying mother. "You could spend the night here," she said.

"I didn't bring an overnight bag. Besides, I need to get back."

"For what?"

I had to pause before replying. I didn't have a job other than modeling, and school was out until Monday.

"I have some reports to write for school," I told Mom. That was sort of true. I had one report to write, but it was almost finished.

"Well, OK." she said in a voice that was almost whining. "I'm glad you came though."

"I am too." And I was, except for that stare of Glenda's from the photo.

Once we got the plates rinsed, Mom retrieved my coat from her bedroom. That seemed to be the signal to everyone that I was leaving, and I was deluged with hugs and questions about why I had to leave, that I was going to miss the Cowboy game.

"Well," I told my step-father, "if past performance is any indication, the Cowboys will jump out in front and lead for almost the entire game before blowing it in the end. I think I can skip that."

Nobody could counter my assessment. The Cowboys were adept at snatching defeat from the jaws of victory. But getting out of the house was an ordeal. Mom and Tammy walked me to the car and even held my car door open, talking as I sat behind my steering wheel.

"Now you are coming for Christmas aren't you," Mom said. "School will be out, so you won't have any papers to write."

"Sure," I said without thinking and almost immediately wishing I had said no. "I'll be here," I continued, but I wondered what excuse I could come up with for not coming once Christmas arrived.

"And call me. I want to know how you're doing."

"Call me too," Tammy chimed in. "And come see us. We aren't far from the ski resorts, you know."

Snow skiing did sound like fun, and I hadn't been in over five years. "I will," I said.

Once I got away and was driving south on US 287, I realized that during my entire time there, no one had ever mentioned Glenda's name. It must have been a conscious effort on their part to avoid it. Yet, I had felt her presence all the same. When I got home, I walked around the house and counted the pictures of Glenda still on the walls. There was one in the living room, and one other, our wedding photo, in the hallway on the way to the master bedroom. I tried to remember how many had been up before the accident and whether I had taken any down or not. I couldn't recall ever removing one, but I did remember how much Glenda hated having her picture taken. I just didn't have many photos of her.

I took the wedding photo off the wall and looked at the two of us.

We were so happy and so oblivious to the world and what it would bring. She had been so beautiful in her wedding dress and had been even more beautiful that night when I got the dress off her in our honeymoon hotel suite in San Antonio. I kissed the glass over her face, said "Happy Thanksgiving baby," and put the picture back on the wall. "And I'm sorry," I repeated for at least the hundred thousandth time.

3

I didn't see Lydia again until January. I modeled for three more classes the week after Thanksgiving before the drawing stopped and the end of semester critiques began. Lydia's name was on the schedule once that final week, but it was for a Wednesday morning. I was in history and English classes during that time.

As expected and as I had told my mother I would do, I finished my classes with a 4.0 grade point average for the semester. On Christmas Eve, I packed a week's worth of heavy winter clothes without having a really clear plan and drove to Mom's. I spent Christmas Day with her and Robert, and I never once looked at the photo of Glenda and me in their living room while I was there.

On the morning of the 26th, I drove to Colorado Springs and stayed at Tammy and Carl's for four nights. We skied at Monarch Ski Resort for two of those days, and I enjoyed myself more than I had in years. Tammy's girls were amazing skiers. Lori had such a low center of gravity that she could zip down the mountain at speeds that made her parents nervous. Jenny, who had been so shy around me at Thanksgiving, volunteered to leave her parents and accompany me on a couple of the expert black diamond ski runs. Neither of us did very well and spent almost as much time sliding down the steep slopes on our backsides as we did on skis. But it was a fun time.

I left Tammy's on the 30th and spent two days meandering the highways of the American Southwest, watching the vast wilderness with its multitude of colors draped in white snow pass by out my window as the miles on my car's odometer kept ticking up. I had turned and started for home before checking into a Hampton Inn in

Santa Fe just before dark on New Year's Eve. I went down to the hotel bar for a few drinks with a hundred dollars in cash in my pocket and wound up spending it all on drinks for myself and the two women I met there. The first one was named Britney, a tall, shapely blonde with God only knew how many dollars' worth of make-up caked onto her face and what had to have been surgically augmented breasts. She seemed surprised when I ignored her attempts to invite herself up to my room. During the eleven o'clock hour, she spied a traveling businessman who seemed more agreeable and vacated the barstool next to me for his table.

A few minutes before midnight, a large but not quite obese woman in jeans and t-shirt took that barstool and ordered a glass of pinot noir in a weary, out of breath voice. She wore no makeup that I could see and had a harried look. Her hair, both color and length, reminded me of Lydia. When she turned her head, I could see a bruise on her right cheek, just below her eye.

"I've got that," I said when the bartender brought the glass of wine to her, putting a ten on the bar.

"No, that's OK," she said with a sigh. "I'm not looking for company."

"Believe me, I'm not either," I told her. "I just wanted to be nice to someone who looks like she could use a little niceness."

She looked at me. I raised my mug of beer and took a drink.

"As long as you understand that you're not getting anywhere with me."

"I don't want to get anywhere with anyone," I told her and sucked the foam from my upper lip.

She waved the bartender on and took a sip of her wine. The bartender took the ten and brought back three ones and two quarters. On the TV screen above the bar a music group I didn't recognize was playing a song I'd never heard before. A box in the corner of the screen counted down to midnight. It passed the fifteen minute mark as the lady thanked me for the drink.

"No problem," I said.

Her name was Rachel, and she had just left her boyfriend. She was in the middle of driving from Amarillo to her mom's house in Tucson.

"Your boyfriend the one that gave you that bruise?" I asked, the alcohol making me feel more outgoing than I had been in a long time.

She touched the bone of her cheek where the bruise was and then looked at her finger tips, rubbing the tips together.

"I should have tried to cover that up," she said.

"I'm sorry," I said, seeing her wistful stare at some point behind the bar and thinking I should just mind my own business.

"He tried to make me get an abortion," she said. "And when I didn't, we had a huge fight. I mean, I grew up Catholic. I couldn't. I mean, it's murder, right? Killing my baby. I could never…"

She was quiet for a moment before taking a drink from her glass.

"Should you be drinking?" I said.

Rachel rubbed her lips together as she set the wine glass on the bar. "A glass of red wine a day is supposed to be good for you."

"Where did you hear that?"

She shrugged. "The Internet."

"I think I would talk to a doctor about that," I said and then told myself that I should just keep my mouth shut. I didn't want to think about Rachel's baby or that the baby's father wanted her to get rid of it.

"He told me that he'd kill me if I ever tried to get any child support from him," she continued. "I told him not to worry, that I never wanted to see his sorry ass again."

By that point, I figured that I had asked too many questions and just kept quiet. We both finished our drinks, and I paid for another round, Rachel switching from wine to ginger ale. The clock on the television wound down to less than a minute, and people in the bar started counting out loud when the seconds got to fifteen.

At midnight, as "Auld Lang Sine" played and drunk people sang, Rachel and I skipped the midnight kiss, clanking glasses instead.

"Happy New Year," we both said in unison.

I saw her focus on my wedding ring as we toasted the New Year.

"Where's your wife?" she asked.

I started to say, "Greenwood Cemetery," but I decided that I really didn't feel like telling that story. "At home," I said instead.

"You're traveling without her on New Year's?"

"She wasn't able to come with me."

After an awkward silence, Rachel said, "Well, I'm sorry I didn't get to meet her."

"Me too."

I downed the rest of my beer and motioned for the bartender to bring me another.

"You wouldn't ever hurt her, would you?" Rachel asked. "Hit her, I mean."

I'm normally a happy drunk, laughing at everything. But this brought me to the verge of tears. Would I ever hurt her? Did I hurt her? There were other ways of hurting a person besides hitting her. I took a deep breath, trying to keep the tears at bay.

"No," I said. "I never hit her."

"I didn't think so. You seem gentle. Like you have a gentle soul, I mean."

"Thank you."

The bartender brought me a fresh beer, and I gave him my last five-dollar bill. I tried to remember how many drinks I'd had. There were the three Manhattans, and at least four beers, probably more. I chugged the first half of my fresh beer and looked at Rachel.

"Don't go back to him," I said. It's funny how alcohol can bring out the honest bluntness. "You can do a lot better."

"I know. I won't go back."

"You promise?"

"I promise."

We sat and drank more. When my beer was empty, I slipped off my barstool and almost fell to the floor. The room was spinning. I needed to pee, but I thought I could wait until I got upstairs to my room.

"You all right?" Rachel asked.

"Yeah. I think I'm going to call it a night."

"That's probably a good idea."

I took a step away from the bar, but Rachel grabbed my arm.

"Your wife," she said. "She's not OK, is she?"

"No."

"I'm sorry. It's none of my business, but you just seemed sad."

"Yeah."

"I'm sorry."

"Thank you."

She hugged me, and I hugged her back.

"Good night," I said.

"Night."

I staggered away toward the hotel lobby and the elevator beyond. Britney and her business man were waiting for the elevator when I got there. She looked at me with contempt as the business man fondled her backside. I smiled at her, and she turned away.

I couldn't remember my room number or even what floor I was on, so I dug into my pocket and found my room key. Britney and her new friend got into the elevator with me, and we rode up together. They got off on three; my room was on five.

"Y'all have fun," I said as they got off.

Britney sneered at me as the elevator closed. When I finally got to my room, I put the do-not-disturb tag on the door, stripped, peed, and collapsed onto the bed. I didn't wake up until almost noon on New Year's Day with a throbbing in my temples and a jagged pain under my forehead. I went down to the hotel gift shop and bought and took four Advils.

I continued toward home after lunch. As I drove past Amarillo, I thought about Rachel's now ex-boyfriend, what kind of man he must be, wondering when his anger and selfishness and violence would catch up to him, because it always did, one way or another. I considered stopping at Mom's house as I approached Wichita Falls but decided against it. I wanted to be home more than anywhere else in the world.

Everything at the house was as I had left it when I arrived shortly before ten PM. The mailbox was empty, which meant that Mrs. Bixby, my next-door neighbor, had been checking my mail just as I had asked her to do. I went in, dumped the clothes from my suitcase directly into the washing machine, threw in a detergent pod, poured in some fabric softener crystals, and started the washer. I sat on the couch in my living room and stared at the TV. The remote was not on the coffee table in front of me, and I didn't feel the urge to get up and look for it. I listened to the silence. After the noise of Tammy's family and the highway traffic of the road, the house never seemed so quiet, so empty. I saw the remote on the TV stand, right in front of the television. I didn't think getting up to get the remote and sitting back down on the couch to watch TV was worth the effort when I could go into the bedroom and watch TV from my bed.

I lay in bed that night with a Harry Potter movie playing on the TV, the one with Kenneth Branaugh playing some prima donna wizard. I muted the sound and stared at the ceiling fan turning slowly above me, wondering whether I was living or just merely existing. My big plans for going to law school were supposed to get me back in the world. I had a large bank account and very few expenses. The house and car were paid for. I had to pay property taxes and utilities. Other than that, I had groceries, gas for the car, and entertainment. I attended my classes and modeled for figure drawing sessions. I was living what should have been a stress-free life. Why, then, did I feel such a heavy weight dragging on me, motivating me to retreat from the outside?

I spent the next two weeks playing Call of Duty on the PlayStation 4 and going to the movies almost every evening until I had seen everything playing in current release. Rather than registering online from home, I drove up to the Denton campus and registered on campus. This consisted of sitting at a computer in the library and doing exactly what I would have done on my home PC. I walked through the art building while I was there, but the doors to all the drawing rooms were locked.

The semester began on a Tuesday, the day after Martin Luther King Day. I needed 21 hours to graduate, so I only carried twelve for the semester. I would take the other 9 either in the summer or the following fall. I wasn't in a hurry. My classes were all either MW or MWF ones, just like the previous fall, so, once again, my Tuesdays and Thursdays were free for modeling. The art classes never used models the first day, so the only gig I had that week was on Thursday, a beginning figure drawing class from 11:00 to 2:00.

I arrived later than usual and must have missed the models from the 8:00 to 11:00 classes. I looked at the schedule and saw Lydia's name down for the other 11 to 2. I took my time changing, hoping I would get to see her. She made it in at 10:55. I was already in my robe and slippers when she knocked and walked in.

"Hi Lydia," I said.

She smiled, and maybe it was just wishful thinking on my part, but her face seemed to brighten when she saw me.

"Hi," she said as she took off her coat. "David, right?"

"Yep. How were your holidays?"

"OK, I guess," she said. "I went to my mom's."

She whipped her shirt off and started unsnapping her pants. Her small breasts jiggled as she moved. "How about you?"

"Great. I got to go skiing for the first time in I don't know how long."

"Awesome!"

Lydia stepped out of her pants and started folding them. Her nude body seemed more muscular than I remembered, and I wondered whether she had lost weight. She turned away from me as she packed her clothes into her gym bag. The lightly freckled creamy white skin of her back as it rounded into her bottom, with two dimples just above each buttock, seized my attention. I caught myself staring, and I turned away, thinking that I really needed to vacate the changing room so that I would be able to safely remove my robe when it came time for me to get into a pose.

"Well, you have a good semester," I said as I grabbed a clean sheet and headed toward the door.

"You too. I'll see you later."

The corridor was clearing as I hurried to class. It was exactly eleven o'clock, and I didn't want to be even a minute late. My slippers made shuffling sounds on the floor as I squeezed between easels and headed toward the model stand. I set my sheet down and started doing a few stretches. The students were still setting up, and I didn't see anyone who looked like the instructor. A guy with red hair and scruffy beard and carrying a spiral notebook walked in and said hi to a couple of people. He dropped his notebook on the teacher's desk and slid an easel aside to get to me.

"You must be David," he said. "I'm Julius."

"Hi." We shook hands.

"We've actually got a few things to go over, so we're not going to need you for probably another twenty minutes or so."

"OK." I disliked having delays in modeling time, but it was part of the job. I made sure I was always ready to go at the start of class time. After that, everything was up to the teacher.

"If you want to wait in the models' room, I can come get you when we're ready."

"All right," I said.

I left the sheet on the model stand and made my way past the easels and back into the corridor. Lydia was sitting in the changing room reading a paperback book when I got there.

"Long time no see," I said.

"Your teacher giving a lecture too?" she asked.

"Something like that. What are you reading?"

I sat down in the chair opposite her. She held her book up so that I could see the cover. It was *Stranger in a Strange Land* by Robert A. Heinlein.

"I read that about twenty years ago," I said. "Good book. A classic."

Lydia folded the corner of the page and closed her book. I cringed. I hated folding pages or abusing books in any way.

"Do you read sci-fi?" she asked.

"I used to. I don't read much of anything anymore. Except textbooks."

"I have to read something for pleasure, even during the semester."

"How are your grades?" I asked her.

"They're good now. They weren't so good the first time I tried to go to school."

"The first time?"

"Yeah," she said, "I went for two years right after high school. When I quit, my grade point average was like 1.6 or something. It was horrible."

"What happened?"

She shrugged. "I just didn't know what I wanted to do, didn't want to be in school, thought I knew more than my mom. I don't know."

"So you quit and came back?"

"Yeah. I just got off of academic probation after last semester."

"How long were you out of school?"

"Four years."

Maybe Lydia wasn't as young as I thought. "How old are you?" I asked.

"Twenty-five. How old are you?"

"The big 4-0," I said.

"You look good for 40."

I smiled and probably blushed. "Thanks."

"So why are you up here taking your clothes off for money?" she asked.

I laughed. I had never thought of art modeling in quite those words. "I used to model during my first attempt at college, and I remembered how much I liked it. So when I came back to school, I started to do it again."

"You've been modeling awhile then."

"On and off, yeah," I said.

"Can I ask you something?"

"Sure."

"You won't get offended?"

"I don't know about that. What's the question?"

Lydia took a deep breath and asked, "Have you ever, like, gotten an erection when you're modeling?"

I'd been asked that question a few times before by people who had never been in a life drawing class, but I had never expected to hear it from a fellow model. The memory of my first meeting with Lydia and the stirrings I had felt when I had been in a pose with her roared back. I had come close then.

"Never a full one hundred percent hard on, no," I said.

32

"I was just asking because you're bigger than most guys."

"Really?"

"Oh yeah," she said with more enthusiasm than she probably intended. She blushed and picked up her book again.

I had never made a habit of comparing myself with other guys, and of course, no one in any of the art classes I had ever modeled for had ever said anything. But Glenda had told me many times that she loved my penis, that it was the perfect size for her. I had dated another girl in high school, and things had gotten serious. We never went all the way, but we had gotten close once. She had taken one look at my erection and put a halt to things. She told me that she didn't want me to hurt her and that she was afraid I wouldn't fit. Being a teenage kid with no experience, I just thought that was a fear common to most girls.

Lydia looked at her book and closed it again. I could feel my arousal building just thinking about her question. That she would even ask such a thing excited me. I knew we were both waiting on drawing teachers, but I decided to see how far things would go.

"There was this time at TWU," I said. "This one girl in class would always focus her drawings on my – you know. Every time I would walk around and look at the drawings, hers would be a big close up of my thing, you know."

Lydia leaned forward and seemed really interested.

"So late that semester, I went in and took a long standing pose. My back was to most of the students, but this girl moved over to the side, so she could see me in profile. And then she started talking to the girl next to her, saying things like 'You have to start with the most important part,' and giggling. Well, I started to get...you know."

"Yeah?" Lydia said.

"Yeah. I couldn't believe that the teacher let her go on like that. But she did."

"And you started getting hard?"

"Yeah. But I don't think I got all the way there. I could kind of show you how it was, if you wanted me too."

"Sure." Her eyes had seemed to light up.

I stood up and slipped the robe off. I wasn't fully erect, but things were definitely on the rise just from the conversation. Lydia gasped and then laughed.

"I got to something like this," I said. "But since my back was turned to most of the people, I got away with it."

Lydia turned at her head to look at me from different angles.

"What do you think?" I said. "This probably wouldn't be appropriate for an art class, huh?"

"No, definitely not now," she said.

I looked down and saw that I was fully erect. I grabbed my robe and covered up.

"Sorry," I said.

"Don't be. That's impressive."

Lydia touched her top teeth with the tip of her tongue. I looked away and sat back down hoping I would be able to cool off before that Julius guy came to get me.

"So what happened?" she asked.

"What?"

"With the class. What happened?"

"I don't know. The semester ended. I never modeled for that class again."

"Was she good? This penis artist of yours."

I laughed. "I think so."

"So your cock and balls might be on display in some gallery right now."

I had to laugh at her frankness, and she laughed with me. There was a knock at the door, and Audrey poked her head in.

"You guys sound like you're having too much fun in here," she said. "Lydia, we're ready whenever you are."

"Hey Audrey," I said.

"David. I'm glad you're modeling again this semester."

"Thank you. I'm sure I'll be in your class soon."

"I hope so," Audrey said and closed the door.

Lydia looked at me and stood up.

"Well," she said, "I guess I'll be going. See ya."

"Yeah. See you later."

Lydia left for class, and I sat in the room alone. She had left her book, and I picked it up and thumbed through it. Her folded page was about two-thirds of the way through it. I set the book down without disturbing her place, stood up and started stretching. Less than five minutes later, Julius knocked on the door and told me his class was ready for me.

I spent the next two and a half hours doing a variety of short poses, starting with one minute gestures before moving to five minute ones. While I was in those poses, I started to feel a touch of remorse, as if I had taken things with Lydia in the changing room a bit too far. She had been sitting in that tiny room with nowhere else to turn, a virtual captive, and I had taken advantage of that. I didn't have any intentions of trying to date Lydia, but I did want us to remain on friendly terms.

During the long break, I went to the changing room, but Lydia wasn't there. I stopped outside the door to the room she was in and could hear music playing. I remembered that Audrey usually gave her classes a break every hour, which meant they got two breaks. Julius had given his class a break at roughly the halfway mark of the three-hour session. Why couldn't our breaks have coincided?

I continued posing after the break, and the class ended with what Julius said was going to be a fifteen-minute reclining pose. I took a position where I could see the clock on the wall. It was one-thirty when the pose started, but Julius didn't call an end to the pose until 1:51, a minute past the time that the class was supposed to end. Audrey usually dismissed her models five to ten minutes early so that her students could clean and pack up. I quickly got Julius to sign my time sheet and shuffled down the hall to the changing room, wondering how Lydia would react when she saw me.

I knocked on the door, didn't hear anything, and slipped inside. Lydia had already gone. I closed the door, wet some paper towels, and started washing the charcoal off my feet. The models for the 2:00 classes would soon be coming in, and I glanced at the schedule to see who they were. I didn't have time to register the names when Lydia burst into the room.

"Hey," she said.

I paused in my foot cleaning and said, "Hi."

She stood there for a second or two as she looked at me. I was in my robe leaning against the wall with my right lower leg perched above my left knee, a charcoal blackened wet paper towel in my hand.

"I left my book in here," she said.

She walked to the far corner and picked it up from the counter. I resumed wiping my foot off.

"How did your class go?" she asked.

"OK. He kept me a little later than usual."

"Yeah," Lydia said and stuffed the Heinlein book into her gym bag.

"Listen," I said, "I hope I didn't go too far earlier with the whole…"

I was interrupted by a knock on the door, and Walter poked his head in.

"Hello. Is everyone decent? Wait, we're always decent even when we're naked," he said as he walked in and set his stuff down on the counter.

"No, it's fine," Lydia said to me.

"What's fine?" Walter asked.

"Nothing. I better get going."

"Bye Lydia," I said.

"Later."

I watched Lydia leave, and I wished that Walter could have been just a few minutes late.

"Who was that?" he asked.

"Her name's Lydia."

"She new?"

"No, she modeled a few times last semester."

Walter had started undressing, so I quickly finished cleaning my feet and got my clothes on. Walter kept talking as usual, something about modeling gigs at SMU in Dallas, but I tuned him out, still wishing I had had more time with Lydia.

4

I saw Lydia the following Monday, but she wasn't anywhere near the art building. I had just settled into my seat in my morning political science class, Public Opinion and Participation, when she took the desk next to me.

"Hi," she said, startling me. I hadn't noticed her come in.

"Hey, what are you doing here?"

"I'm taking the class."

"What? Why?"

"I decided to major in political science."

I couldn't think of anything to say. Her presence was a jolt. She was wearing a black Led Zeppelin concert t-shirt over a gray sweatshirt and camo pants.

"What about the class prerequisites?" I said.

"I already took a couple of poli-sci classes a few years ago," she said.

"A few years ago?"

"Yeah, you know. The first time I went to college. One of them was the only B I got my whole freshman year. So, I figured, why not major in it."

After the other things we talked about during our previous conversation, I had forgotten about Lydia's academic history. I had intended to apologize for any indiscretion I might have committed the next time I talked to her, but now I wondered whether I needed to. Lydia knew I was majoring in political science before she changed her major. I wondered just then whether she might be a stalker and had to laugh at such a thought. Lydia had no way of knowing that I would have been in this particular class. And why would anyone want to stalk me anyway?

"What's so funny," Lydia asked, and I realized I had laughed out loud.

"Nothing," I said. "I guess I'm just happy to see you."

Lydia smiled. "Good."

Dr. Brady entered the room and set the stack of books she had been carrying on the desk at the front of the class. I'd never taken a class from her before, but I had listened to her introduction as she explained the course syllabus on the first day of the class the previous Wednesday.

"Good morning everyone," she said.

Lydia, who had been facing me, turned and gave her attention to the instructor. The class started with an abbreviated rehash of the first session. Lydia was not the only late registrant who needed a syllabus and course introduction. Dr. Brady gave a short lecture during the last twenty minutes and issued a reading assignment.

Lydia turned to me after Dr. Brady dismissed the class and said, "I hope I didn't freak you out, showing up in your class like this."

"No," I lied. "You didn't."

"I didn't even know you were in this class. I mean, I knew you were a poli-sci major, but I didn't know... You know?"

"Yeah," I said. "But I'm glad you're here."

"Me too. I'm just glad I know someone in the class."

There was a major assignment on political protests listed on the syllabus that could be done with a partner or as part of a small group. It occurred to me then that Lydia would probably want me as her partner. When Dr. Brady had mentioned it, Lydia had glanced at me. However, Lydia didn't say anything about it then. She gathered her books and jumped up from her desk.

"I've got another class in eight minutes," she said, "and it's all the way over by the library. So I'll see you later."

"OK," I said, just getting up from my own desk. She was gone before I could stand up.

I had the following day, Tuesday, off, no classes or modeling gigs. It probably wasn't the best day for me to have off since it was the four-year anniversary of Glenda's accident. I spent the day at home cleaning, doing laundry, and studying. I should say, trying to study. The day Glenda died was on my mind so much that I wound up just staring at the text on the page rather than reading anything. She and I had been talking on the phone when it happened, and the sound, that almost unearthly squealing, smashing, crunching sound instantly followed by dead silence on the line was something that I couldn't get out of my mind. It was like a virus, infecting every part of my being. All my life, I have been conscious of dates on the calendar, remembering D-Day every June 6th, Pearl Harbor every December 7th, Glenda's birthday every May 30th, and a host of other dates. I tried to block out my memory of the accident, but every time I saw or thought of the date, January 29th, it came roaring back.

My phone rang four times throughout the day. Each time, I looked at it and saw "Mom" on the screen. She would want to know how I was holding up, and I didn't feel like talking about it. She left voicemails after the first two calls, but I didn't plan on listening to them until the following morning. I ended the day sitting on my living room couch watching a marathon of The Big Bang Theory and drinking an entire bottle of Red Moscato.

I went to Public Opinion class Wednesday morning with a foul taste in my mouth and a throbbing pain in my temples. Lydia was already there when I arrived, her Heinlein paperback sitting on top of her notepad on her desk. I took my regular seat next to her and thought how strange it was that I considered it my regular desk after only two classes.

"Morning," Lydia said without enthusiasm. Her mouth was curled into a frown or a grimace, her eyes dull and downcast. I thought I was the one with the hangover.

"Morning."

I pulled my textbook and spiral notebook out of my backpack. Lydia sat with her shoulders slumped and her chin almost on her chest.

"You OK?" I said.

"I don't know. I guess so."

"What's wrong?"

Lydia turned and faced me.

"I modeled for a 2 to 5 class yesterday," she said in a voice barely above a whisper. She looked down and didn't offer anything else.

"And?" I said. My head was pounding.

Lydia pulled a folded paper from the middle of the paperback. She handed it to me. I unfolded it and read: "Dear Lydia: I love drawing your naked body so much. U R so hot. I want u so bad it hurts. Be at the Drafthouse Friday night. Please." The note had been typed and printed from a computer. There was no signature. I thought about making a joke about her having a fan club, but I saw how upset she was.

"Where did you find this?" I asked.

She held up the Heinlein. "In my book."

"And where was the book? Was it in the class with you, or was it in the changing room?"

"I left it in the changing room during the break."

"But you had it in the class with you before that?"

"Yes, I think so," she said.

I looked down at the folded sheet of paper. If it had been placed in her book while it was in the changing room, then anyone could have put it there. The changing room is never locked. In fact, there's a sign on the inside of the door telling us not to ever lock the door. But whoever it was would have had to have known that the book was hers. So it had to have been someone who had seen her with the book.

"How long have you been reading this?" I asked, picking up the copy of *Stranger in a Strange Land.*

Lydia shrugged. "I started it last week, right when school started."

"And you don't have any idea who might have left the note?" I asked.

"I don't know."

I looked at the paper again. There was no date on it. But since it was done on a computer and printed out, I doubted that whoever it was did it on a whim. He would have had to have printed it out and carried it with him until he spotted a way to get it to Lydia. The strange part of that was that yesterday had only been the second figure drawing session of the semester for those Tuesday-Thursday classes.

"You didn't model for that class Thursday, did you?" I asked, although I knew that Chloe would not have scheduled the same model for the same class for two consecutive sessions unless the instructor had requested that.

"Nope."

"It's advanced figure drawing, right?"

"I don't know. I didn't pay attention."

"Was it in the same room where we modeled together, or was it in the other one?"

"Same one."

"OK, so it was advanced then." I felt like a detective interviewing a witness. "Tell you what," I said, "I just happen to be modeling for that class tomorrow. I'll try to pay really close attention to everyone, and then I'll go to the Drafthouse Friday night."

Dr. Brady rushed in before Lydia could say anything else. I peeked at my phone and saw that she was three minutes late.

"Good morning everyone," she said, her voice way too cheery for someone as hung over as I was.

Dr. Brady kept that cheery tone all the way through her lecture. My headache subsided over that hour, so I didn't mind it much. When she dismissed the class, Lydia turned to me looking much more upbeat than she did at the start of the class.

"So you'll really come to the Drafthouse with me Friday?" she said.

"No, I said I would go. I don't think you need to be there."

"Sure I do. He's got to see me. And if he sees me with you, maybe he'll back off."

"And what if he doesn't?"

"Then we'll beat the shit out of him."

I couldn't help but laugh. Lydia did not laugh with me.

"Seriously?" I said. "This guy's probably someone who is so socially inept that he doesn't know how to talk to women. I don't think you need to risk a felony assault charge for him."

"OK, we won't beat the shit out of him. But you need to talk to him. Scare him."

"Are you sure you want to go?"

"Yes."

We packed up our books and started walking out of the class. Lydia didn't seem in as much of a hurry as she did Monday. I checked my phone and saw that Dr. Brady had let us out a few minutes early.

"Did that note scare you?" I asked.

She considered that for a moment and then said, "No. It pissed me off. I mean, what the fuck is wrong with this guy?"

"I told you, he's probably just socially inept. Probably a computer nerd or something like that." I started to say that I was a computer nerd myself, so I should know. But then Lydia might associate me with this person, and for some reason, I didn't want her doing that.

"OK. You just want to meet there?" she said.

"Sure. What time? The note didn't say."

Lydia's eyebrows raised. "Oh! Well. How about eight then?"

"I can do that," I said.

Lydia reached out, drew her hand back, and then reached toward me again, taking my hand. "Thank you."

"No problem," I replied, feeling uncomfortable by her gesture but also feeling uncomfortable because I liked it. "It'll do me good to get out of the house."

Lydia kissed me on the cheek, let go of my hand, and looked away bashfully. "Later," she said as she hurried away.

I stood in the same spot for a moment, watching her bound away. I hadn't expected a kiss on the cheek. What did it mean? "If he sees me with you," she had said. Was I supposed to pretend to be her date? Was I her date? What had just happened? I shook my head and started toward the Student Union. I had an hour break until my next class. Lydia was far too young for me to even consider dating. I was taking driver's education when she was busy trying to get her head through a birth canal. But she hadn't asked me to go to the Drafthouse. I had offered. And the kiss wasn't really a kiss but more like a little peck. I was clearly reading too much into things. I pushed those thoughts aside and concentrated on my school assignments.

I modeled for two classes the next day, an 8:00 to 11:00 and the 2:00 to 5:00. I wasn't thrilled with the three-hour break. UNT is in Denton, and I lived in Haslet which was about a 45-minute drive south. It didn't make sense to drive home, stay for an hour, and drive back for the second class.

The 8 to 11 session was uneventful. It was a beginning figure drawing class early in the semester, so I did a lot of dynamic short poses. I was tired when it was done, but it was a good kind of tired. No body parts had gone to sleep in class, and my circulation was good.

The weather was nice for the end of January, so I took a long walk between classes, stopping by my car to leave my modeling bag. I even walked off campus and took a look at the Drafthouse. It was a bar in an older building on Oak Street, not far from the art building. I walked around the building and checked the alley in the back. There was nothing remarkable about the place. The Drafthouse was open for lunch, so I went inside and ate a sandwich. The NFL Network was playing on all the televisions, with the show hosts talking about the big Super Bowl matchup. I stayed and watched some of it after I finished my sandwich. I didn't have anywhere else to be. But I got bored with the talking heads after just a few minutes. There are only so many ways to analyze an upcoming football game.

I retrieved my bag from my car and got back to the art building before 1:30, sitting on one of the benches down the hall from the two figure drawing rooms. Three students were already sitting cross-legged on the floor, their portfolios against the wall next to them, waiting for access to the advanced figure drawing room. They were all female, so I ruled them out as suspects.

I watched people walk up and down the corridor. Most of them had drawn me in a class at some time, but only two or three students acknowledged me in any way. Those acknowledgements were nothing more than a nod or an eyebrow raise. Modeling completely nude in front of a classroom full of people is an unusual job, and people don't know how to react to it, especially if they've been in those classes. Several times, I thought I heard whispers between people after I've passed by them in the art building.

At 1:40, the door to the drawing room opened just enough for Rochelle, her sarong wrapped tightly around her body, to slip out. She shuffled down the hall away from me and toward the models' changing room. The three girls sitting on the floor stood up. They were joined by two guys carrying portfolios. The newcomers both engaged the girls in conversation, and I heard laughter. One of the girls took a sketchbook out of her portfolio and started flipping through the pages so the other four could see. While they were looking at and talking about the sketches, the door to the drawing room burst open, and several students rushed out.

I figured that it was time for me to start getting ready for class, so I started toward the changing room. As I walked, a lady in a bathrobe emerged from the beginning figure drawing room and almost ran into me. I had never seen her before.

"Sorry," she said.

"It's all right," I said with a smile. "I think we're going to the same place."

"Oh yeah?"

Rochelle exited the room just as we got to it.

"Hey David," she said. "How are you?"

"Good. Did you have a good break?"

"Yeah, it was great. Went skiing."

"Really?" I said. "Where at?"

"Crested Butte."

"Ah. I skied at Monarch a couple of days."

"Awesome. I'd love to chat, but I gotta go."

"OK. See ya," I said.

The lady in the bathrobe had gone into the changing room while I was talking with Rochelle. I gave a single knock on the door and went in. She was still in her bathrobe, sitting in one of the chairs and texting on her iPhone.

"Hi again," I said.

She was tall and thin and looked a little older than most of the female models I had seen at UNT.

"Hey," she said.

I set my bag on the counter, unzipped it open, and dug my robe out of it. I snuck a peek at the model schedule on the wall and saw the name Brenda W. listed for both the 11 to 2 and 2 to 5 beginning figure drawing sessions. I took my jacket off, set it on the counter, and pulled my t-shirt over my head.

"I'm David, by the way," I said as I folded the shirt and set it on top of the jacket.

She didn't answer as I stepped out of my tennis shoes.

"Sorry," she finally said, looking up from her phone. "Texting my babysitter. I'm Brenda."

She offered her hand, and we shook. I leaned my backside against the counter and started removing my socks.

"Are you new here?" I asked.

"Here, yes. I've been modeling for three years, mostly in Dallas."

"Really? Where at?"

"SMU, UTD, Brookhaven College, Creative Arts Center. Lots of places."

I took my jeans off as she spoke, folding them and placing them on my shirt. Taking a cue from Lydia, I had forgone the underwear. Brenda laughed.

"This is so weird," she said.

"What?"

"Just everybody using the dressing room at the same time."

"Yeah," I said, putting my robe on, "this is the most unusual place I've ever modeled. They have so many classes going at once, all the time."

"Where else have you modeled?"

"Mostly on the Fort Worth side," I told her. "TCU, UTA, Texas Wesleyan, Tarrant County College." It had been fifteen years or more since I had modeled at any of those places, although I had resubmitted my name to TCU. They just hadn't called me yet. Nearly all of the other schools in the area only offered one or two life drawing classes a semester.

Her phone chimed, and she looked at her incoming text. She sighed and started typing something. I put my house shoes on and picked a fresh sheet from the stack.

"Sorry," she said again.

"Babysitter?"

"Yeah."

"How many kids do you have?"

"Just one," she said. "She's two and a half."

"I'll bet that's fun."

"She is a handful."

"Wait," I said. "Your daughter's two and a half, and you've been modeling for three years?"

"Yeah. A friend of mine was teaching figure drawing at SMU, and she really wanted a pregnant model. I let her talk me into it, and you know. I loved it. So, I kept doing it even after Sarah was born."

"That's cool," I said. "I always love hearing about how people got into this job."

"How did you get into it?"

I glanced at the clock and saw that it was almost time to get to class, and I wanted to get there with enough time to look at each student and try to figure out who might have left Lydia that note.

"Same way I get into everything," I joked as I backed out the door, "trying to impress a girl."

Brenda smiled.

"Have a good one," I said.

"You too."

Every easel was occupied when I got into the room. The instructor was a lady about my age named Robin. I had worked for her a few times before.

"Hi David," she said with a smile when I walked in.

"Hey Robin." I thought about telling her about the note Lydia got since it had apparently been placed there during her class, but I didn't see a way to do that out of earshot of any of her students.

"We're going to skip the gestures and do two twenty minute poses and then a long pose for the rest of the class after that. Is that OK?"

"Fine with me," I said.

Robin had never spent a lot of time talking or taking roll. I had heard her on several occasions tell her students that every minute of drawing from a model was precious to an artist. So when the clock ticked over to two o'clock, I already had the robe off and was getting into a pose. That first pose was a standing one with a bit of a twist. But my head was turned so that I was facing the middle of the class.

The model stand was against the wall rather than in the middle of the room, and I could see every student without having to turn my head. I counted ten females and eight males. Of the eight males, two of them looked like they might be awkward with women just from the way they dressed and wore their hair. The other six guys were more mainstream in appearance and seemed to have a good rapport with the girls around them. But I didn't rule them out. I examined each of them, while avoiding direct eye contact with anyone, trying to make their faces familiar enough that I would recognize them if I saw them at the Drafthouse Friday night.

The long pose that ended that session was a challenge. I was seated on a stool with my right foot on the model stand and the other up on a block. The stool wasn't well padded, and I kept losing feeling in my left foot. But when the pose wasn't so uncomfortable, I thought about the changing room. The note had to have been left in Lydia's book when it was in that changing room. It would had to have been folded at least twice to fit inside the book which would have made it so thick that she would have noticed it when she carried the book to the changing room during her break. In all the time I had modeled at UNT, I had never seen a student even try to go into that changing room, unless, of course, that student was also a model as well. I think the students were warned multiple times never to go in that room over the course of their time here.

But I had just been in that room with someone I had never seen before. She had been another model, but there had been no one to check her in and make sure she was allowed access to that room. Still, she had been a model. Just then, a thought occurred to me. What if one of the other models had put that note in Lydia's book? I started trying to count all the models that I had met or seen in that room. I didn't think one of the women would have left the note unless it had been done as a joke. And who would even have thought of such a joke? Lydia was still new, and none of the other models I had talked to even knew her. She wasn't a student in the art department like a lot of the other models; she was in political science.

The male models were a mixed bag. Walter and I were the only ones I knew of who were above the age of a typical college student. And Walter certainly didn't have a problem talking with women. He didn't have a problem talking with anyone. Getting him to shut up was the problem. One of the other male models had dreadlocks down to his shoulders and a piercing on his lower lip. I had talked to him only in passing. Another guy had tattoos on his neck and the side of his face. I could only remember seeing him twice, but I don't think I had ever heard him say a word to anyone. There were at least two other male models I had seen, but I had never matched names to faces. Still, I thought I would recognize them if I saw them at the Drafthouse.

My list of suspects was expanding rather than shrinking. The pose was causing my foot to tingle by then, so I stopped thinking about Lydia and that note. Whatever happened would happen, I thought, but I did expect Friday night to be an interesting evening.

5

The Drafthouse was much louder at 7:30 PM on Friday than it had been at lunch on Thursday, with music that could be heard from the street. I looked through the front window, but I didn't see many people inside. Lydia had not yet arrived. I considered waiting outside for her, but I had gotten there so early that I would have had to stand outside for longer than I cared to. The temperature was hovering just below freezing, and the wind was enough to rub my cheeks raw. One of the things that used to get on Glenda's nerves was my tendency to arrive everywhere early. She had been habitually late, so we usually balanced each other enough to get most places just on time. I felt a familiar twinge of despair as I realized how incomplete I felt without Glenda, even after four years. I pushed that feeling aside as I walked into the Drafthouse and told myself to concentrate on other thoughts, like trying to find someone I recognized from the art department, someone who might have left that note for Lydia.

Most of the tables were empty, but I decided to sit at the bar. A seat at the end was available, which was perfect because I could see the front door from it. I unbuttoned my coat but didn't take it off and ordered a Coors Light. The bartender brought me the beer, and I paid cash. I took just a sip, intending to make that one beer last. The drive from Denton to my home in Haslet took forty-five minutes in great weather, and the weather report for that night had mentioned the possibility of sleet. I refuse to drive even tipsy, and in this weather, drinking more than one or two beers would have been an even worse idea than in good weather.

I watched the people in the bar and everyone who walked in

through the front door. I didn't see a familiar face until Lydia walked in five minutes before eight, wearing a hoodie and jeans. She stopped just by the door and scanned the place. I thought about waving to get her attention, but I wanted to wait and see if anyone approached her. Lydia's face brightened into a smile when she finally saw me in my corner, and she walked over to the bar.

"Well, nobody accosted you when you came in," I said.

She looked around at the people in the building. "No, not yet."

"How are you?" I asked.

"I'm all right. How about you?"

"I'm good. Do you want to get a table or sit at the bar?"

"I'm thinking a table."

I slipped off my barstool and followed her to a table near the door. Any newcomers to the Drafthouse would be sure to see us. A waitress came by as soon as we got seated.

"Can I get you anything, hon?" she said to Lydia.

"Can I get a vodka tonic?"

"Do you have your ID?"

Lydia had already been reaching into her purse. She got her wallet, pulled her driver's license out, and showed it to the waitress. I tried to remember the last time I had been carded.

"OK," the waitress said. She looked at me. "How about you?"

I still had more than half a beer left. "I'm okay."

"All right. I'll be right back with that vodka tonic."

When the waitress had walked away, I asked Lydia, "Don't you have a thicker coat?"

She looked down at her hoodie. "Yeah, but I didn't feel like wearing it."

"Aren't you cold?"

"It's OK in here," she said, rubbing her hands together.

We sat in silence for a moment. I kept looking at the door every time someone passed by the window outside, but none of them entered the bar.

"So where is this mystery person?" I said.

Lydia shrugged. "The note didn't specify a time."

"Well, we shouldn't sit here all night. The weather is supposed to get bad, and I have to drive all the way back to Haslet."

"I didn't watch the news."

"Fifty percent chance of sleet after midnight."

"That sucks," Lydia said. "Why is it always sleet and never snow? I love snow."

"We live in Texas."

Lydia's vodka tonic arrived. "That's four-fifty," the waitress said as she set the drink down.

I started to pull some money out of my jeans pocket, but Lydia had already given her a five and waved her on.

"Thanks, hon," the waitress said.

Lydia took a sip of her drink. "Mmmm."

"You know," I said, "I modeled for that class yesterday, and nobody there seemed like the type to leave that note."

"Yeah, I was thinking about that. I was trying to remember if anyone left the room between the break and the end of class. You know how Robin doesn't let anyone in or out when the model is posing?"

"Yeah."

"I don't think anyone did leave. I mean, I would have remembered it if anyone had because Robin would have made a big deal out of it."

"Agreed." I took another sip of beer. "How well do you know the other models? Besides me, that is."

Lydia shrugged. "I don't know. Not much. That day with you was the only double model class I've had. I've seen a few of them in the changing room, but I haven't really talked to any of them much."

"You don't know any of them well enough that they would try to play a very bad joke on you?"

Lydia laughed. "No," she said.

The door opened, letting in a gust of cold air, and Lydia shuddered. A young guy stepped in, stopped, and looked around. The door closed behind him. He seemed to look right over us. I heard, "Hey Bobby!" from the pool table area. Bobby nodded to them and headed off in that direction. Lydia was holding her arms against her chest.

"Are you sure you want to sit here?" I asked.

"It's OK," she said.

"You just look like you're freezing."

"I'll be OK."

We sat in silence for a moment. I took another small sip of beer. I'd had it so long that it was no longer cold. I didn't mind it much after that blast of cold air from the front door. A cup of hot chocolate sounded good right about then.

"Did you tell your wife that you were going out with a college girl on a Friday night?" Lydia asked.

"What?" I saw that she was looking at my left hand, at my wedding ring. "No."

"So what'd you tell her?"

I looked down into my beer bottle and shook my head. When I looked up, Lydia's light, happy expression had turned serious.

"I'm sorry," she said. "It's none of my business."

I shook my head.

"She's not…"

I nodded.

"I'm sorry."

"It's been four years now," I said. "I don't know why I still wear the ring. I guess I feel naked without it. That sounds weird huh? Coming from a nude model."

Lydia smiled. "No," she said.

"Well, I guess I should stop wearing it. So people don't assume, you know."

"I think you should stop wearing it when you're ready to stop wearing it," Lydia said.

She moved her hand over mine, and I saw a spark fly from her fingertip and felt a jab of static electricity jerk my arm when she touched me. Her hand immediately retracted, and we looked at each other.

"Wow," she said, and we both laughed. The tension that had started to build was gone.

"You don't have shag carpet in your house, do you?" I asked.

"No. I don't know where that came from."

I took a sip of my beer and tried to remember what I had been saying. Lydia watched me with those green eyes that had first captured my attention.

"Anyway," I said, "I don't think a student left that note. I have never, ever seen a student go in that room. Other than models, that is."

"But that doesn't mean they don't."

"That's true. But it would have taken a lot of balls for someone to have gone in and messed with your stuff like that." Models not only used the room for dressing and undressing, but it was a lounge and a place to fill out timesheets. The weekly schedule was posted on the wall next to instructions for filling in all the account codes on our timesheets. Any one of the models could have walked in at any moment for something.

"Maybe," she said.

The door opened, and we were subjected to another blast of Arctic wind. Several people walked in, all of them bundled up in hats and scarves. They stopped just inside the threshold and started unwrapping. Lydia and I watched them, but none of them looked familiar. Lydia was shivering.

"Here," I said, taking off my coat. I had on a sweatshirt under it and a t-shirt underneath that.

"I'm OK, really," she said.

I stood up and put my jacket over her shoulders. "Put it on," I told her.

She uncrossed her arms from her chest and put my jacket on. It was way too big on her, and she had to push the sleeves up to get her hands to emerge from them. The door opened again, and a middle-aged couple entered. They walked straight to the bar and didn't look at us.

"Is that better?" I asked.

"Yes, thank you."

We sat in silence for a while, sipping our drinks. The Drafthouse got busier and busier as the evening wore on. Lydia and I watched each person as he or she entered. Nobody looked at Lydia with anything resembling recognition or expectation.

"How did she die?" Lydia asked once her glass was empty.

I finished my beer in one gulp. I should have been used to people asking by then.

"Car accident," I said.

I didn't plan on offering any more details than that. Reliving it on the anniversary earlier in the week had been difficult enough. But Lydia didn't ask any more follow up questions. It seemed that she could sense my pain. For that, I was glad.

Our waitress came by and asked if we wanted another round. Lydia and I both said yes. I pulled my money out of my pocket before the waitress could get back.

"I've got this," I told Lydia when I saw her rummaging in her purse.

"You sure?"

"Yeah."

The waitress brought our drinks, and I paid for them, giving her a three dollar tip. Lydia and I drank and watched.

"How long do you want to sit and wait for this guy?" I asked.

"I don't know. I wonder if he's already here and just afraid to come over because of you."

"Why? Because I look so scary?"

Lydia giggled. "No. But I'm glad you're here." She paused, took a drink, and then said, "Maybe he's intimidated by your stunning good looks."

I laughed as I thought about my previous Friday nights, spent either playing Call of Duty against anonymous people in anonymous places via the magic of cyberspace or going to a movie by myself.

"I seriously doubt that," I told her. "But I am glad I'm here too." And I was, even if we were on what I thought was a wild goose chase. This guy wasn't going to show up. And if he did, we would never know it. "So how did you wind up modeling for art classes?" I asked her, both to make small talk and because, as I had told Brenda the day before, I was always interested in hearing how people got into this unusual job.

Lydia shrugged. "I saw an ad for it in the school newspaper, and I thought it would be a perfect job for me." She lowered her voice, leaned forward, and said, "I'm kind of an exhibitionist."

"No!" I said, feigning shock.

Lydia giggled again. "And it pays better than any other work-study job. How about you?"

"Well," I began, "when I first went to college, I stayed in a dorm."

"What college?"

"UT Austin. I was eating lunch one day, and this girl was sitting across from me. She was cute but a little strange. I don't remember her name. But I remember that she was a big Grace Jones fan. You know Grace Jones, right?"

Lydia slowly shook her head. "She was in Jefferson Starship, wasn't she?"

"No, that was Grace Slick," I said. "Grace Jones was this really weird Jamaican musician. She had like a crew cut or flat top. Very athletic looking. If you ever saw the last James Bond movie that Roger Moore did, she was in that."

Lydia was shaking her head. I waved as if it wasn't important.

"Anyway, there were a few other people around, and this girl was talking to us. She mentioned that she drew naked people in her art class. Well, that got a lot of reactions. One guy asked her if she got to draw hot chicks."

"What did she say?" Lydia asked.

"I don't remember. But a couple of us chimed in and said that we would like to be models for her class. She laughed and told us to go for it. As far as I know, the other guy never did. But I wanted to impress her by following up and doing what I said I was going to do."

"Yeah, right," Lydia said. "You wanted to impress her by showing her your big cock."

"Lydia!" I exclaimed and instantly realized that that was the first time I had addressed her by name. It sounded strange in my voice. "It's not that big," I said more quietly.

"Yes, it is," she said, glancing down toward my crotch.

"Whatever. Anyway, I went down to the art office the very next day and applied to be a model."

"And...?"

"And three weeks later, I modeled for my first art class."

"Was that girl in it? The Grace Jones fan?"

"Yes, she was."

"And was she impressed?"

"I don't know. She didn't have much to do with me after that. Actually, she didn't have much to do with me before. I had just thought she was cute."

"So you never asked her out?"

I shook my head.

"Why not?"

"I don't know. I've never asked out any girl who had drawn me in an art class. It just seems unprofessional."

"What was your first time like?" Lydia asked. "Were you nervous?"

"Are you kidding? I was terrified. I showed up in class with nothing I needed. Nobody had ever told me what to bring, so I didn't even have a robe. I had to undress there next to the model stand and get up there naked. I almost chickened out."

"What made you nervous?"

"Everything. I was worried about getting an erection. I was worried about some gay guy hitting on me. I was even worried that they really didn't draw naked guys, that they just figured that I knew I was supposed to wear a speedo or something, and that when I stripped down to nothing, they would haul me off to jail for indecent exposure or something."

Lydia was laughing. "But you went through with it?"

"I did. And when the class was over, I didn't want to have to put my clothes on. It was so exhilarating, so liberating, like I had been freed from bondage."

Lydia laughed. "That's fucking awesome!"

"I know, right! Apparently, I did a good enough job that I got put on the schedule for the rest of that semester. The teacher did tell me I should buy a robe. So I did."

I was almost out of breath from talking. I looked at Lydia and smiled, realizing how comfortable I had gotten with her. It couldn't have been the beer. I wasn't even halfway through my second one. As we talked, I tried to remember the last time I had been that comfortable with another human being. It had been before Glenda's accident. I didn't want to think about that, to think about Glenda, any more that evening, so I just concentrated on Lydia. We talked for two hours, mostly about experiences we'd had modeling. Since Lydia had just started the previous semester, she didn't have as much to say. So I was doing most of the talking. Eventually, we had forgotten about the note in her Heinlein book and about why we had gone to the Drafthouse in the first place.

I was on my third beer when I noticed that the bar had thinned out. I checked my phone and saw that it was past 11:15.

"Holy crap," I said. "It's after eleven."

I looked out the window, but I didn't see any rain, sleet, or snow falling yet.

"We should probably go then, huh."

"Yeah," I said. I tried to remember how many drinks Lydia had had. I had paid for three of them. "Are you OK to drive."

"I didn't drive," she said.

"You walked?"

"Yeah. I don't live very far."

"How far?"

"Five blocks."

"I'll give you a ride," I said.

"You sure?"

"Of course."

I was parked on the street just a hundred feet or so from the front door of the Drafthouse, but the cold wind was so rough that I sprinted to the car. Lydia jogged and slid into the passenger seat as I started the motor.

"Nice," she said.

I drove a five-year-old Prius, so I didn't know what she was complimenting. Maybe she was impressed that I could unlock and start my car without getting my keys out of my pocket. But I didn't ask her what she meant. My teeth were chattering too much to make small talk. I switched the car into drive and pulled into the street.

"Where to?" I asked.

"Take the next right," she said.

Lydia directed me to a small multiplex. The building didn't look like much, and I imagined the landlord just couldn't keep up with the maintenance required for a place for college students, given that many of those students partied like they were away from home for the first time.

"You don't have to park," Lydia said. "Just drop me off in the front."

"I should walk you to the door."

"It's too cold for that."

I stopped the car, and Lydia leaned over and kissed my cheek.

"Thank you for coming," she said.

"No problem."

"See you Monday."

She got out, and I watched her bound to her door, fumble with her keys, and disappear into her apartment. Once I saw her lights go on inside, I pulled away and started for home. I'd had three beers, but they had been spaced out over three and a half hours. I was feeling perfectly sober, but relaxed. The evening had been more fun than I could have ever expected. I had been comfortable around Lydia. When was the last time I had been comfortable around anyone? When was the last time I had been comfortable, period? But Lydia was way too young for me, just a girl really. She could be a friend, I thought, nothing more. Surely, she felt the same way. Or did she? I recalled all the little things she had said about my looks and my anatomy. She had been suggestively flirting with me, and at the time, those things had gone straight over my head.

I was on I-35W passing the Texas Motor Speedway when my cell phone rang. I looked at the screen but didn't recognize the number.

"Hello," I said after accepting the call.

"I'm so sorry," Lydia said. "I seem to have stolen your coat."

I laughed and started to wonder how she got my number before remembering that every model had been e-mailed a copy of the contact list so each of us could try to find our own replacements in case of emergencies.

"That's all right," I said. "You can give it to me on Monday."

"I don't want you to freeze this weekend."

"I'll be OK. I'm not going anywhere. Maybe the grocery store."

"OK. Thank you for going tonight."

"No problem. I'm just sorry we didn't find the guy."

"You probably scared him off."

"Maybe. Good night Lydia."

"Good night David."

I arrived home at five past midnight, rushed into the house, turned the thermostat up, used the restroom, undressed, and got under the thick blankets of my bed. I turned the TV on and started watching a sitcom rerun. I don't remember the end of that episode, sleeping soundly all night. The sleet, just like Lydia's mystery note writer, never showed up.

6

The high temperature the following Monday afternoon made it all the way up to seventy-three degrees, so I didn't even need the coat when Lydia gave it back to me after our Public Opinion class. But the calendar had only just turned to February, and I knew that another cold front would be blowing through all too soon. Texas winters are like that.

I saw Lydia often over the next few weeks, but never outside of either our political science class or the art department building. We talked every day, excluding weekends, but never for more than five minutes at a time. She never mentioned the note she found or whether she had received any more. And apparently Lydia had earned the trust of the model coordinator because she was modeling as much as any of the other models on the roster, averaging at least twelve hours a week. My light class schedule allowed me to model more than the previous semester, and I even had a few Monday and Wednesday late afternoon sessions. I looked forward to every art class, and I was usually first in line whenever one of the other models needed a substitute. I even skipped my British lit class once to fill in for Rochelle when she was feeling sick.

The first Friday in March, Lydia turned to me as soon as our Public Opinion class ended and asked me if I knew anything about Ecstatic Dance.

"Ecstatic dancing?" I said. "I don't think so."

"It's like yoga, except it's dancing," Lydia said.

"Never heard of it," I said as we walked out of the room and into the corridor.

"There's a dance in Dallas this weekend, and I was thinking about going. Would you like to go with me?"

"I don't know," I said. "What do you do at these things?"

"Dance, I guess."

"You've never been to one?"

Lydia shook her head.

I held the door open and she walked out of the building and into the bright sunshine. I followed.

"How did you find out about these things?" I asked.

"Facebook."

"Ah." I had a Facebook account, but I hadn't logged into it in years. Glenda still had a Facebook page too. People had left notes and messages on her Facebook wall in the days and weeks after the wreck. I finally couldn't stand seeing them. I'd had thoughts about deactivating her Facebook account, but when I tried to log in as her, none of her regular passwords worked. So, I had just quit going to Facebook altogether.

"I've wanted to go for a while," Lydia said, "but I never had a ride."

"Do you not have a car?" I asked.

"Yeah, but it won't start, and I haven't had the money to get it fixed."

"It won't start? Where is it?"

"In the parking lot of my apartment building. But it would have to be towed, and I haven't been able to get it done. So?"

"OK," I said.

"Really? You'll go?"

I had nothing better to do. But that was the story of my life. If I wasn't scheduled for an art class, then I never did have anything better to do. "Sure," I said. "When is it?"

Lydia jumped with excitement. "Sunday afternoon. Starts at 1:00."

"OK. So I should pick you up at 11:30?"

"Yes! You remember where I live?"

"Yeah."

"Thanks." She kissed my cheek and took off for her next class. I stood in that spot for a moment watching her walk away. Just when I was thinking that we shared so many things in common despite the fifteen year difference in our ages, Lydia had proposed something that had the potential of being well outside my comfort zone. Perhaps that age difference was bigger than it seemed.

I modeled for a Friday night painting group that evening, the first modeling gig I'd had outside of UNT in over fifteen years. I had begun to think of modeling as my profession. I wanted to expand my opportunities, so I hadn't turned the group of artists down when the group leader emailed me. The session was going to consist of one three-hour long pose, with breaks every half hour. I posed nude, although some of the artists had talked about past costumed poses while setting up, making me think that I should look into getting some costumes. Most of the people in attendance were either professional artists or hobbyists. There wasn't an instructor, but the group leader did keep time for the breaks and was in charge of making sure I had gotten back in the correct position after each break. It was a fun and relaxed session, with classical music playing the whole night. During the pose, I kept thinking that I should just quit school and try being a full-time model. The world had too many lawyers as it was. Then I thought of the long stretch of holidays, when colleges and art schools let out in early December and didn't start back up again until mid-January. Modeling hours were almost non-existent during that time of year. The available hours in summer weren't great although better than during the winter holidays, but those summers lasted almost three months. Once the money from the insurance and accident settlement was gone, would I be able to make enough as a full-time model? I didn't see how. Of course, if I quit school, that settlement money would last a lot longer. But not long enough, I thought.

I was paid one hundred dollars in cash for the three-hour session. On the way home, I figured that, without the settlement money, I would need to make two thousand a month to be comfortable. With the various schools paying different rates, I would need to do eight to ten three-hour classes every week to make that much money. Such a schedule was certainly doable during the regular semesters, but impossible during those holiday periods and summers. Could I save enough during the long semesters to make it through those slow periods? I was happier in my working life than I had ever been, doing nothing but modeling, but I just didn't see any way to make it a permanent thing. Between undergraduate school and law school, I figured I had three and a half years to really enjoy myself before I had to consider a long-term career move. So I told myself that I had just better enjoy this time while I had it.

Throughout the day Saturday while working on a couple of school assignments, I wondered what I should wear to the Ecstatic Dance thing the next day. I got on my computer after returning from dinner at a nearby Subway and Googled Ecstatic Dance. I clicked on the first site in the list and found a dark photograph of an altar, a dozen or so candles illuminating several idols depicting what looked to me like Buddha, a large gold colored goblet, and a few other indiscernible items. Below the photo was a list of guidelines for Ecstatic Dance. There were, apparently, only three. 1. Move however you wish. 2. No talking on the dance floor. 3. Respect yourself and one another.

I scrolled down and read more details about the practice, about how it was a freeform movement space and how participants were to "dance as manifestations of light." The authors of the site did recommend wearing "loose comfortable clothing that you can move in." Nothing I read on that website or any of the others in the Google search results gave me any desire whatsoever to attend a dance. But, I had promised to take Lydia, and I wasn't planning to let her down.

I left Google and logged into Facebook for the first time in years. My profile photo was one of Glenda and me. I should change it, I thought, but I felt a stab of sadness. There were three numbered red flags at the top right of the screen, indicating that I had 27 friend requests, 18 messages, and 99+ notifications. That was a little much. I clicked on the Change Profile Picture link and selected an old one of me at a Ranger game. It had been taken by Glenda the summer before the wreck. Satisfied that my profile looked OK, I closed the browser and went to my game room to play Skyrim on the Playstation 4 until I fell asleep.

I pulled up in front of Lydia's apartment at 11:20 the next morning, put the car in Park, and listened to the radio play "Love Shack" by the B-52's as I texted Lydia that I was outside. She bounded out about five minutes later, wearing a blue t-shirt with the caption "Keep Calm and Don't Blink," the white outline of the Doctor Who TARDIS just above the caption, and a black skirt that only went down to her knees. The temperature was in the mid-50s with sporadic rain.

"Hey," she said as she slid into my car and shut the door.

"Hey. Aren't you cold?" I asked.

"A little." She turned the heater up and settled back into her seat, her hands between her knees.

I had worn workout pants and a Dallas Cowboys t-shirt under my jacket.

"We're going to be working up a sweat though." When I didn't start driving right away she looked at me and said, "I'll be fine."

"All right," I said and slipped the car into Drive.

The drive to Dallas was long, but since it was Sunday, there wasn't as much traffic as usual. I told Lydia about modeling for the artists' group Friday night. She was interested in getting gigs outside of UNT, and I told her that I would give her name and number to any artists or instructors I met. Lydia had watched the latest Terminator movie on disc over the weekend. I told her that I had seen it when it was in the theater, and she launched into a long and minutely detailed explanation of all the errors, impossibilities and time paradoxes created by the plot of the new movie as compared to the previous ones.

As we entered the Dallas city limits, I handed my phone to Lydia for her to type in the address into my Maps app and let the female voice give directions from the phone's speaker. Lydia was quiet as she looked out my window at the Dallas skyscrapers. The dance thing (I didn't really know what to call it) was held in a large yoga studio just south of downtown. My phone directed me through an open gate and into the enclosed parking lot.

"Is this a bad part of town?" Lydia asked, looking at the metal fence surrounding the property.

"I don't know. I don't know Dallas very well. I usually try to avoid it."

I parked the car, grabbed my phone from Lydia, and closed out of the Maps app. Lydia looked around at the six or seven other cars in the lot and at the front door of the yoga studio. She seemed to be shivering.

"You OK?" I asked.

She snapped her head around toward me as if I had just woken her. "Yeah. I'm fine," she said, looking back toward the door.

Another car drove into the parking lot. It was parked quickly, two spaces down from our spot, and two fit young women wearing light jackets, yoga shorts, and leg warmers hurried inside.

"We don't have to go in," I said, hoping that Lydia would give me the go ahead to drive back toward Denton.

"No," she said. "I want to go."

"OK."

I decided not to wait for her, and I opened my door and stepped outside. I walked around the back of my car as Lydia opened the passenger door. She stepped out as I held the door open and shivered slightly in the cool misty air. After closing her door, I started toward the yoga studio entrance.

"We should get inside before you catch a cold," I said to Lydia when she hesitated, still standing by the car.

She looked past me at the building and nodded her head.

"Why are you so nervous?" I asked.

She forced a smile and said, "I don't know. It's silly."

Lydia brushed past me, and we walked into the building together. I decided to let things be and not push her. She had so badly wanted me to bring her to this that I couldn't understand why she would be so hesitant.

We were greeted by the strong smell of patchouli incense as soon as we walked in the door. Some kind of altar was set up near the entryway, with burning candles, incense sticks, and what looked like a couple of birds' wings. A middle-aged woman, her graying hair braided into two long pigtails, greeted us.

"Welcome," she said in a soft voice. "Welcome. I'm Amanda. And you are?"

She was looking at me, so I said, "I'm David. And this is Lydia."

"Wonderful. And how did you hear about Ecstatic Dance?"

"Facebook," Lydia muttered in a quiet voice.

"Wonderful! If you could sign in here."

Amanda pushed an open spiral notebook toward us, a pen lying on top. Lydia picked it up and wrote her name, paused, looked at me, and wrote mine.

"We do ask for a ten dollar per person donation for the dance," Amanda said.

I looked at Lydia and raised an eyebrow. She hadn't said anything about money. But I dug into the pocket of my exercise pants and pulled out a twenty. Amanda took it from me, smiling, and slipped it into a brown envelope.

"You can put your shoes in one of the cubbies there," she said pointing. "You can wear your socks, but I recommend going barefooted. There's a better connection to the earth and the elements with bare feet."

I saw Lydia smile at this. She exhaled, and her shoulders seemed looser. "Awesome," she said.

"We'll get started in just a few minutes. Feel free to stretch if you need to. We start in a circle before moving into the dance."

Just then, the door opened behind us, and Amanda turned to greet the new arrivals. Lydia and I wandered around the edge of the studio, looking at the Buddhist artwork on the walls and at the barefooted people gathering in the middle of the room and whispering among themselves. We both removed our socks and shoes and stored our footwear in the cubbies. I removed my jacket and stuffed it into the cubby with my shoes. Lydia kept looking to me, and I tried to hide my displeasure at the place. I didn't want to do anything to ruin her enjoyment of this thing, whatever it turned out to be. Amanda called everyone to order in her soft voice, using hand gestures to get everyone into a circle.

We all sat on the floor cross-legged and held hands as Amanda talked about setting our intentions and that once the dance started it was a non-verbal space. Instead of listening to her, I counted the people in the circle. Including Lydia and me, there were fourteen of us, nine women and five men. Lydia sat next to me, and I was soon distracted by how high her mini-skirt had risen when she sat down. I looked at the guy across from us, about mid forties and wearing loose paisley harem pants and a tie-dyed t-shirt with a peace sign on it. He seemed to be staring intently at Lydia's crotch. I thought back to the day I had met Lydia and how she had told me in the changing room after class that she never wore underwear. The guy was probably wondering if he was really seeing what he thought he was seeing. I had to suppress a laugh as Amanda continued with her introduction, which had turned poetic, almost into a chant, the beat of a drum reverberating throughout the yoga studio. I turned and saw a guy I hadn't noticed earlier, sitting in the corner pounding on the drum between his legs with the palms of his hands.

People started swaying from one side to the other with the beat, letting go of hands whenever their movements became more pronounced. Amanda stopped chanting, jumped to her feet, and scurried over to a stereo console. Music, slow and twangy, filled the studio, and the guy on the drums adjusted his drum beats to complement the music. The circle broke apart as people rolled back, writhing and curling on the floor. Lydia and I seemed to be the only two people still holding hands, but she let go when she lay back and scooted herself toward the wall to give herself room to move without bumping into me or anyone else.

The only thing I was feeling was a sense of being out of place, and the only way I knew to let those feelings out with my movements was to get up and walk out of the building. But I didn't want to disappoint Lydia. I was the only person still sitting up, so I leaned over and lay on my side, watching the writhing, undulating bodies of some of the ecstatic dancers. The music changed, the beat quickening, and the people started rising to their feet, still moving and dancing, although a couple of them could have been mistaken for having the spasms of an epileptic seizure.

Lydia was on her hands and knees, moving like a slow bucking horse. I struggled to my feet, standing up stiffly, without all the flowing movement, graceful or otherwise, of the other dancers.

Most of the other people were undulating their bodies with their feet planted on the floor, trying to emulate a slow fountain or a flowing river. Lydia rose to her feet and did the same. I swayed back and forth just a bit, feeling silly. The music changed again, the tempo growing a little faster than before, and people started moving around, stepping around each other, some of them dancing together, intertwining their arms and legs. I moved toward Lydia, wanting the safety of her presence before someone I didn't know tried to wrap herself around me. Lydia glanced at each of the other dancers, pausing only to smile at me as I approached.

I tried to remember the last time I had tried moving to music beyond just tapping my foot. There had been a dance at one of the dorms during my first stint as a college student, twenty years before. My girlfriend at the time had laughed and told me that I was a terrible dancer with no rhythm. That was discouraging enough that I never went to another dance again. I felt grounded and stiff now, my feet not wanting to leave the floor, as I tried to move like most of the other people in the studio. Lydia kept tugging at the bottom of her t-shirt as she moved, pulling it so tight that I could see the outline of her nipples under the fabric.

When the music shifted into something faster and harder, the dances became more energetic, with people jumping up off the floor. Lydia bounced with them, her small breasts jiggling with each beat. I tried to dance too, but I couldn't bring myself to bounce so that both my feet were off the floor at the same time. Lydia kept glancing around, her gaze never staying in one place for more than half a second. I saw her take a deep breath, close her eyes, pull her shirt over her head and toss it aside. She kept dancing, her breasts exposed and her eyes closed. Before I could get over to her to ask her what she thought she was doing, she unzipped her mini-skirt, let it fall to her feet, and kicked it toward her shirt.

I stood looking at Lydia's naked body as she opened her eyes and gazed at me. She smiled and increased the pace of her dancing, turning as she bounced and stepped. The other dancers started to notice. Some of them turned toward her, and others moved away, to the other side of the studio. I was struck by how pure she looked compared with all the other dancers, how everyone else could have been described and defined by what they wore, while every contour of Lydia's body was visible, moving without restraint. She turned back toward me and, just as I was about to say something to her, motioned for me to take off my shirt. Her motions reminded me that we weren't supposed to talk on the dance floor. I wondered if anyone had thought to include remaining clothed in the rules. As if in answer to my unspoken question, Amanda scurried around the edge of the dance floor, picking up Lydia's discarded shirt and mini-skirt and stepped to Lydia's side. Lydia stopped dancing as Amanda said something I couldn't hear into her ear. Amanda led her off the dance floor and over to the area in front of the shoe rack.

"The studio owner probably wouldn't like it," I heard Amanda whisper in a soft voice as I approached.

Lydia threw her clothes on, almost stumbling and falling as she stepped into her skirt, grabbed her shoes, and ran out the door, not looking at anyone or anything but the floor directly in front of her. I took my jacket and my socks and shoes from the cubby, said "Sorry," to Amanda, and followed Lydia outside. She leaned against the hood of my car, putting her shoes on. The concrete felt cold against my bare feet as I walked over, putting my jacket on, shifting my footwear from one hand to the other to get my arms into the sleeves, and stood beside Lydia. I didn't know what to say, but before I could utter something, Amanda rushed outside.

"You don't have to leave," she called as she scurried over to my car. "Please stay."

Lydia shook her head without looking at her and stepped over to the passenger door.

"Really," Amanda said.

Lydia tried to open the door, but my car was still locked. I reached into my pocket, found my key fob, and pressed the button to unlock it.

"And believe me, I can understand the appeal of dancing nude," Amanda continued. "I went to a clothing optional dance in Oregon last year, and it was an amazingly freeing experience. It's just that people here, in Texas, the Bible belt, aren't ready for something like that. Especially when it hadn't been advertised as clothing optional."

Lydia had gotten into the car and shut the door by the time Amanda finished, and I held up my hand to her.

"It's all right," I said. "I think she's feeling a bit embarrassed, so I'm going to take her home."

"All right," Amanda said, looking longingly at Lydia sitting in my car with her chin down on her chest. "I can talk to some of the others about maybe having a clothing optional dance one day. If there's enough interest..."

Amanda trailed off, and I opened my driver's side door. Lydia turned away when Amanda bent down as if to say something to her.

"Well," Amanda said, standing back up. "Please feel free to come back. If she still has a desire to dance nude, we could even talk about it in Circle, and see how everyone reacts."

I nodded, said "Thank you," and sat down as Amanda hurried back inside.

Sitting on the side of my seat, facing away from Lydia, I put my socks and shoes on without saying anything. A headache was starting, and I doubted that I had any Tylenol in the car. Once I finished with my shoes, I turned around, closed my door, and started my car. I turned my head to look at Lydia, but she was facing away from me, her head against the window. I backed out of the parking space and started driving toward Denton.

"Did you plan on that?" I finally asked when we had passed downtown Dallas. "Is that why you were so nervous when we got there?"

Lydia didn't say anything, but she did turn away from the window. I glanced over and saw that she had been crying.

"It's all right," I said, and I would have patted her thigh if she had been wearing more clothes over it.

"You must think I'm some kind of a freak," she said after a few minutes.

I was thinking about the first time we met, both of us naked in front of a class, of my demonstration of male anatomy to her in the changing room in January, and of watching her dance naked in the yoga studio when I said, "We're both freaks."

She smiled and laughed. "I can't believe I did that."

"It was certainly unexpected."

"It felt amazing. At least for just a little bit."

"But why?" I asked.

She shrugged. "Because. Everything I read said that you were free to dance and move how you wish. That your dance was supposed to be a reflection of you, uninhibited. I guess they didn't really mean it."

"They probably didn't expect anyone to want to dance naked," I said.

"I guess." She gazed out the window as I drove past the interchange with LBJ Freeway.

"So, why did you want to do that?" I asked.

"You know how freeing it feels in art class when you first take off the robe?"

"Mm-hm," I murmured.

"And during the gesture poses when you're moving every minute? And then, you have to get into a longer pose where you can't move, and it feels like you're confined again? Like your freedom just got taken away?"

"I never thought of it that way."

"I wanted to feel that freedom and keep moving. To dance completely free. I thought the people at that place would be OK with it."

"You should have tried going to a nudist resort or something," I said.

"I don't even know where one of those is. And besides, it's different when everyone else is naked than it is when you're the only one. You know. You've been modeling longer than I have."

"Yeah," I replied.

I could see her point, but showing up at your very first Ecstatic Dance and taking off all your clothes seemed a bit too extreme. At the Drafthouse that night we had tried to find her mysterious letter-writer, she had leaned toward me and told me in a soft voice that she was an exhibitionist. I had acted as if she had been joking, but I realized then that modeling could certainly be one outlet for that, especially in the mind of the person modeling. Today I had seen the full extent of Lydia's exhibitionism, and I realized that she hadn't been joking at the Drafthouse. I thought about the guy who had been staring up her skirt during the opening circle and wondered what he might really have been thinking at the time. I felt a sudden and urgent sense of responsibility to Lydia, to protect her from herself and from those who would take advantage of her.

My headache had eased but not dissipated by the time I parked in front of Lydia's apartment. The two of us sat in the car for a moment after I put it in park. Lydia stared out the window at the building in which she lived. I finally turned the car off and stepped out. I walked around and opened Lydia's door. She didn't move. I offered my hand

and she took it.

"Are you mad at me?" she asked as she got out.

"No, of course not" I said.

I walked her to her door.

"I'm sorry for ruining your Sunday," she said as she fumbled around in her purse for her keys.

"It's OK. It was actually kind of fun, especially seeing everyone's reactions."

Lydia got the key out, unlocked her door, and stepped inside, turning on the living room light. She stopped and looked at me when I didn't follow her.

"You coming in?"

"I don't think I should," I said.

Lydia grabbed my hand and pulled me inside. I didn't resist.

"It's all right," she said as she closed the door and turned the deadbolt.

"You want something to drink?" she asked.

"Sure. Dr. Pepper?"

"I just have Diet Coke. They're in the fridge. I'll be right back. I need to go pee."

She disappeared into the back of the apartment, leaving me standing alone in what passed for her living room. The ceiling was stained from past leaks, and the paint on the walls was peeling in places. Lydia's living room furniture consisted of a brown and red couch that was worn around the edges, a love seat that didn't match, and a coffee table that looked to be older than I was.

"Make yourself at home!" Lydia called from the back.

In the kitchen, the smell of bleach was strong although not overpowering, and I wondered how much time Lydia had spent cleaning her apartment in anticipation of today and the possibility of inviting me inside after the Ecstatic Dance. In the fridge was an unopened gallon of milk, a half a pound of hamburger meat, and a twelve pack of canned Diet Coke. Lydia had various condiments in the door. It looked like the fridge I had when I was twenty years old. I took one of the Diet Cokes and went back to the living room just as Lydia walked in. She was naked.

"That's much better," she said, smiling.

My first thought was that I should leave, but I stopped myself. She and I were both nude models and had seen each other without clothes on several occasions. Lydia had been nude the very first time I saw her. I also thought that if her being nude around me, where she would be safe, satisfied some need or desire she had, then I was going to help her do that.

"Absolutely," I said, probably a little too enthusiastically.

"Cool!"

She padded into the kitchen, her bare feet slapping the linoleum once she left the carpet of the living room, and opened her pantry. "Are you hungry? I can cook some Hamburger Helper."

"What kind?"

"Cheeseburger macaroni."

"Ooh, that's the best kind."

Lydia smiled and pulled a skillet out of the cabinet next to the stove. She had gone from crying from deep embarrassment to happy and lighthearted in just a few minutes. It was as if she had left her foul mood back in her bedroom with her clothes. I wondered if she might not be bi-polar. She cooked the Hamburger Helper, and we sat at her kitchen table and ate and talked until it started getting dark outside, moving into her living room after the food was gone. We never mentioned the Ecstatic Dance session, and we never talked about her lack of apparel. Her nudity was a non-issue. We did talk about art teachers and some of the other models. At one point, I asked her if she had received any more notes. She paused a moment as if she didn't know what I was talking about before saying that she hadn't. And she said that she still had no idea who had left the one she got in January.

We were on the last two Diet Cokes when she yawned, and I checked the time on my cell phone.

"It's after seven," I said.

"Holy shit!" Lydia said.

"I had better get going. I've got some reading to do for British lit."

"You could stay here," Lydia said.

She and I exchanged a glance. "I mean, you could sleep on the couch."

"I'd better not," I said.

I stood and gathered the empty Diet Coke cans from the coffee table to throw away. Lydia stood by the front door, one hand on her belly rubbing lightly in a circle just above her pubic mound. I could imagine exactly what she would be doing about five minutes after I left. Somehow, I think that's exactly what she intended me to imagine.

"I'm sorry the dance didn't go like you'd planned," I said.

"This was nice though. Just sitting around and talking." She smiled, and I really did give serious thought to spending the night and not just on the couch.

"Yes, it was," I agreed.

"Thank you for letting me be comfortable."

"You're more than welcome. It is your house after all."

"Be careful driving."

"I will. Good night Lydia."

I put my hand on the door knob. Lydia stood on her toes, put her hand on the back of my head, pulling me toward her, and kissed me on the mouth. I felt her small, firm bare breasts pressed against my chest. My hands touched her bare hips for just a moment as we kissed. Lydia drew back and smiled. "Good night," she said.

I thought about that kiss all the way home. It was the first time our lips had touched. Regardless of my paternal inclinations toward her, I hoped that it wouldn't be the last.

7

Dr. Brady explained our public protest project in detail the Monday after spring break. I had spent the time off from school working on the house. The idea of selling my house so that I could model full time prompted me to spend spring break landscaping the front yard and doing a thorough cleaning inside. The house was paid for, so whatever price I could get would all go straight into my reserve funds. I could put off law school and start modeling for colleges and art groups all over the area, building up a clientele and a reputation for dependability and professionalism. By the time the week ended, the house looked so nice that I hated to think of parting with it.

Lydia and I didn't get much of a chance to talk the week after the Ecstatic Dance debacle. Our modeling schedule did not coincide, and she always had to rush out of our Public Opinion class to get across campus for her next class. I didn't see or hear from her at all during spring break.

I was more than happy to be back at school once the break ended. I had a full schedule at UNT that first day with my regular classes and then a late afternoon modeling gig. We spent all of our Public Opinion class beginning our protest planning assignment. Dr. Brady split us up into groups of three or four to plan and organize a protest of some kind. The protest didn't have to be carried out, but we did have to plan the place and the time and make at least two signs. It could be on any issue currently in the news. We also had to have a plan for recruitment if our protest depended on having a large crowd. Our reports also had to include plans for contacting the media and the expected media coverage. Lydia was ecstatic to learn that she and I would be working together on the project. A thin blonde girl named

Crystal, who looked like she should still be in high school, would also be on our team.

Once Dr. Brady had thoroughly gone over the details of the assignment and answered questions, we had twenty minutes of class time left for a preliminary planning session with our teammates. Lydia, Crystal, and I put three desks in a circle in a corner of the room and started brainstorming. Since I was, by far, the oldest person in our group, I took charge of the meeting.

"The first thing we need to do is decide on an issue," I said. "What are the big topics right now? We have Trump and the wall, immigration in general, the national debt, gay marriage, abortion, global warming…"

"Climate change," Lydia said.

"Climate change. What else?"

"Prayer in schools," Crystal said.

Lydia shrugged. "Animal rights?"

"Yeah, animal rights," I said.

"You know, a few years ago, some models did a nude protest against wearing fur," Lydia continued. "The slogan was like, 'I'd rather wear nothing than fur' or something like that."

I couldn't help but smile. It was just like Lydia to think of something that involved nudity.

"I've read about those," I said. "So you want to do a naked protest?"

"Umm, no," Crystal said.

"It would be fun," Lydia said. "And part of this assignment is to try to get as much media coverage as possible, right? Naked people tend to get a lot of coverage."

"Yes, they do," I agreed, "but it's not always good coverage."

Lydia shrugged, a huge smile on her face. The two of us were almost laughing out loud.

"You guys know each other?" Crystal asked.

"We work together sometimes," Lydia told her. "In the art department. We model."

"Oh," Crystal said.

"Naked," Lydia added.

"Ohhhh. So you're serious about the naked thing."

I waved my hands as if trying to move that topic off the table. "Let's figure out what we're actually going to protest about before we decide on what kind of protest. Now, is there anything that anyone has really strong feelings about?"

Lydia slowly shook her head.

"I think kids ought to be able to pray in schools," Crystal said. "The whole separation of church and state thing is so out of proportion." I noticed the cross on Crystal's necklace and the little Bible in her stack of textbooks.

"OK, we have school prayer. Lydia?"

She shrugged. "I don't care much about that," she said.

"What do you care about?" Crystal asked.

"I don't know. I just think people ought to be able to do what they want."

"Like prayer in schools?" Crystal said.

"If they want," Lydia replied.

"OK," I said. "Let's think about this. We are doing this for a grade, so we want it to be impactful and thoughtful. Prayer in schools sounds like a topic from the sixties or seventies. No offense. I think we should do something current, the most polarizing, controversial topic we can find."

"And what is that?" Lydia asked.

"What would you say it is?"

She shrugged. "Guns."

"Ok," I said. "Guns. Gun control. How about you Crystal? What do you say?"

She was quiet for a moment. "Abortion," she finally said.

"Abortion," I repeated. Abortion had been in the news lately with the State of New York just passing a law expanding abortion access. "And what's your opinion on abortion?" I said, even though I knew I didn't need to ask.

"I am one hundred percent pro-life," Crystal said.

"Good. I am too. Lydia?"

She shrugged. "I don't know. I've always thought of myself as pro-choice."

"Pro-choice. Why?" I asked.

Lydia shrugged. "Because I think a woman should be able to have control over her own body."

I didn't want to get into a debate on abortion with Lydia since I knew I wasn't going to change her mind in time to do this assignment. But I still thought abortion would be our best topic even if we didn't all agree.

"How firmly pro-choice are you?" I asked.

"I don't know. Pretty firm, I guess."

I sighed. "Since we don't all agree on abortion, do you have another topic to suggest?"

"Wait," Crystal said and turned to Lydia, her face set in a determined scowl. "What about the baby? When that baby is there, it doesn't have a choice. What about that baby's body?"

Lydia rolled her eyes. "First of all, it's not a baby yet. It's a fetus. And it's inside the woman's body. She should have the ultimate decision about her own body."

"She had that decision before she hopped into bed with a guy. Once that baby is there, it's alive. And abortion kills—"

"Crystal," I interrupted, "I agree with you, but I don't think we want to get into this kind of debate now."

"No, if we are going to do something meaningful and important, it should be this. If she doesn't like it, maybe she should switch teams."

I turned to Lydia, and I could see that she was fighting to hold her tongue.

"Lydia," I said, "would you be willing to take a minor role in a pro-life demonstration?"

"Even though I don't believe in it?"

I sat contemplating for just a moment. Images of Lydia nude on the model platform, dancing at the yoga studio, and in her apartment cooking Cheeseburger Macaroni Hamburger Helper flashed in my mind as I thought about her first suggestion about the naked fur protestors.

"What if we did the protest naked," I said.

"What!?" Crystal exclaimed.

"We do a naked pro-life protest," I replied.

"That sounds like something the pro-abortion people would do."

"Pro-choice," Lydia asserted. "Nobody is pro-abortion."

"It does sound like something the pro-choice people would do," I said, "and that's why I think it would make an impact."

Lydia didn't say a word, but I could tell by the smirk on her face that she liked the idea.

"I don't understand," Crystal said. "What would be the point of being naked?"

"Let's look at it this way. When you think of a naked person, what does it make you think of?"

"Freedom," Lydia said.

"Pornography," Crystal said.

"What else?"

"I don't know," Crystal replied. "Cold, poor, ashamed, vulnerable."

"Vulnerable," I repeated. "As in defenseless. Like a baby. Like an unborn baby about to get ripped out of its mother's womb."

Lydia and Crystal were both quiet for what seemed like a long time. I was hoping that Lydia would go along with the idea. I personally had no problem protesting abortion. Glenda and I had struggled through so many months of fertility treatments that the thought of a couple or a woman getting pregnant and then ending the pregnancy by murdering the baby just ripped at my heart. Didn't these people know that there were thousands of couples like Glenda and me who would have loved that child? When we looked at adoption and the high costs associated with it, I thought that the process would have been much easier and cheaper if abortion had been illegal. The law of supply and demand would have forced the costs down. But I wanted Lydia to go along with it because I really wanted to work with her on this project, although I couldn't explain why.

"How would it work?" Lydia asked.

"I don't know yet. Would you be willing to do it given your views on abortion?"

"Where would this protest be?"

"I figured it would be on the street in front of an abortion clinic somewhere," I replied.

Lydia was quiet but nodded her head.

"Awesome!" I said.

"Wait," Crystal whined, "what just happened? There is no way I'm going to let anyone but my future husband see me naked."

"You won't have to," I said. "Lydia and I will handle the actual protest. We'll need you for support, to help with the signs, et cetera."

Crystal was shaking her head. "This is in theory, right? We're not actually going to do this."

"I don't know," I said. "I think we would get a better grade if we did carry it out."

"I can't do this. It's wrong."

"What's so wrong about it?" I asked.

"Going naked in public, that's what's wrong. It's indecent."

I pointed to the Bible in her books. "Could you look up Isaiah chapter 20 and read the first three or four verses?"

Crystal looked at me with exasperation before pulling out her Bible and thumbing to Isaiah. I watched her mouth move as she silently read the verses. I've never been great with finding passages in the Bible, but when I started modeling for art classes twenty years ago, I looked up some things to use to defend the job amongst my church friends. I had always remembered Isaiah 20, where God told Isaiah to go naked and barefoot throughout the land for three years as a warning to Egypt. When Crystal was done reading, she closed the Bible and put it back in the stack.

"See?" I said. "Public nudity does have legitimate and godly uses. And what could be godlier than trying to protect the unborn? Besides, if we show up at an abortion clinic and just walk around with signs, who's going to care? People do that every day anyway. Doing it naked makes it unusual, makes people notice. And makes people think. And you know what's wrong with people's perceptions of pro-life protesters?"

"What?" Crystal asked.

"That they are all a bunch of Bible-thumping religious extremists. That they are all holier-than-thou, don't drink, never have sex until they're married, Jesus freaks."

"But I am a Jesus freak," Crystal said. "And proud of it."

"I know. And it's so easy for people on the other side to target that. They get people to criticize the protestors rather than really think about the issue. Because the pro-abortion argument is all built on lies. The biggest one is that that baby in the womb isn't really a baby, that it somehow isn't a human being yet."

I could see that Lydia was about to say something, so I held my hand up to stop her and shook my head.

"Another lie is that to be pro-life you have to be a religious zealot. This kind of demonstration will blow that lie out of the water."

The more I tried to convince first Lydia and then Crystal about the merits of this project, the more I convinced myself that our protest was important and that it was something that had to be done.

"OK," Crystal said. "But I'm not getting naked."

"You don't have to," I said. "We'll need you to help with our clothes and to bail us out of jail, in case we get arrested."

"You really think they would arrest us?" Lydia asked, a note of concern in her voice.

"This is the middle of the Bible belt, so I'm pretty sure they would. We need to plan on it, anyway."

The three of us sat quietly for a moment, contemplating our plan.

"I can't believe we're actually going to do this," Crystal said. "You two are crazy."

I wrote down available meeting times that would fit each person's schedule. We decided to meet in the Student Union building that Thursday evening at 5:30. I had an art class that day that ended at 5:00, so I knew I would already be in Denton. Crystal lived in a dorm and Lydia's apartment was within walking distance of the campus. Neither would have a problem getting there.

The two girls both had to get to other classes when the period ended. I spent the next hour in the library, looking at top results from a Google search of "nudity in protests." There were supposedly 865,000 hits, but I clicked on a just a few links in the first two pages. Some of the articles were loaded with large color photos of nude protesters. I felt a bit self-conscious looking at those on a public computer in the middle of the university library, and I wound up hitting the Back button without even reading the articles on a few of them.

After my last class ended, I did a long reclining pose for an advanced figure drawing class, giving me time to think. What had seemed like such a good idea, a necessary idea, now seemed crazy. Lydia and I would get arrested for indecent exposure, and no one other than the witnesses at the scene would know why. Our message would get lost, and there was a very real danger of getting placed on a sex offender list for life. The more I thought about the legal aspects of what we proposed doing, the more I thought that I should consult a criminal attorney before we did it. I left campus feeling defeated and confused, a far cry from the elation I felt that morning at the possibility of being able to do something meaningful and impactful.

If I changed my mind about doing this insane protest, Lydia would throw a fit. The only consolation I took was that, for our grade, we didn't have to carry out the protest after planning it. I wondered how differently the police and courts would treat a woman arrested for public nudity rather than a man. It occurred to me that I was risking a lot more than Lydia was. I therefore felt that the go/no-go call was mine.

A drawing instructor at the University of Dallas had booked me to model the following day, my very first time to ever work there. I arrived at the Irving campus almost two hours early to ensure that I would be able to get all the paperwork done, forgetting that I had already faxed in part of it the week before so that their Human Resources department could do the background check. As I parked my car, I thought about how funny it was that the University of Dallas was in Irving and then remembered that the University of Texas at Dallas was in Richardson. I was a lifelong resident of Fort Worth and its surrounding cities within Tarrant County, but I would never even consider living in Dallas. I took satisfaction in noting that at least two large institutions with Dallas in their names also didn't want to be in Dallas. Even the most famous of Dallas institutions, the Dallas Cowboys football team, played their home games not in Dallas but in Arlington.

The class went well, and I wound up with three more bookings for the semester. During the long pose at the end of the class, I thought about the lawyers I knew. I had worked with several at the firm that had represented me in Glenda's wrongful death suit against Trinity Ironworks. But I had never gotten to know any one of them well enough to ask about something like this protest project. Besides that, they only handled civil cases. My questions were regarding criminal law.

I went further back and thought of Greg Duplantis. Glenda and I had attended the same Bible study class with him and his wife. I had lost contact with him over the past four years since Glenda's wreck. Now that I thought about it, I had lost contact with everyone from the church since then. I couldn't even remember Greg's wife's name. But I did remember that Greg was an attorney. I didn't know what kind though. Our previous interactions had all been at church functions.

I googled Greg's name as soon as I got home from modeling and found that he worked for the Tarrant County District Attorney's office. Great, I thought, maybe he would become the prosecutor on my case. Still, I clicked on the email link on his department profile page and started typing.

"Greg," I wrote, "it has been way too long. How are you? I hope you don't think it strange that I am writing you out of the blue after so many years. Life without Glenda has been a struggle, but I think I'm finally beginning to emerge from the fog. I was wondering if you were available for lunch one day this week. I'm taking classes at UNT now. I have a school assignment that I have a couple of hypothetical questions about, and I think you may be the person to answer them. My schedule varies from week to week, but I'd love to arrange something."

I used my auto signature at the bottom of the email which included my cell phone number, looked over what I wrote, and hit send. My phone rang twenty minutes later. I answered it even though I had just gotten into a Call of Duty match online.

"Hello."

"Hello, David? Greg Duplantis here."

I found what I hoped was a decent hiding place for my Call of Duty avatar and muted the TV.

"Hey Greg, how are you?"

"Good, good. It was awesome to hear from you."

"Yeah," I said. What was I supposed to say, that I too thought it was awesome that he got to hear from me?

"Listen, I'm getting ready to go into court, but I wanted to see if you could do lunch on Thursday."

"Yeah, I could do Thursday."

"You know where La Familia is, just off Seventh Street?"

"I do," I said. It had been one of my favorite places once upon a time.

"How about 11:20 there. Beat the lunch rush."

"Sounds great to me."

"All right," Greg said. "It'll be good to see you. Just the other day, Carol was talking about Glenda, and we were both wondering how you were doing."

Now that Greg had mentioned his wife's name, I wondered how I could have forgotten it. "It'll be good to see you again too."

"See you Thursday then."

"Looking forward to it."

I ended the call just in time to see my Call of Duty match finish. My team had lost, and I had finished in last place. Thursday, though, was the perfect day to meet for lunch. I would catch up on school work in the morning, have lunch with Greg and hopefully get my questions answered, drive to Denton, model for my 2 to 5 class, and then meet with Lydia and Crystal in the Student Union.

Dr. Brady spent the entire hour lecturing during our Public Opinion class on Wednesday. Lydia basically said hi and bye to me once class was done and took off across campus. Crystal walked beside me when I left the classroom.

"You can't actually do this," she said to me.

"I'm having second thoughts myself," I told her. "But I'm going to talk to a lawyer tomorrow."

"Good."

"It would be nice to be able to report actual results rather than speculation."

"Then we need to change our plan," she said.

"We'll talk about that tomorrow."

I smiled and walked toward the Jack in the Box adjacent to the campus. Crystal continued on to wherever she normally went after Public Opinion.

8

I arrived at La Familia a few minutes after eleven on Thursday. I peeked inside, but Greg wasn't there. It had occurred to me that I might not recognize Greg from a distance after not seeing him in over five years, but no one in the restaurant looked even close to how I remembered him. The restaurant host tried to seat me, but I told him I was waiting for someone. I stepped back outside and walked over to the art supply store two doors down. Inside was a bulletin board covered with business cards of artists and art dealers. I saw one model's card, a female whose name I didn't recognize. I should print business cards of my own if I were serious about modeling full-time.

I nodded to the guy behind the register at the art supply store and stepped back outside. I saw Greg a couple of minutes later, getting out of a new Jaguar that he parked in a just vacated spot right by the entrance to the restaurant, wearing a gray suit and blue tie. I felt underdressed in my jeans and t-shirt. If Greg only knew how underdressed I would be from 2:00 to 5:00 that very afternoon, I thought with some amusement.

"David," he said when he saw me, "how are you? You look great."

"Thanks," I said, shaking his hand, knowing that he was lying. "I think you've got me beat though."

He looked down at his suit and shrugged.

"Part of the job."

I nodded toward his Jaguar. "It must pay well."

Greg laughed but didn't say anything. We went inside and got seated. We started with small talk before the waiter came and took our order. Chips and salsa arrived soon afterward, and we both dove in.

"You said you were doing a school project," Greg said.

"Yeah. I'm working on a political science degree. Pre-law."

"That sounds great."

"One of the classes I'm taking is on public opinion. We have a unit on public protests, and we have to plan a hypothetical protest and write a report on what we think would happen."

"Yeah."

"I came up with the idea of doing an abortion protest outside a clinic. The people doing the protest would have signs saying 'naked and defenseless' and 'protect the defenseless.'"

"As long as they stay on public property and not set foot on the clinic's property, I don't see an issue with that."

"And they're naked when they are doing this."

"OK," Greg said, drawing the K sound out.

"If the protestors are arrested, what happens to them?"

"Depends on the prosecutor," he said. "And most prosecutors do try to gauge public opinion on minor cases that get any press. That would be a strange case. The people who would tend to agree with the protestors would be very disapproving of the nudity. And the people who would be OK with the nudity would strongly disagree with their position. So I don't know what they would be trying to accomplish."

"Well," I said, scooping a huge bite of salsa on a curved chip and tossing it into my mouth. Once I finished chewing, I continued. "What could the prosecutor do? What does the law give him power to do?"

"You mean, would they be charged with indecent exposure?"

"Yeah, something like that."

Greg ate a salsa covered chip and shook his head. "Indecent exposure requires some proof of sexual gratification. The law reads that a person has to be exposing him or herself to sexually arouse or gratify someone. That someone could be the offender or the person or persons who see him. I think a prosecutor would be hard pressed to prove that in the case of your protestors."

"So what are we looking at then?"

"Disorderly conduct. Class C misdemeanor and a max fine of 500 dollars."

"500?" I asked. "That's it? No jail time? No sex offender registration?

"Well, if the protestors are arrested, they would see the jail. But they could also just receive citations." He paused to eat another chip. "Do you remember that music video that was shot in Dallas a few years ago?"

I shook my head.

"The girl doing it stripped down to nothing in Dealey Plaza. Once she was naked, she dropped to the pavement right were the bullet hit JFK's head."

I vaguely remembered reading something about that, but it had been awhile.

"She wasn't arrested the day of the shoot. But after the DA saw the video, he went and found witnesses who were there and who would swear out a complaint against the singer. She wound up having to pay the 500 dollar fine for disorderly conduct."

The libertarian in me was appalled. Why would a district attorney spend time and money trying to find so-called victims for what seemed to be an unnecessary prosecution? Who had actually been victimized by the singer's nudity? I didn't know who she was or even what point she was trying to make in the video, but I didn't care. She should have been allowed to make that point. Wasn't that what the First Amendment to the Constitution was for?

"Interesting," was all I could manage to say.

"So even if your protestors are able to get away from the scene without an arrest, they may not be getting away."

"I see. And this singer—she didn't have to register as a sex offender or anything?"

"Oh, no. A class C misdemeanor is—well, a speeding ticket is a class C misdemeanor."

Our waiter brought our plates to our table and set them down in front of us. I was reminded why La Familia used to be my favorite Mexican restaurant as I took my first bite of brisket taco.

"What are the chances," I said once I had washed the bite of taco down with a drink of water, "that the protestors get a jury who approves of what they did and doesn't want to convict them?"

"That's something called jury nullification," Greg said. "It's not something that we prosecutors like all that much."

"Jury nullification?"

"Yeah. Basically, the jury agrees with the facts of the charges that a defendant violated the law or statute but, for whatever reason, disagrees with the law or doesn't believe it should be applied in that particular case."

"I see."

"This is all hypothetical," Greg said, "right?"

"Yeah. It's for a class assignment."

"OK. I don't want you to think I'm giving legal advice."

"Oh no," I said. We both took another bite of food before I steered the conversation in another direction by asking how Carol was.

The rest of the lunch was friendly. Greg caught me up on people in the church that I hadn't even thought about in several years. And of course, he invited me to both the service and our old Bible study class that Sunday.

"I don't know," I told him. "I quit going because the place reminded me of Glenda. It just... I couldn't go any more."

"That's understandable," Greg said. "If you ever need anything, you let me know, OK?"

"I will," I said, knowing that I never would unless it was to ask for legal help.

I objected to Greg picking up the tab for lunch, but not that strongly. Once he had paid, we walked outside together.

"Greg, it was really good to see you again," I said, extending my hand.

Instead of shaking, he embraced me in a bear hug.

"You too David," he said. "We'll be praying for you."

I thought about telling him to be careful what he prayed for, but I didn't because he would, of course, ask what I meant by that.

"Thank you," I said. "And thank you for lunch."

"Any time."

I left La Familia a few minutes before 12:30. Construction had Interstate 35W down to one lane on the north side of Fort Worth. The backup was over three miles. I spent most of the time in traffic checking the clock and trying to figure out if I would be better off taking an alternate route. I stuck with it and got through the construction zone, but I didn't walk into the UNT art building until 1:55. The elevator was notorious for its slow, rattling ascents, so I bounded up the stairs, and almost ran to the changing room. It was already empty. I stripped, throwing my clothes into a pile rather than folding them, donned the robe, grabbed a sheet, and shuffled to class. I was modeling in advanced figure drawing. The door to the beginning figure class was still open when I walked past, and I caught a glimpse of Lydia sitting on the edge of the model stand. She had already stripped, leaning back on both hands, legs apart with one foot on the stand and the other on the floor, flashing her most intimate feminine body parts to everyone in the room and anyone who happened to walk by in the corridor. I was already a couple of steps past the room before I realized what I had just seen. I backed up and waved at Lydia, both to say hello and to let her know that she was flashing the world. She smiled and waved back but didn't make any move to cover herself. I thought about closing the door, but I didn't want to step on the toes of the drawing instructor. I couldn't remember who was teaching that class. Come to think of it, I didn't remember seeing Lydia's name on the schedule. She must have been substituting for someone.

I continued to my own class. Robin wanted me to do one long three-hour pose, but she had arranged pillows and padding on the platform so I would be comfortable. I took a reclining pose, staring at a point on the ceiling and thought about Lydia. She must have some undiagnosed clinical disorder regarding her exhibitionism, I thought. Modeling for art classes was probably the safest outlet possible for such a thing. I wondered if she hadn't tried dancing in a strip club somewhere. But she wasn't built like a typical stripper. Her breasts were small and looked like they could have belonged to a young overweight boy rather than a fully-grown woman. She was a little thick in the waist although I wouldn't have ever thought of her as fat. Her thighs were thick compared to the rest of her body, but I thought they made her that much more attractive. Her rounded backside was her best feature, at least from the neck down. It was her sandy hair, her winning smile, her button of a nose, and, most of all, her sparkling green eyes that made her beautiful.

My heart was thumping a little too rapidly, and I realized that I was fully exposed in an art class. I took a peek down and saw with some dismay that my arousal had become visibly noticeable. I tried to think of other things, but images of the little demonstration of male anatomy that I had given Lydia thrust itself into my thoughts, the way she had watched me and the way I had felt about it. Things were getting worse. I didn't want to have to ask Robin for a break. My thoughts went to my old standby of Nelson Cruz running back, extending for the catch that would secure a World Series championship for the Rangers, and the ball zipping by just out of his reach and bounding off the wall back toward the infield. I replayed that twice, trying to push all thoughts and images of Lydia out of my mind before I made the connection of the name Nelson, Cruz's first name and Lydia's last name. Lydia had been sitting on the edge of that platform with her legs spread, saying "look at me!" I thought of the guys in the corridor ahead of me when I had been walking toward this class. Had they seen? Were they talking about Lydia? Nelson Cruz reached for the ball again and missed it again, over and over.

After about five minutes of Nelson Cruz, I sighed. The crisis was over. Blood was returning to less conspicuous parts of my body. Robin asked if I needed a break.

"What time is it?" I asked.

She looked at the clock on the wall, which was out of my field of vision in that pose. "It is two-fifty."

Had I really been in the pose for over forty-five minutes? "I'm OK," I said. "When were you going to give the class a break?"

"Can you go 20 more minutes?"

"Sure," I said.

The pose was easy. There was nothing strenuous about it, and I wasn't losing feeling in any hands or feet. My thoughts returned to Lydia, but I managed to keep them more paternalistic rather than physical. In terms of modeling, I felt like I was her mentor. She and I had shared the model stand on only her second modeling gig. When she had had questions about modeling after that, she had asked me. Therefore, I also felt protective of her. But how could I protect her from her own behavior? Not only was I concerned about her safety, but now I worried about her losing her modeling job for flashing people out in the hall. Of course, when I modeled here fifteen years ago, there were a few instructors who had left the classroom door open for most of the class, while I was posing. I never worried about it because it was just art students in the halls. But the people in charge of the art department now seemed stricter about keeping models from being out in the open. At least, that was the impression I got from the way the current teachers ran their classes.

Of course, if anyone complained about Lydia's display to the corridor, it was the instructor who was more likely to get into trouble. Models are expected to be a little strange. It takes a unique person to remove all of his or her clothes and then try to stay in one position for long periods of time when it was the nature of the human body to be in constant motion of some kind. The aches and loss of feeling that I got in some poses were enough to convince me of that. Yet, we continue on, both because it is our job and because we want to see ourselves portrayed in the artwork. I wondered if Lydia cared about the drawings of her or if she modeled just to expose herself to groups of people. I thought of Maria, who was so shy about dressing and undressing in front of any of us in the changing room. What had been her motivation for modeling? Her name had not been on this semester's model's contact list. Had she gotten what she wanted out of her modeling experience?

When the break arrived, I donned the robe and walked back to the changing room. The door to the beginning figure class was closed when I passed by. I checked my phone. There were twelve new emails. Eleven of them were junk. The one that wasn't was from the gallery manager of an art center in Arlington. They were starting Saturday morning figure drawing sessions in April and wanted to know my availability to model. I typed a quick message telling her that my Saturdays were free and that I would love to model for her group.

When I put my phone away, I grabbed a timesheet and filled it out. I looked down at my feet when I was finished. I had been in such a hurry to get to class that I had left my slippers in my modeling bag. The bottoms of my feet were black with charcoal dust. I wet some paper towels and washed and dried them. By the time I was done, it was almost time to go back to class. I put my slippers on, grabbed my timesheet, and walked down the corridor back to class. I wondered what kind of pose Lydia was doing as I passed by the closed door of the other drawing room.

The rest of the class passed, and I almost fell asleep in the pose. I've never quite let myself fall all the way asleep while modeling, but I got pretty close in that class. Robin had been very good in setting up the platform, and the pose was one of the most comfortable long poses I'd ever done. She kept the students drawing, and me in the pose, for as long as she possibly could before calling an end to class. I stood up and worked the kinks out. Even the most comfortable pose can make a body stiff after over an hour. The students started clapping and applauding.

"Yes," Robin said. "Very good job David. Thank you."

I must have blushed. I wonder what I must have looked like there, totally comfortable being naked but blushing because of the accolades I was getting. Instead of covering up and shrinking away, I decided to play it up. I put one hand across my belly and one behind my back and took a bow. This drew some laughter from the students.

"Thank you," I said to the class.

I put my robe and slippers on, took my timesheet from the

instructor's desk, making sure that Robin had signed it, and started for the door.

"Really," Robin said, "that was very good. So many models here can't hold a pose."

I thought about that for a second. Most of the UNT models were young students. I was trying to be a full-time professional model, and Robin's comments gave me encouragement.

"Thank you," I said again. "I always try my best."

"Yes, you do."

I headed toward the changing room and saw that the other figure class had been dismissed. When I got to the changing room, Lydia was sitting fully clothed in one of the chairs looking at her phone.

"Hey David," she said, when I walked in.

"Hi Lydia. How are you? How was your class?"

"It was fun," she said.

"I'll bet. I saw you before it started."

"Yeah, I know."

I kicked off my slippers, picked them up, and put them in my bag.

"That was quite a view," I said.

"Thank you."

I took my robe off and stuffed it into the bag.

"I hope you don't get in trouble for it."

I almost laughed at the thought that I was criticizing her for being naked, while I stood there naked. She was smiling at me when I looked at her.

"I won't," she said. "The door was only open for half a minute. You just got lucky."

"Yes, I did. But it wasn't anything I hadn't seen before."

"But still, you stopped."

"I didn't say I was tired of seeing it." As soon as I said it, I wondered why I was encouraging her. Maybe my present state of dress, or undress, was affecting my thinking. I looked down and saw myself in the beginning stages of arousal. Lydia was watching and apparently enjoying.

"You really are hung like a horse," she said.

I grabbed my pants and put them on.

"What can I say," I said. "You bring out the best in me." Stop flirting with her, I told myself. What was wrong with me?

Lydia laughed and stood up as I put my shirt on.

"Are you ready for our meeting with Miss Goody Two Shoes?" she asked.

"Yes, I am. Oh, and I talked with a lawyer friend today."

"Really? So we're really going to do this?"

"I don't know about that yet. We still need to talk about it. But Crystal did tell me on Wednesday that she didn't think she could be a part of it."

"That Bible verse you showed her Monday didn't change her mind?"

"I guess not."

"What did it say?"

I sat down to put on my socks and shoes. "God told Isaiah to go through the land completely naked and barefooted for three years as a sign against Egypt and Cush."

"Really? I guess I need to read more of the Bible."

"You should," I said.

"How did you know where that was?"

"I grew up in a very conservative Baptist church," I told her. "When I first started modeling back when I was 20, the few people who knew about it were not amused. So I armed myself. If I could show them where, in the Bible, nudity wasn't condemned, they would leave me alone."

"Did they?"

"I don't know. The subject rarely came up. No one wanted to talk about it."

"That's cool."

"Yeah," I said. I got my shoes on and my modeling bag packed and slung over my shoulder. "You ready?"

"Yep."

We walked across campus together, the sun still bright in the sky. Daylight Savings Time was in full force now, and the afternoon sunshine was lasting a lot longer. Leaves, bright green, were sprouting on the trees. Lydia and I seemed to be the only people walking toward the middle of campus. Everyone else looked to be heading away for the day.

"I saw that we are on the schedule together next week," Lydia said.

"Really?" I hadn't checked my email since the break in class.

"Tuesday morning, 8 to 11."

"Awesome," I said.

"We should do some really cool interactive pose."

"Like what?"

"I saw a Rodin sculpture once, called *The Kiss*," Lydia said. "We could do that."

I'd just gotten out of a class where the mere thought of Lydia had almost caused me great embarrassment. How would my body react to a three-hour nude embrace with her, in front of an entire class?

"We'll have to see what the teacher wants us to do," I said. "Do you remember who it was?"

Lydia pulled her phone out and looked it up as we walked.

"It's Audrey," she said.

I remembered how pleased Audrey had been with the way Lydia and I had posed together the previous semester, and I wondered if she had requested that the two of us be matched up again. Audrey just might go for Lydia's *The Kiss* idea, I thought.

Even though we had agreed to meet at 5:30, Crystal was already sitting at a table eating a sandwich when Lydia and I walked in at ten after five. She saw us before we saw her and waved us over.

"Hey guys," Crystal said.

Lydia was looking at her sandwich. "That looks good," she said, setting her backpack in a chair. "Are you going to get anything to eat?" Lydia asked me.

The brisket taco lunch at La Familia was sitting heavily in my system. "I'm not hungry."

"All right. I'll be back."

Lydia took off for the food line, and I sat across from Crystal.

"And how are you?" I asked her.

"I'm good. Busy though. The semester is starting to wind down."

"How many hours are you taking?"

"Eighteen."

"Damn," I said. "I'll bet you are busy."

Crystal took a bite of her sandwich and washed it down with a drink from her straw.

"Have you talked to her?" she asked, motioning toward Lydia with a nod of her head.

"About the project? Not much."

"She's crazy."

"I know. But I'm crazy too. You have to be a little crazy to do the job we do," I said, echoing the thoughts that I'd had in class.

"Why do you do it?"

"Because I can. And so many people either wouldn't or couldn't. Some of the people who would be willing to take off their clothes couldn't hold a pose to save their lives. But most people just wouldn't be able to be nude in front of a whole class for three hours. I love the job, actually. I guess I'm a bit of a narcissist."

"You'd kind of have to be," Crystal said.

Lydia came back with a chicken salad sandwich, a bag of chips, and a fountain drink. She set her food on the table, dropped her backpack from the chair to the floor between her and me, and sat down.

"So where do we start?" Lydia said as she unwrapped her sandwich.

"If we are really going to do this," I said, "we need to discuss the possible consequences. I had lunch with an old lawyer friend of mine today."

"Did you tell him what you're going to do?" Crystal asked.

"I presented it to him as a hypothetical scenario for a report I was writing for class. Which is true. Except for the hypothetical part."

"What did he say?" Lydia asked.

"He said that for the charge of indecent exposure to apply, there would have to be evidence of sexual gratification. Or the intent to sexually gratify someone. Or something like that. But we'll be protesting the killing of defenseless babies. They couldn't prove any kind of sexual intent on our part in a million years."

As I said this, I thought of Lydia sitting on the edge of that model stand with her legs spread. I only hoped that if and when we got out there, she would behave in a solemn manner, as if she really were protesting the legality of abortion.

"So what," Crystal asked. "They're just going to let you protest naked?"

"No, I doubt it," I replied. "He said that we would probably get charged for disorderly conduct which carries a maximum fine of five hundred dollars. Then he told me about some singer who stripped down in Dealer Plaza for a music video."

"Erykah Badu," Lydia said. "I saw that video."

Of course, Lydia would know all about it, I thought. She was probably jealous of the singer for getting to walk around naked in public like she had.

"They, like, issued her a citation after the fact," Lydia said.

"Yes. My friend said the DA had to go out and find a witness to file a complaint."

"Sounds like a PR stunt," Lydia said.

"The video sounds like a PR stunt," Crystal chimed in. "How many more people heard her name because of what she did?" She looked at Lydia and said, "Had you ever heard of her before?"

"No," Lydia replied, "I hadn't."

"Well, the whole point of our doing this protest nude is to get attention from people who would have ignored us otherwise," I reminded them.

Lydia and Crystal both took bites of their sandwiches. I thought about going to get myself a drink, but Lydia offered hers to me. I smiled and took a sip from her straw.

"Thanks," I said.

"So, what about kids," Crystal said. "What if there are children nearby when you start to strip down?"

Lydia and I looked at each other. She shrugged.

"Honestly," I said, "it's not kids we need to worry about. It's the parents of the kids. I don't think seeing a naked person is going to hurt a kid one iota, but our society has ingrained us into thinking that we need to protect children from seeing certain things, whether those things are really harmful or not. I actually think it would be healthy for kids to see a nude adult, especially if they have an honest parent who would answer their questions."

"Are you serious?" Crystal asked, giving me an incredulous look.

"I agree," Lydia said. "People in America are too uptight."

"Have you ever been outside America?" Crystal asked.

"No. But I read a lot."

"The main thing is," I said, "are we willing to pay the 500-dollar fines if we get cited or arrested?"

Lydia looked down at her sandwich. "I don't have five hundred dollars."

"But if you had to work extra hours to make it, would you be willing to part with it for this cause?"

"Sure," she said.

"OK," I said. "Crystal. We would need you as our support person. Handle our clothes and bail if we need it. Are you in?"

"Oh my God," she said. "I guess so. I mean, I need the grade."

"Let's plan all the details, and then we'll see where we are," I said. "Does that sound good?

They both nodded. Lydia got her spiral notebook from her bag and wrote down all the necessary information. We talked about signage, what we wanted them to say and how we wanted them to look. The time and location of the protest became the biggest point of discussion.

By the end of our meeting, we had come up with two possibilities for a place. One was the Planned Parenthood in Fort Worth. I didn't want to do it in Tarrant County just because I didn't want to have Greg Duplantis involved in any way. The option I liked was an abortion clinic in North Dallas near LBJ Freeway and Greenville Avenue. Part of the assignment was to have a plan to get media attention for whatever protest each team was doing. I argued that doing the protest in Dallas would increase our chances of getting coverage. We decided to put Crystal in charge of contacting the television stations and the newspapers. We thought about talking to radio stations but decided that the more visual media outlets were better suited. Besides that, there just wasn't enough time to contact every media source in Dallas.

It was decided that I would look at the calendar and determine when a good day for the protest would be. The project was due on April 22nd, so I had three Saturdays from which to choose. April 20th was out of the question, and I ruled out April 13th because I didn't think that gave us enough time to write our reports and prepare our presentation. That left March 30th and April 6th. The 30th was just a little over a week away, and I didn't know if we would be ready that soon. So I was pretty much counting on April 6th if the weather cooperated. Of course, a naked protest in foul weather would make our point even more, being defenseless against the elements.

We left the Student Union at a little past six. Crystal took off one way, and Lydia and I walked toward the art building. She stayed beside me until we reached the edge of the campus.

"You want a ride home?" I asked her.

"Sure."

We walked to my car, but I was parked so far away that by the time we got there, I thought that she might have had a shorter walk if she had just gone straight home.

"So, do you think we'll really get arrested?" she asked me once we got seated in my car.

"I don't know," I said.

"Have you ever been arrested?"

"No. You?"

"No," Lydia replied.

"I hope we don't. Maybe we should set a time limit on the protest. Like fifteen minutes or so. If we stay there long enough, we will get arrested. Maybe we could get away with it if we leave after fifteen minutes."

"Do you think that's enough time to get our point across?"

"It depends," I said. "I've never done anything like this before."

"Me neither. Exciting, isn't it. I'm excited."

I thought of her emerging from her bedroom naked after the Ecstatic Dance session and of her sitting naked on the model platform earlier that day. "I'll bet you are," I said.

I pulled up in front of her apartment building and put the car into park.

"My apartment is a mess," she said softly.

"That's OK. I've got to get home."

She leaned over and kissed my cheek.

"You're the best," she said.

"Thanks."

"I mean it. You're like the only real friend I got. I live alone here because my roommates… Well, I didn't get along with any of them."

"Well," I said, feeling my heart open, "the problem must have been theirs."

We sat looking at each other for what seemed like a very long time. I certainly felt something for this girl, but I couldn't explain what it was. I was incapable of loving her; I knew that. But still, being around her was such a relief. I hadn't been able to relax around anyone in such a long time, not even my own family. And yet, I was constantly letting my guard down around her, even flirting with her when I kept trying not to.

"Thanks for the ride," she finally said and got out of the car. "See you tomorrow."

I watched her to her door. Once she was safely inside, I drove home.

9

I did see Lydia the next day, in our Public Opinion class, but she left so quickly that I didn't get a chance to talk to her. Crystal walked out of the room with me and told me that she had a list of newspaper and TV contacts ready, one of whom, at the local FOX affiliate, was her second cousin. All she needed was a time and place.

"Is April 6th OK with you? 9 AM?"

"Sure," she said.

"In Dallas. You'll have to drive. Or I guess you could drive my car if you had to. If the police'll let you have it if we're arrested," I added.

"I can drive."

"OK. Don't send anything until I make sure that date is OK with Lydia," I said.

"This is crazy." Crystal shook her head. "You're really doing this."

"Unless I chicken out at the last minute."

"I doubt that'll happen," Crystal said. She started walking away from me. "See you Monday."

"Have a good weekend."

I finished my Friday in regular fashion, eating lunch and going to my afternoon classes.

The next morning, I drove to the abortion clinic in north Dallas. I parked at a nearby Whataburger, went inside, and ate two breakfast burritos. When I was finished, I walked around the area, leaving my car in the Whataburger parking lot. There were three pro-life protestors on the concrete median of Greenville Avenue across from the entrance of the clinic. One of them was an older lady carrying a rosary. She seemed to be silently praying as she followed a bearded man about her age. The man was carrying a sign with a photo of an unborn child. Lydia would call it a fetus. The caption on the sign was, "I AM A PERSON." A teenage girl in jeans and sweatshirt followed the woman. "Christ the King Church" was stenciled on the girl's sweatshirt.

I waited for traffic to clear and then crossed to the median.

"Good morning," I said to the man in as friendly a voice as I could muster.

He stopped walking his picket circle and said, "Good morning."

"I like your sign," I said, not knowing how to start the conversation.

"Thank you. I have extras if you'd like one."

I looked around at the traffic passing by us on both sides.

"Maybe next time," I said. "Are you out here every day?"

"No, just Saturday mornings. There are others who come at other times."

"Do you ever get bothered by police?"

"No. We don't see many police."

The young girl stepped forward and said, "We had a lady throw a bottle at us last week."

"We've had a few incidents from the pro-aborts," the man said, gesturing for the girl to be quiet.

"What kind of incidents?"

"Insults, things thrown at us, horns honking, people spitting on us. That sort of thing. Nothing we can't handle."

"Do you ever report those incidents?" I asked.

The man laughed. "If we were dependent on the police, we wouldn't be here. We are prepared to suffer just like our Lord and Savior Jesus Christ suffered for us."

"Well," I said, "I hope nobody tries to nail you to a cross."

My attempt at lightness seemed to fall flat with the family. They gazed at me with expressions ranging from a frown to neutral curiosity. I looked around at the median and thought it would be a good place for our protest in two weeks. I hoped these three wouldn't be in the way.

"What time do you usually get here?" I asked.

"We start at eight AM," he said.

"That's when the abortuary opens," the woman added.

The entrance to the parking lot was across the northbound lanes. People turning left into that parking lot would have to sit right next to the picketers as they waited for traffic to clear.

"Do you ever have any women see you and decide not to go in?" I asked.

"Yes, a few. And we counsel them and pray with them if they let us. I have cards for adoption services and for our church."

"It's always a blessing when a young lady turns away from murdering her child." the woman said.

I looked over at the parking lot, but it was obscured by tall hedges. I wondered if anyone was having an abortion right then, her legs in a pair of stirrups, the baby inside her not even knowing that he or she has been sentenced to an execution. The thought made me shudder.

"How would you feel about an extreme protest if it would draw more attention to pro-life issues?" I asked the man.

"We are not pro-life," he replied. "We are abolitionists. Abortion should be outlawed in every case. No exceptions. Each child is a human being with a God given right to life. It doesn't matter if that child was conceived in an act of rape or in the back seat of some boy's car."

I was nodding. "Awesome! But how would you feel about an unconventional protest?"

"How unconventional?"

"Unconventional enough to get attention from people who might not have ever considered the pro-life – the abolitionist position."

The man had a skeptical look on his face.

"My name is David," I said.

"Russell." We shook hands. "This is my wife Mary and our daughter Rebecca."

I waved at them, and they waved back. They seemed nice enough, but I decided to forget about talking to them about the protest. They could just be surprised like everybody else.

"Would you like to walk and pray with us?" Mary asked.

"Sure," I said.

I fell into line behind Rebecca. We walked up the median to the next turn lane, then back down to the abortion clinic entrance.

"Rebecca," I whispered.

She looked back at me.

"How old are you?" I asked.

"Fourteen," she whispered back.

"Where do you go to school?"

"I'm homeschooled. We're supposed to be in prayer."

"Oh yeah. Sorry."

I walked in silence for another twenty minutes. I heard four cars honk, but I don't know if they honked in agreement or in opposition to us. Nobody threw anything at us while I was there. I checked my phone and saw a text from Lydia. She wanted me to call her.

"Russell," I said, stepping out of line and going around Mary and Rebecca, "I've got to go."

"All right," he said. "Thank you for walking with us."

"No problem."

"And God bless you. Can we pray for you?"

"Ummm, sure," I said.

The three of them gathered around me and each of them put a hand on my shoulders.

"Our heavenly Father," Russell began, "we pray for our new friend David and for his love for all your children, born and unborn. We pray for your guidance for him as he goes forth into the world. We ask that you be with him in all his endeavors. We thank you for dying for us, for redeeming us by your blood, and we accept that gift in all humility. We ask for the forgiveness of our sins as we forgive those who have wronged us. We pray for these babies who you created and who will never live to see a birthday. And we pray for the women who have made the horrible choice to kill their babies, that they will seek you Lord, and that you will forgive them. We thank you for the gift of your son, and it is in his name that we pray. Amen."

"Amen," Mary, Rebecca, and I all echoed, in unison.

"I hope we get to see you again," Mary said.

"Oh, you will," I replied. She would be seeing ALL of me soon, I thought, and I had to stifle a laugh. "Thank you."

"God bless you," Russell said again as I started to dart across the northbound side of Greenville.

I looked back at them once I got safely across the street. One of them had to have a cell phone. It was the twenty-first century after all. One of them would call 911 as soon as Lydia and I stripped down, I thought. I wondered how long it would take police to arrive. I watched them do two circles around the median before I turned and walked back to my car at the Whataburger.

Once I got into my car and away from all the traffic noise, I called Lydia. She answered after one ring.

"Hello."

"Hey Lydia, David. What's up?"

"I was bored."

"You were? Did you get the signs done?"

"Yeah, and they look really good too."

"Awesome. I went to where we're going to do the protest. I was there when you texted in fact."

"How does it look?"

I decided to be honest. "Scary. We would be in a median in the middle of a very busy street."

"So we'll be seen by a lot of people."

"Yep."

"Awesome!" she exclaimed.

"There will probably be some other pro-life protesters there, and I don't know how they will react to a naked couple."

"You'll have to give them that Bible verse you gave Crystal. What was it?"

"Isaiah chapter 20."

"Yeah, that."

"I'll have to remember to do that," I said.

"Are you busy?"

"No, not anymore. Why?"

"I was wondering if you could help me with my car."

"Sure," I said. "And you can show me the signs you made."

"Yeah, awesome."

"I'm about an hour away."

"Cool. See you then."

She ended the call, and I started my car and drove out of the Whataburger parking lot. I drove past the abortion clinic and Russell's family of abortion protestors. I tried to wave when I drove past, but none of them saw me.

I parked in front of Lydia's apartment forty-five minutes later. Dallas traffic on a Saturday morning was lighter than I had expected it to be. Lydia, wearing tight blue jeans that highlighted her pleasantly wide hips and a vintage Pink Floyd concert shirt, emerged from her apartment before I could get out of my car. She walked over to a white nineteen-ninety-something Chevrolet Corsica with a registration sticker that had expired eight months ago and popped the hood from under the steering wheel.

"Hey there," I said, walking up to the disabled vehicle. "So this is your car?"

"Hi David," she said and gave me a hug. "Yeah. I managed to get the battery posts disconnected early this morning. I thought, maybe, if we could get it out, we could take it up to Pep Boys and get it tested."

I looked and saw that everything was disconnected except the bolt holding the battery in its slot.

"Do you have a wrench set or anything?" I asked her.

"All I have are these," she said, handing me a pair of pliers.

I've never been one to try to work on my own vehicles. I always hated getting my hands dirty too much to have become an auto mechanic. Somehow though, I managed to get the battery out of Lydia's car with those pliers. We put it in the back of my Prius.

"Pep Boys?" I asked, closing the hatchback.

"Sure. Let me just check my apartment."

Lydia made sure her front door was locked.

"I'll show you the signs I made when we get back," she said as we got into my car.

"That reminds me. April 6th. Are you doing anything that morning?"

"What day is that?"

"Saturday. Two weeks from today."

"Nope. Is that when we are going to do the protest?"

"I think so," I said, and I pulled out onto the street.

"Miss Goody-Two-Shoes is OK with that?"

I laughed. "You shouldn't be so hard on her. She's young."

"And sheltered."

"This experience will be good for her then. I remember my first year at college. I was eighteen and had never even had a beer. Talk about sheltered."

"She's not a freshman, is she? That's a 4000 level course."

"I never asked her," I said. "She looks like she ought to still be in high school though."

"I wonder how she'll react when she sees you naked," Lydia mused. "You may be the first naked man she's ever seen."

That thought had never occurred to me, but now that Lydia had mentioned it, it seemed like a possibility. The Pep Boys wasn't far from Lydia's apartment, and I pulled into the parking lot while thinking about Crystal's likely lack of experience with nude men. We had the battery tested, and it was dead. Lydia paid for a replacement with a wad of fives and ones from her front jeans pocket. When she came up just a little short, I threw in a ten.

"Well, that was embarrassing," she said in the car on the way back to her apartment.

"Don't worry about it," I said.

"I'll pay you back as soon as I get my next modeling check."

"Don't worry about it."

We got the battery installed into her Corsica. Once I got it mounted, she insisted on connecting the cables to the posts herself. I stood back while she did her best at tightening them with her pliers. Once she was done, I checked them. They were tight.

"You ready to try it?" I asked her.

She made a show of crossing her fingers and got into the driver's seat. The engine fired up immediately when she turned the key.

"Yes," she squealed. "Oh my God, that's such a fucking relief."

I watched the engine run for a minute and then closed the hood. Lydia turned the car off, got out and hugged me tightly.

"Thank you so much," she said while I was tight in her embrace.

"No problem," I said. "How long has your car been broken?"

She sighed. "Four months."

"And all it was was a dead battery? Why didn't you check it before now?"

"Well, something's just come up, and I need the car to do some stuff."

"OK," I said. I stifled my curiosity and didn't ask her to explain.

She finally let me go, and we stood together in front of her apartment for an awkward moment.

"You were going to show me the signs?" I said.

"Oh yeah." She started for her door, then stopped and looked at me. "Now my apartment is a mess. Just saying."

"That's OK."

Mess was an understatement. The place looked like a typhoon had hit it. There were clothes strewn all over the floor and piled on her couch and love seat. I looked toward the kitchen and saw that almost all of the cabinet doors were standing open. The shelves were empty, but there were dishes piled all over the counter.

"Are you moving?" I asked.

Lydia ignored me as she picked clothes up from the floor and threw them on top of the pile on the couch. She grabbed two signs leaning against the wall in the hall toward her room and held them in front of her. They were done just as we had discussed at our meeting. One of them had a picture of a fetus. Above the picture was the caption, "Naked and Defenseless." Below it was "Laws Should Protect the Defenseless." The picture looked like the same one that Russell had

had on his sign that morning. The other sign had the same captions but had a photograph of a newborn baby. They were both on poster boards that were stapled to wooden sticks.

"Those are awesome," I said.

"Thank you."

I took one and tried to hold it up as I would be doing during the protest. The top of it hit the ceiling and knocked off some of the popcorn stuff from it.

"Oops. Sorry," I said.

"That's OK."

I held it lower, feeling the weight of it.

"Can you take them with you?" Lydia asked.

"You sure?"

"Yeah, I got a lot going on here."

I looked around. "I see that."

"Trying to do some spring cleaning."

"OK. I'll just put these in the car."

I took the signs outside and put them in the back of the Prius. When I went back into the apartment, Lydia had disappeared into the back. I walked over to the kitchen table and saw a pile of papers, markers, and other school work. And on the corner of the table underneath part of a piece of poster board was a sheet of paper with "Notice of Eviction" printed at the top. I pulled it out and saw that it was dated today. Lydia had five days to vacate the premises.

A toilet flushed in the back. I looked up and saw Lydia standing at the edge of the living room. Her face seemed to fall when she saw what was in my hand.

"Yeah," she said, sighing heavily.

"You got this today?"

"Yeah."

"Where are you going to go?"

"I don't know. A hotel for now, I guess."

"If you can't afford this place, how are you going to be able to afford a hotel?"

"I don't know."

She sat down at one of the kitchen table chairs, put her hands over her face, and sobbed. I stood there, watching her cry, for what seemed like a long time. I knew what was going to happen before I even gave any thought to it. I had taken upon myself to be this girl's protector, and I wasn't going to let her go to a seedy motel or, more likely, live in her car. She hadn't even been able to pay for her car battery at PepBoys.

I sat down in one of the other kitchen chairs and took her hands in mine, pulling them away from her face. Her cheeks were red and streaked with tears.

"Let me help you," I said. "Can I help you?"

Lydia nodded without saying anything. I looked around at the mess of her apartment.

"How much of this stuff is yours?" I asked.

"The clothes. The dishes. My TV and computer."

"What about the furniture?"

Lydia shook her head. "Apartment was furnished."

"Not very well," I said.

Lydia managed to crack a smile through her tears. "Tell me about it. This stuff is crap."

"Tell you what. I live alone in a house with three extra bedrooms. One of them has a bed in it. You can stay there until you figure out what to do."

"Are you serious?"

"Sure."

For the second time in less than ten minutes, she grabbed me in a tight embrace.

"Now, we'll have to come up with some ground rules," I said as I tried to get myself out of her grip.

"Anything."

She stood looking at me, waiting.

"I'll have to think of them first," I said.

She broke into a belly laugh at that. I wanted to shake my head. What was I doing? Lydia was a young, impressionable girl with who knew how many emotional problems and who obviously had feelings for me. I was setting her up for a huge heartbreak. But I couldn't help myself. She was in such need of help, and I could not just leave her hanging.

We spent the next two hours boxing up her belongings and stuffing them into both of our vehicles. Everything fit with room to spare. She made one last sweep through the apartment, threw the key onto the kitchen table, and walked out, leaving the front door unlocked.

"You have my number in your phone in case you get lost?" I said.

"Yes."

"Do you have enough gas to get to Fort Worth?"

Lydia looked at her gas gauge and said, "I think so."

I had given her my address, and she had punched it into her map app on her phone. I wondered how she was able to pay her cell phone bill, but I didn't ask her about it. Perhaps she put the phone bill at a higher priority than rent and food.

"Remember," I said. "The 287 exit and then the Bonds Ranch road exit off of that."

"Got it."

"OK. I'll see you at the house."

I drove much more slowly than usual and checked my rear-view mirror often. Every time I looked, she was right behind me. It was mid-afternoon when we got to my house. I parked on one side of the driveway. Lydia parked on the street in front of the house. I jumped out of my car and motioned for her to use the other side of the driveway. When she saw me, I saw her mouth the words "Are you sure?"

"Yes!" I exclaimed, waving more forcefully.

She parked next to the Prius, and I opened her car door for her.

"Yes, you can park in the driveway," I said. "I don't want to have to carry your stuff all the way across the front yard.

"Oh, OK. I just didn't want your neighbors to wonder why you have an old clunker like mine in your driveway."

"I don't care what my neighbors think."

Lydia got out of her car, and we stood facing each other for an awkwardly long moment. She looked at the lawn and at the front of the house.

"Looks nice," she finally said.

"Thanks. Come on in, and I'll show you the inside."

"Cool."

I had forgotten to open the garage, so I reached into my car and hit the remote. The door rumbled up, and I led the way inside. The garage opened into the laundry room.

"You can wash your clothes here," I said.

"Oh my God!" Lydia said. "I won't have to go to the fucking laundry mat anymore."

The other end of the laundry room opened into the kitchen. Lydia's eyes were wide when she entered, looking around like a kid in a candy store.

"This is the kitchen," I said. "The dining room is right across here."

I led her through my large one-story house, showing her the living room and game room.

"Oh my God, you've got a pool!" she exclaimed when she looked through the back window of the game room after giving the sixty-inch LCD TV with surround sound merely a cursory glance.

It was a small pool, shaped like a kidney bean. The winter tarp was still covering it. I usually didn't take it off until late April or early May. Lydia stood at the window, looking at the back yard.

"Here," I said, opening the back door. "We can go out."

"Cool!"

She followed me out and looked at the eight-foot-tall wooden privacy fence.

"You could so totally skinny dip out here."

"Oh, I do," I admitted. "I haven't worn a bathing suit in five years." I also hadn't been swimming anywhere except my own back yard in all that time.

"That's awesome! I can't wait for it to get warm enough to swim."

Lydia's staying at my house was a short-term plan. Her being here into the summer was not at all on the radar. I thought about saying something then, but I decided that we would talk about it when we sat down to go over the ground rules.

"Come on, I'll show you the rest of the house," I said.

We went from the game room to the master bedroom, the room I had once shared with Glenda. I had kept the king size bed and had gotten used to sleeping by myself in its huge space. I never bothered to make up my bed in the mornings, so the covers were turned down as I had left them when I got up.

"This is my room. Sorry for the mess."

"What mess?" Lydia said. "You just saw my apartment."

I had seen it, and I made a mental note to bring that up when we went over the conditions for her staying here. I showed her the master bathroom, and she took a big interest in my elongated walk-in shower.

"That is fucking awesome!" she said. "Can I shower here?"

"Sure," I said. "As long as I'm not using it at the time."

"Why not? It's big enough for both of us."

She smiled and laughed, lifting her eyebrows at me.

"We'll see," I said.

I showed her the other two bathrooms, the bedroom that I used as a study and where my desktop computer was, the empty room that would have been a nursery if Glenda and I had ever had a child, and the guest room, where Lydia would be staying.

"Here's your room," I said.

The bed was a double, not the single twin bed she had had at her apartment. The closet was of the large, walk-in variety and was empty. I had kept a small chest of drawers in the room. I couldn't remember if anything was in them, so I pulled a couple of drawers open and was pleased to see that they were also empty.

"This is awesome," Lydia said. "How do you keep the place so nice?"

"I try to keep everything organized. I have to keep on a regular vacuuming and dusting schedule, but I fall behind sometimes. I am a little OCD about having a clean kitchen though."

"That's good."

I walked to the kitchen with Lydia not far behind.

"Do you want something to drink?" I asked.

"What do you got?"

"Diet Coke and Coors Light."

"I'll take a beer."

I took two beers out of the fridge and handed one to her. I sat at the breakfast table and motioned for her to sit.

"I cannot begin to tell you how much I appreciate this," Lydia said.

"It's no problem. But like I said, we need to establish some ground rules."

"OK," she said, leaning forward.

"The most important thing is, this isn't permanent. You need to get on your feet and get yourself independent."

"Absolutely," Lydia said a little too enthusiastically.

"Second, your area, meaning the bedroom and that bathroom next to it, need to stay organized. They don't need to be spotless, but I don't want them looking like your apartment did this morning."

"I was just getting ready to move out. It normally didn't look like that."

"I know. I just want to put that on the record though. Your space will be your space. I'm not going to intrude, but I don't want anything illegal going on."

"I don't even smoke pot," Lydia said. "It burned my lungs the times I tried it, and I didn't even feel anything. 'This is stupid,' I thought. So I never tried it again."

"Good," I said. I didn't bother mentioning that Glenda had started smoking it after we ended the fertility treatments and that I still had an ounce or so of hers that she had left buried in the bottom drawer of her side of the dresser. I didn't know if it was still any good after four years. But, like everything else that had belonged to Glenda, I was reluctant to throw it away. "Likewise," I continued, "I need my space. Although I did tell you that you could use my shower."

"Cool."

"I'll have to give you a spare key to the front door until I can get another garage door opener ordered." The opener that Glenda had used had been demolished in the crash. I remembered seeing pieces of it in what was left of the car when I went to the police vehicle pound to collect any personal belongings before the insurance company sold the car for scrap. In the end, there had been nothing worth saving from the car. I remembered the stains of the blood splatters throughout the inside of the car, blood that had once pumped through the body of the one person on the earth who should have been the most precious to me.

"David?" Lydia said, and I jolted back to the present.

"Sorry," I said, feeling overwhelmed. How could I let Lydia stay here when everything about her presence reminded me of Glenda? What was wrong with me? This was never going to work.

But what would Lydia do if I just suddenly changed my mind? I couldn't send her away now. I had gotten myself into an impossible situation. I couldn't let her live here and keep my sanity, but I couldn't send her away either.

"Are you OK?" Lydia asked.

"Yeah," I said.

"You sure? I mean, are you sure you want me here?"

"Yes," I said. "It's just strange. The last woman to spend a night under this roof was my wife. It'll be all right."

"I'm not trying to replace her."

"That's good," I said and then wondered what I even meant by that. "I mean, I know."

"You must have loved her a whole lot."

"Yeah, I thought I did. I mean, I must have. Yes, I did."

Why was I having such difficulty talking? The pain and emptiness of coming home to an empty house in the days immediately after her funeral came flooding back. I had embraced that emptiness, knowing that her death was ultimately my fault and that I was getting what I had deserved.

Lydia was looking at me, an expression of grave concern on her face. I gave her my best smile and patted her hands.

"We should go unload your stuff," I said.

10

We separated the boxes with Lydia's dishes and stacked them in a corner of the garage. I already had a fully stocked kitchen as far as dishes, cookware, and utensils were concerned, so we wouldn't need Lydia's. We made a huge pile of Lydia's clothes in the laundry room, and she went to work on just washing all of them rather than try to separate what had been clean from the dirty clothes. I left her alone in the house for an hour or so in the early evening to make a grocery run and to buy a bunch of clothes hangers for her to use. Once we finally got everything done, at eleven PM, both of us were too tired to cook dinner. We went to a Denny's and ate a late supper. Or, since we both ordered Grand Slams, perhaps it was an early breakfast.

Arriving back home after our late-night meal was just a bit strange. We entered the house through the garage. We stopped in the kitchen and stood looking at each other for a moment. The awkward silences seemed to be getting more and more common.

"Good night Lydia," I finally said.

"Good night."

I turned and started for my bedroom.

"David," she said.

I stopped.

"You have no idea what this means to me. Thank you."

"You're welcome Lydia."

I got to my room and took off all my clothes, just as I had done every night I had spent in my house since Glenda died. I brushed my teeth and used the toilet. When I came out to get into bed, I turned and saw Lydia in the hall. It hadn't even occurred to me to close the door. She was still in her jeans and t-shirt and on her way back from the kitchen, having gotten herself a glass of something to drink.

"Good night," she said as she waved to me.

"Night."

I thought about closing the door, but I left it open. We'd seen each other naked more than once, so why close doors on each other now? I slid into bed under my sheet and blanket, turned on the TV, and switched off the light on my night stand. I channel surfed for a while, settling on one of the Back to the Future movies. The clock on my night table read 1:17 when I finally turned the sound down low and set the sleep timer on the TV. I turned on my side and stared out past my open bedroom door and down the hall. Sleep did not come for a long time, despite my physical exhaustion. I remember the television switching itself off. I had set the TV timer for an hour, so I knew it was 2:17 AM.

Eventually, sleep must have come because I woke up Sunday morning to full daylight. I looked at my clock and saw that it was after 11:00. I got up and stumbled to the restroom, relieved myself, and wandered toward the kitchen. I could smell something cooking, which didn't make sense to me in my groggy state. I was about to call out Glenda's name when I rounded the corner and saw Lydia standing in front of the stove looking down at a saucepan, an open can of Spaghetti-O's on the counter. She was as naked as she had been the very first time I saw her, and I realized with some amusement that I was naked too. I was about to turn back to my bedroom and get something to put on when she saw me.

"Good morning," she said.

Now that she had seen me, and since she was naked herself, it would have seemed rude to have gone to cover myself.

"Good morning," I said.

"I found a can of Spaghetti-O's in the pantry. I hope you don't mind."

"No," I said. I remembered seeing the can occasionally and sometimes wondering how long it had been there. "How did you sleep?"

"Awesome," she said. "I've had so much shit to worry about the past month, and you made it go away, at least for a little while."

"Good," I said, glad to hear the phrase a little while. "So, just out of curiosity, how are you paying for school?" I asked.

"Student loans pay for my tuition and books. Modeling and

working at Whataburger paid my rent and food and stuff."

"You work at Whataburger?"

"Well, not anymore," she said.

"Ah."

"Yeah."

"What happened?" I asked.

"Got in a fight with a customer."

"A fight?"

"An argument."

"So you got fired?"

"No, I quit before they fired me."

"Good," I said. "Always say that you resigned from there on job applications."

"You want some?" Lydia asked, holding up the pan of Spaghetti-O's.

"I'll pass."

Lydia tossed an oven mitt on the table, set the pan of Spaghetti-O's on it, sat down with the spoon she had used when heating it, and started eating.

"First thing you need to work on is replacing that income you had from Whataburger," I said.

"Mmmm-hmmm."

"That means finding another job."

"I know. I worked graveyard shift at Whataburger. Where am I going to find another job like that?"

"How many hours did you get there per week?"

"About thirty, I guess."

"And how many hours a week do you get modeling?"

"Nine. Maybe. Sometimes only six."

"You may not like it, but you may have to give up modeling for a different job."

"I make eighteen an hour modeling. I was only getting eight-fifty at Whataburger."

"I'm not saying you have to quit modeling now, but you need to keep all of your options open when you look for another job. You may find one making ten or twelve an hour working during times that you might have been modeling. Except that you would get a set number of hours every week. You don't get that modeling. And we've only got another month or so of modeling left in the semester. It'll probably take you that long to find something."

"I know," she said and took a bite of Spaghetti-O's.

"Have you been looking?" I asked.

"Sure. I put applications in at 7-11, Denny's, and IHOP."

"For graveyard shift?"

"Yeah."

"You need to expand your search."

"OK," she said.

I knew how she felt though. I loved modeling as much as she did, although perhaps for different reasons.

"You should start looking today," I said.

"It's Sunday."

"So? Places are open on Sundays. Fill those applications out and get them in."

"Fine. I'll go up to Denton and look for a job." She threw her spoon into the sauce pan, got up and walked toward her room.

I felt bad, pushing her like that, but she couldn't stay here indefinitely. I just couldn't let that happen.

"You don't have to get hired today!" I yelled to her, getting up and following her. "You just need to try. That's all."

I stood at the open door to her room. Lydia had gone into her bathroom. She came back out holding bottles of shampoo and conditioner.

"I can use your shower, right?" she said.

"Sure. Be my guest."

Lydia tramped down the hall, barefooted and bare-assed, past my bed and into my bathroom. I followed her into my room, noticing that she hadn't closed the bathroom door, and lay on my bed. I listened to the water from the shower, heard her lather her hair and rinse it. The water slapped against the ceramic tile of the shower floor, and I imagined her ringing water and soap out of her hair. I heard the squirt of the body wash dispenser and the sound of scrubbing. I imagined her washing her armpits, her breasts, between her legs. I looked toward the bathroom, but I couldn't see the shower around the open door. At some point, the variety of sounds diminished to a steady thumping. Lydia made the first moan a minute or two after that. I listened more intently, and I could hear her rapid breathing. It increased in speed. I heard another moan, then a grunt. I looked down and saw myself fully erect.

"Oh fuck," I heard her whisper.

I was tempted to do exactly what she was doing, but I didn't want her to catch me. Instead, I got up and went back to the kitchen, my erection bouncing with every step I took. I just hoped it subsided before Lydia got out of the shower. The pan of Spaghetti-O's was still on the table. I ate what was left, thinking that it didn't taste half bad, then started rinsing the pan and spoon. Lydia walked past me in the hall, the towel slung over her shoulder, and stopped.

"That shower is amazing," she said and then noticed what I was doing. "Hey, let me do that."

"It's alright, I got it," I said, looking down at myself. Thankfully, my arousal had subsided. I then wondered why putting pants on hadn't occurred to me. "I'm sorry if I seemed harsh earlier."

"No, you didn't. You're right; I need to get a plan or something."

All the sauce from the Spaghetti-O's had been rinsed from the pan, so I put it in the dishwasher.

"I'm going to go to Denton and put in some applications," she continued.

"So you're going to stay in Denton over the summer?"

"Yeah, I'm taking classes both sessions."

"That's awesome. You can put me down as a job reference if you need to. We are co-workers after all."

I smiled at Lydia. Her bare skin glistened from the shower she had taken. I watched a drop of water fall from a strand of her wet hair, roll down her shoulder and over her breast. It paused for a half a second on the tip of her nipple before falling all the way down to her thickly muscled thigh. When I looked back up to her face, she was grinning.

"Well, I'd better get ready," she said.

I nodded. Lydia disappeared into her room. By the time I got out of the shower, she was dressed in a red blouse and black skirt. Her legs were bare, but they were smooth and shaved. I couldn't imagine them looking any better in hose. She sat in the living room, thumbing through several papers.

"You look nice," I said.

"Thanks," she said, looking up at me. "So do you."

I was still naked. "Haha."

"I hope you don't mind. I borrowed your computer to print out some resumes."

We had unloaded Lydia's computer, television, and DVD player into my study but hadn't hooked anything up. She didn't have a printer, but I was going to try to hook mine up to her PC via the wireless LAN once I finally got a desk or table for her computer.

"No, that's great," I said. "Can I see it?"

"Sure." Lydia handed me one of the pages.

She still had her apartment listed as her address. That was probably a good idea for now. Potential Denton employers might question why she had a Fort Worth address. She had her high school listed as Lubbock High school, class of 2012. The resume reflected her college experience, first at Texas Tech, then at UNT. The most recent job she had listed under experience was figure model at the University of North Texas College of Visual Arts and Design.

"Are you sure you want to put your modeling on here?" I asked, wondering what a potential hiring manager might think about such a thing.

"Yeah. It's one of my jobs. I didn't put that it was nude and most people won't realize that unless I tell them."

I nodded. She didn't have many jobs listed. Besides the Denton Whataburger job, there were positions at a Wendy's and a Wal-Mart, both in Lubbock. The Wendy's job had lasted five years, which I thought would appeal to a potential employer. I handed the resume back to her.

"What are you going to say in an interview if they ask you about the modeling job?"

"I'll just say that I took and held poses for college drawing classes. That the job depended on reliability and dependability."

"Ok. Good. Do you have your references?"

She handed me another page from her stack. I saw my name listed first, followed by the UNT model coordinator and another person from Lubbock. Complete addresses, phone numbers, and emails were listed for each.

"Awesome," I said, handing the sheet back to her. "You're going to do fine."

"See. You don't have to baby me."

She stood up and kissed me on the cheek.

"See you later," she said.

Lydia left via the front door. When she was gone, I got on the computer and ordered another garage door opener. Lydia wasn't staying long – couldn't stay long – but I figured that it would be good to have a spare opener. I spent the rest of the afternoon finishing a paper for my British lit class and playing Call of Duty online. I never got dressed and never went outside. It was like almost every other Sunday afternoon since Glenda's wreck.

Lydia returned to the house around 6:00. I had put a frozen lasagna in the oven, and the smell of Italian spices wafted through the house. I was in the game room when I heard the door open. I left the PlayStation 4 controller on the table, Call of Duty still running, and hurried to my bedroom to at least throw a pair of shorts on. Yes, we were nude models, but I thought we had been a little too relaxed with the nudity. Lydia was a very attractive girl; I couldn't lie to myself about that. I didn't trust myself to keep things platonic amidst such constant nudity, with her sleeping under the same roof. She deserved someone capable of loving her, and that someone wasn't me. I found a pair of flannel pajama bottoms and I virtually jumped into them and hurried back to my Call of Duty game. I had already been killed and re-spawned twice by the time I got back.

Lydia bounced into the game room about ten seconds after I sat down with the PS4 controller.

"How did it go?" I asked.

"Good. I put in three applications. Went to four other places, but they require applications over the web."

"Awesome," I said as I shot two members of the opposing team on my TV.

"Nice," Lydia said.

She watched me play the rest of that round and looked at my stats with me. They were not great, but they weren't awful.

"Cool," she said. "I've got to get out of these clothes."

"Yeah, I wanted to…"

I turned, but she had already gone back to her room. I exited the game and turned the PS4 off. I figured that the lasagna should be ready by then, so I went to the kitchen, checked it, and started serving our plates.

"I hope you like lasagna!" I called.

"Love it!"

"Well, it's ready!"

"Awesome," Lydia said, bouncing into the kitchen, naked once again.

I set out plates at the breakfast table. Lydia looked in the fridge, got us each a beer, and sat down. I sat across from her.

"Lydia," I said, "do you think it's a good idea to run around naked all the time?"

She shrugged. "Sure. You don't?"

"Not really, no."

She blew on the bite of lasagna on her fork to cool it. Something stirred in me at the sight of her puckered lips.

"Why not?" she asked and put the bite into her mouth.

"Well..." I stuttered and stopped. How could I put this?

"I mean, you were naked for a long time this morning. I don't know why you have those PJ pants on now. It's kind of hot in here."

I decided to drop it. I'm sure she was used to being naked at home as often as possible. She had told me as much that day we met, when we had teased Maria, the shy model. I didn't know how to tell her what I was thinking without hurting her feelings. And like her, I was used to a good deal of household nudity when I was home.

"It is hot in here," I said.

I got up from the table, went into the bedroom, peeled the pajama pants off, and went back to the kitchen.

"Is this better?" I asked.

"Much."

We ate and talked, and nothing else was mentioned about our nudity. After dinner, we both played Call of Duty and drank beer until ten o'clock before calling it a night. I was feeling a little tipsy by then, which I hoped would help me get to sleep after waking so late that morning.

"I guess we can ride together tomorrow," I said.

"That would be awesome."

"Can you be ready by 7?"

"Sure."

"All right then. I'll see you in the morning."

Sleep came easily, thanks to the beer, but I had to get up at two AM to pee, also thanks to the beer. Sleep was difficult after that. At some point, I did doze and dreamed that Glenda had come home and found Lydia and me naked together. She had fallen to her knees, crying, asking me why I had betrayed her like I had. I got up and rushed over to comfort her, but the floor had turned to mud. Each step became more difficult as I sank deeper and deeper. The mud was like quicksand. I was in it up to my neck by the time I woke up, sweat covering my body. It was four–thirty by then, and I gave up any hope of going back to sleep.

I grabbed the remote and turned on the television. As I flipped through the channels, I realized that there were way too many infomercials on at that hour. I settled on Kill Bill Volume 1 since the movie was almost to the showdown scene at the House of Blue Leaves.

There was nothing like seeing a hot blonde in a yellow jump suit slicing 88 ninjas to blood spurting ribbons at five o'clock in the morning.

When the movie ended, I didn't wait for the alarm to sound. I got up, showered, shaved, and brushed my teeth. When I got out of the bathroom, Lydia was sitting on my bed, waiting for her turn in the shower.

"Good morning," she said.

"Morning," I replied. "It's all yours."

"Cool."

She left the door open again, but she showered quickly and apparently skipped the masturbation. I was dressed in my blue jeans and t-shirt, my typical college attire, and was sitting at the breakfast table eating a bowl of corn flakes when Lydia emerged fully dressed and ready to go.

"There's cereal in the pantry," I said.

"I'm not hungry."

She sat down across from me and watched me eat. I didn't say anything. I was never a big morning talker. I was starting to get uncomfortable when she finally said something.

"I'm glad I'm here."

I smiled at her. "I'm glad you're here too."

"Thank you for being nice to me. People usually aren't."

"Then you haven't been hanging around the right people."

She was silent as I continued to eat my cereal.

"My mom's kind of a bitch sometimes," she finally said.

"I'm sorry."

"And her boyfriends are usually scumbags."

"Didn't you have a step-father?" I asked, remembering a conversation we'd had the day we met.

"Yeah. Four of them."

I stopped eating for a moment, thinking of all of her strange behavior, her social awkwardness, getting naked at Ecstatic Dance, my shock when she walked out of her room naked later that day in her apartment, and seeing her sitting on the edge of the platform with her legs apart flashing everyone in the hall in the art building.

"Did any of them—," I started to ask, but stopped. I had wanted to ask if any of them had abused her, but I thought that might be too forward and might bring up something painful. "Did you get close to any of them?"

"No, not really. I didn't get close to anybody."

"What about your dad? Your real dad. Where is he?"

She shrugged. "When Mom didn't get an abortion, he bailed. At least, that's what I've always been told."

"I'm sorry."

She shrugged. "Oh well. You learn to live with it. I mean, everyone has a fucked-up past to one degree or another. We've all got shit behind us that we'd rather forget."

"Yes," I agreed.

Lydia's mention of abortion made me think of our protest project. We would be seeing Crystal in class today. I wondered how she might react to the news that Lydia had moved in with me. Probably not well, I thought.

"Hey, let's not mention your moving in here to Crystal," I said, "at least until after the protest."

"Oh, I wasn't going to tell little Miss Goody Two Shoes anything," she said. "She might back out of the whole thing."

"Yes, she might. And we need her."

I finished my cereal and moved a package of pork chops from the freezer to the fridge to cook for dinner that night. Lydia and I left the house at 7:05, arrived at the university at 7:50, and went our separate ways. The only class we shared was that Public Opinion class, and we didn't get to talk much after that due to Lydia's cross-campus class. Crystal stopped me just as soon as class was over though.

"Are we settled on a day and time?" she asked as I packed my books into my bag.

"Yes," I replied. "April 6th at 9 AM at that north Dallas clinic."

"OK. Are you sure you're going to go through with it?"

"Yes."

"OK. I'll email that to my cousin. And to the other contacts."

"What are you going to tell them, exactly?"

"That there's going to be a nude protest outside the clinic that morning."

I had an image of one of those reporters forwarding that email to someone at City Hall and then seeing the police waiting for us when we got there, killing the protest before it ever started.

"Don't say nude," I said. "Say that we are having an unusual and groundbreaking secular protest against abortion and that the methods used in the protest will make it newsworthy. Something like that."

"Do you think that'll work?"

"I don't know." It didn't matter anyway. If this were a protest for the sake of protesting and not a class project, we would have had a real publicist handling the media contacts. But just having a plan for it was enough for the assignment.

"OK," Crystal said. "What do we do if no one shows up?"

"You'll have my camera to take pictures. We can just write our own story."

"What, you want me to take pictures of the two of you naked?"

"Sure."

"You're not afraid of naked pictures of you being out there?"

"If we were afraid of that, we wouldn't be doing this. And we wouldn't be modeling for art classes. With every cell phone in the world having a camera, do you know how easy it would be for someone to snap a quick picture in drawing class? So I just quit worrying about it."

"Don't they have rules against that?" Crystal asked.

"Sure they do. But since when does everyone follow every rule? I just don't worry about such things. Besides, with the NSA spying on everyone, there may be nude pictures of everyone floating around soon."

I laughed as I said the part about the NSA, but Crystal's facial expression turned to one of pure horror. She didn't get any of my humor.

"Are you serious?" she said.

"No, not really," I said with a laugh.

We walked outside, and I held the door open for her.

"Listen," I said, "whatever happens with the protest just have fun with it."

"I'll try. I really need to get an A in this class."

"We all do. But we might as well try to have fun getting those A's."

"OK, I'll try. See you Wednesday."

"Bye," I said and watched her walk away. I thought of those years that Glenda and I had gone to church, trying to display an air of propriety that we could never actually fulfill. Crystal was trying, but nobody was perfect.

I ate lunch alone, attended my afternoon classes, and waited for Lydia to finish her day. Her last class ended at 5:00. I was sitting in my car reading a massive Anthony Trollope book for my British lit class when Lydia arrived.

"Sorry," she said.

"That's all right. Gives me a chance to catch up. Too many distractions at home."

Of course, the biggest distraction at home right now was currently sitting in the car with me.

"Have you thought about tomorrow?" Lydia asked.

"What's tomorrow?" I said, but I remembered before I finished the question.

"We're modeling together, 8 to 11."

"Yeah, I remember. What do I need to think about?"

"Our pose. *The Kiss*. Remember?"

Yes, I remembered now. She had wanted to do a pose from the Rodin sculpture. I had meant to look up a picture of that piece, but I had forgotten.

"Oh yeah," I said.

"Do you want to try it?"

"I guess so," I said, hoping I wasn't committing to something impossible. "We may have to modify it for comfort if we're going to do it for three hours."

"Sure. I want to make it fun."

"I bet you do," I said. I glanced over at her as I pulled out of my parking space. She had a mischievous grin on her face.

On the drive home, I told Lydia about my conversation with Crystal. "Pictures, yes!" she said when I mentioned Crystal having my camera for the protest. She seemed far too excited about the whole thing. But then again, I had come up with the idea because of her.

After a couple of silent miles on Interstate 35, I said, "You know, you said this morning that your mom almost aborted you."

"No, my sperm donor wanted her to abort me."

"Your sperm donor?"

"I refuse to call him my father, biological or otherwise."

"I would think that someone who was almost aborted would be pro-life."

"I said the asshole wanted Mom to abort me. She never even considered it. Or so she tells me."

We drove in silence for a couple of minutes before Lydia asked me, "Does it bother you that I'm pro-choice?"

I thought about that for a moment. "It bothers me that legal abortion exists at all. I look at it kind of like slavery, a societal injustice of massive proportions. But on a more personal level, I do wish you believed in our protest cause."

"I can't help what I believe," she stated and let it go at that.

I didn't bring the topic up either, although we did talk more about the logistics of the protest. She spent most of the time speculating about how it would feel to be so exposed in public. I talked about what to expect if we were arrested by the police.

"Whatever happens," I told her, "do not, under any circumstances, make any jokes about being naked. They could misconstrue it as sexual and use it against you. In fact, don't say anything to them except, 'I want to talk to an attorney.' Got it?"

"Got it," she said.

We arrived at home a little before six. I glanced at Lydia as I thought of that word, home. I told myself to keep thinking of her as an extended guest, but right now, this was the closest thing to home she had. Hearing her call her biological father a "sperm donor" in such a callous way made me feel even more protective of her. During the fertility treatment years with Glenda, I had yearned to be a father to at least one child, to give that child the kind of paternal love that I felt I had lacked. That Lydia's father had turned his back on her and helped make her so callous toward the very idea of him left a dull ache in my gut. I wanted to hate the man, but that wouldn't do me any good. I would never know who he was or why he did what he did.

When we got inside, I found a recipe on my phone and started cooking the pork chops I had taken out of the freezer that morning, coating them with flour, setting them in the pan with heating olive oil, and covering them with a layer of sliced Yukon gold potatoes and a top layer of sliced onions. I poured a beef broth mixture over that and covered the pan to let it cook for about thirty minutes. At some point during that half-hour, I realized that I hadn't cooked for another person in over four years. Other than simple Hamburger Helper type things and prepared frozen dishes, like the previous night's lasagna, I hadn't cooked even for myself in all that time. I had forgotten how much I enjoyed it.

"Smells good," Lydia said when she walked into the kitchen after the pork chop dish had been simmering for twenty minutes.

I was just starting to microwave some bagged frozen broccoli.

"Thanks," I said.

I was mildly surprised to see her still in the clothes she wore to school.

"Where have you been?" I asked.

"Studying. I have a test in biology tomorrow. What are we

having?"

"It's a pork chop dish that I haven't made in a very long time."

Lydia grabbed a Diet Coke from the fridge. "Call me when it's done," she said. "I have to pass this test."

I finished heating the broccoli and served two plates. There wound up being more food than I thought, so both plates were loaded. And there were two pork chops still in the pan along with a bunch of potatoes and onion.

"Lydia!" I called. "Dinner!"

We ate, and Lydia talked about cellular mitosis and what an asshole her biology professor seemed to be. She surprised me by eating everything I had served her.

"Damn, that was good," she said.

"You want some more?"

"Yes, I do, but I better not. I don't want you to think I'm a pig."

"I won't think you're a pig."

"I still better not. We're modeling in the morning, and I don't want to feel fat."

"Oh yeah," I said. "Do you want to ride together?"

"I'd love to, but I have two classes after we get done. I don't want you to have to wait for me."

"I'll be fine. I need to do some studying of my own, and I usually do that better away from the house."

"OK." She rinsed her plate and fork and put them in the dishwasher. "I do need to study more. That test is right after our drawing class."

"Go study then. I got this."

"Thanks." She kissed me on the cheek and hurried back to her room.

I put up the leftovers, did the dishes, and wiped down the counter. After grabbing a beer from the fridge, I went to my room, stripped off my clothes, and fired up Call of Duty in the game room. I didn't expect to see Lydia for the rest of the night since she seemed really worried about her test. After a couple of hours of playing, I realized that I missed hearing her voice. When was the last time I had missed anyone except Glenda? I thought about our class in the morning and that we would likely be holding each other in an intimate embrace for three hours. The thought was both exciting and comforting. She really was beautiful in her own special way.

And yet, I wanted so much more for her than I could give. She needed to be loved unconditionally, and I knew I just wasn't capable of that. I thought I had loved Glenda like that, but I had failed her with my selfishness. I didn't want to fail Lydia or anyone else like that again.

I played Call of Duty until ten-thirty and then went to bed. As I lay down, I thought of Lydia again. *The Kiss* was the name of the sculpture. I had failed yet again to look for a picture of it, but I assumed that she and I would be in a kissing position. Would our lips be touching for the duration of the pose? I thought of her lips as they had touched mine that night in her apartment after the Ecstatic Dance session. They had been soft and gentle and pleasant, and after she had kissed me, I remembered not wanting to leave. But I knew I'd had to leave, and so I had. Now Lydia was living under my roof, and I wanted her. But I knew it was a selfish want because that was my nature. She needed more than the sexual desire of a selfish man, so I pushed any thoughts of her aside. I turned the television to the MLB Network, set the sleep timer and tried to relax as the commentators on TV talked about that day's spring training games.

11

The alarm blared at me at six AM. I considered hitting the snooze button, but I realized that Lydia would have to shower after I did. I turned the alarm off and, remembering that today was a modeling morning, bounced out of bed and into the bathroom. I showered quickly, and once again, Lydia was sitting at the foot of my bed when I stepped out.

"Good morning, partner," she said with a grin as I dried myself.

"Morning."

Lydia jumped up and walked past me to start her own shower. Her bare hip brushed against my thigh.

"How did the studying go?" I asked as she turned the water back on. "Are you going to ace that test?"

"I hope so," she said.

Lydia stepped in, closed the glass door, and immediately started washing her hair. I stood at the sink to brush my teeth and shave, but I spent a great deal of time watching her in the mirror. She seemed to be dancing to some inner music, although at one point, I could hear her singing.

We both dressed quickly, and I drove us to Denton. She spent the duration of the drive with her biology textbook and notes in her lap, whispering things to herself. I left her to her studying and drove in silence.

Lydia and I walked into the models' changing room at 7:45. She set her books on the counter and stripped down to nothing in about five seconds. She then stood there naked, folding her clothes and reciting things for her test. I looked at the schedule on the wall and saw that

Walter was doing the other figure drawing class. I stripped almost as quickly as Lydia had done, put my robe and house slippers on, and stuffed my clothes into my bag.

"Let's go to the class before Walter gets here and talks our ears off," I told Lydia.

She got covered, and we grabbed clean sheets and headed to the room. Lydia brought her Biology textbook with her. Audrey wasn't there yet, but several students were setting up their easels. The platform was against the back wall. The bench that Lydia had sat on during our first class together was in the far corner of the room.

"We should move that onto the platform," I said to Lydia.

"Yes," she agreed.

Lydia grabbed one end, and I grabbed the other, and we carried the bench to the model stand. After we set it down, I pushed it to the edge of the platform against the wall. The front part of the platform was still free in case Audrey wanted to start with any short poses. Audrey burst into the room as I stepped down onto the floor.

"Good morning," she said in a loud voice to everyone in the room. Taking a quick look at what we had done on the platform, she said, "You guys are awesome!"

Audrey set her stuff down on the instructor's desk, greeting a couple of students as they arrived. Lydia and I sat on the front edge of the model stand and waited for instructions.

"Do we need newsprint?" someone asked.

"Yes," Audrey replied, "we are going to start with some gestures."

Audrey walked over to us. "Is that all right with you? You guys did such awesome gestures together last semester."

"Sure," I said, and Lydia nodded. I wondered how our gestures would be this time, now that Lydia and I knew each other.

We waited about five or ten minutes while everyone got set up. We had been early anyway, which was the norm for me. Finally, Audrey said to the class, "We are going to go ahead and start with two-minute gestures. But there are two figures, so you can only spend one minute on each."

Lydia and I got up while Audrey was talking, removed our robes and slippers, and stepped onto the platform. Audrey bounded to us and said, "I'm going to announce when one minute is up so they can switch to the other figure, but these will be two minute poses. I'll just say 'change' when we need you to change."

"Sounds good," I said.

Lydia and I looked at each other, and I lifted my eyebrows as if to say, let's give them something special. And we did. When Audrey said "Go!" Lydia and I took a pose with our feet touching but both of us falling away from each other. We held each other's forearms to keep ourselves from falling over completely.

"Wonderful!" Audrey said.

We did at least ten gesture poses, all of them interactive in some way. We did one as if I were dipping her during a ballroom dance. We locked arms in another pose, like wrestlers in combat. For the last pose, Lydia stood with right arm stretched toward me. I got on one knee and took her hand, only realizing after Audrey had started her clock that it looked like I was proposing to Lydia. Her eyes sparkled when I snuck a peek up at her.

"Time," Audrey called. "I could do these all day, but we need to move on to a long pose. Get out your good paper." Audrey turned to us. "That was awesome guys."

"Thank you," Lydia and I both said, in unison.

"Do you have any ideas about the long pose?"

"Actually," Lydia said, glancing shyly at me, "I was thinking something like Rodin's *The Kiss*."

"Really?" Audrey said and looked at me. "Are you sure you want to get that close?"

"Well, we live together now," Lydia said in a matter of fact voice.

Audrey's eyes grew wide. I felt like I should say something about our relationship still being platonic, but I held my tongue. "That's awesome guys." She motioned to the bench on the model stand. "Let's see what kind of pose we can get."

Lydia pulled a folded sheet of paper from her biology text and opened it. A photograph of Rodin's sculpture had been printed on it. At first glance, it appeared that the woman was on the man's lap which couldn't have been done for very long. My legs would have lost feeling and circulation in about fifteen minutes. But when I looked more closely, the woman was merely sitting beside the man, her right leg draped across the left side of his lap. The woman's left arm was up around the man's neck, pulling her mouth to his. The man's right hand rested on the woman's hip. The woman's left foot was directly on top of the man's left foot.

"Let's try it," I said softly to Lydia.

Lydia grabbed one of the clean sheets we had brought, and together we spread it out over the bench. I sat down first, my back against the wall. My left arm and her right would be against the wall somehow if we managed to get close to the pose in the sculpture. Lydia sat down to my left and put her leg over my lap. She put her other foot on top of mine, just like in the photograph. I put my right hand on her hip and the bare softness of her skin did something to me that made me glad that her leg was blocking the students' view of my loins. Lydia reached up with her left hand and let it rest as our lips touched. We then froze.

"Can you do that for another thirty minutes until break?"

"I think so," I said, not sure.

Lydia nodded, her lips brushing mine.

"OK," Audrey said, "if you need a break before that, just let me know. I'll go set the timer."

I looked into Lydia's eyes and was surprised to see her looking into mine. I wanted to turn away, but I couldn't. Audrey stepped onto the platform and said, "I want to go ahead and mark you." She put masking tape around our feet and where our legs rested on the cushion of the bench. "That ought to be good. I'm not going to put tape on you, so you'll have to remember where you are touching each other."

"OK," I managed to say from the side of my mouth.

As the pose continued, Lydia's lips gradually parted until I felt what I thought was her tongue on my lips. If I hadn't been in a pose, I would have pushed her away. But I didn't. I couldn't. Her tongue pushed its way between my lips and caressed my tongue. Her eyes seemed to stare into the deep dark pits of my soul. I had a sudden fear that she was pulling all of my darkest secrets out of my heart and that she would run from me when this pose was over. As much as I thought that needed to happen, I didn't want it. I wanted Lydia with me all the time: at home last night, naked here and now on the model stand, and protesting in the middle of Greenville Avenue in less than two weeks. I licked the tip of her tongue and pushed my own between her lips. We were locked in a full-fledged French kiss now, our first, as we were being studied by eighteen college art students.

My erection pushed against Lydia's leg, the one draped over my lap, and I wondered how I was ever going to get up from the pose when Audrey called for a break. Lydia responded to the force of my erection with even more involved tongue wrestling, and I realized that, in her exhibitionist fervor, she had planned this naked make-out session in front of an entire class. And I had gone along with it like the dimwit I was. Making my arousal even more profound was the fact that Lydia and I had never been physically intimate, so this was all new and exciting. I was experiencing feelings I hadn't felt in years and thought I would never feel again. I wanted to move the hand that was on her hip up and down her body, feeling of her breasts, her legs, her back. But I didn't. As difficult as it was, I remained professional and held the pose. The students couldn't see our tongues wrestling with each other.

I saw a tear well up in the corner of Lydia's right eye. It rolled slowly down her cheek and into our mouths. The salty taste mixed in with our saliva. The back of my neck was sticky with sweat from the heat of her arm around it. As the pose continued, I felt the sweat build on my thighs, where Lydia's leg touched my skin. Her hip was feeling wet, and my hand almost slid off several times. My arms tired as I strained to hold the hand in place. My feet started to tingle as the lack of blood supply took its toll.

The timer finally buzzed until Audrey turned it off.

"OK, let's take a ten-minute break," she said.

Lydia detached her mouth from mine and wiped her face with the back of her hand.

"Holy shit," she said softly to me, so no one else could hear.

She moved her leg slightly and looked down at my lap. My erection had subsided thanks to the pose's increasing discomfort. She threw her feet to the floor and stood up on slightly wobbly legs. I held her back to give her support. I knew I wasn't ready to stand up yet with the tingling going on in both of my feet.

"That was amazing," Audrey said. "You'll have to walk around and look at the drawings. They are really looking good."

I stretched my legs onto the bench and laid back to let the blood flow return gradually. If I tried to stand up right away, the blood, aided by gravity, would rush back. I would feel a painful sensation in the bottoms of my feet, as if thousands of needles were piercing the soles. I used the spare sheet to wipe the sweat from my body. By the time I was ready to stand, Lydia had put on her robe and was sitting in the corner, studying her biology book. I wanted to talk to her after what we had just experienced, but I knew she was stressed about that test. So I left her alone.

Audrey's ten-minute break stretched out to fifteen as the students were slow coming back to the room. Audrey finally corralled everyone, and Lydia and I resumed the pose. The eye contact between us remained as intense as it had been for the first part of the pose, but we weren't as adventurous with our mouths. Audrey called for two more breaks during the class, for which Lydia and I were grateful. Lydia spent her break times studying. Once I got the feeling back in my feet, I walked around the room and looked at the drawings. They were some of the best I had ever seen by UNT students. Whatever Lydia and I were doing seemed to really inspire them.

Audrey dismissed us at 10:35, fifteen minutes before the official end of class. She was having the students turn their drawings around so that everyone could look at and critique them. When Lydia and I had gotten our robes on, our timesheets signed, and our sheets gathered, the students congregated around the model stand to look at their work. I wanted to stay and listen to what they had to say, but Lydia was heading out the door with her biology book under her arm. I didn't want her to get away without being able to wish her luck on her test, so I followed her to the changing room.

Lydia was throwing her clothes on by the time I got there.

"That was fun," I said.

"That was amazing. And to think, we get paid for that."

"Yeah, that is strange to think about."

She sat down to get her socks and shoes on. I slipped my robe off and grabbed my pants. I noticed Lydia watching me as she tied her shoe.

"Good luck on your test," I said.

"Thanks. I'm glad she let us go early. Gives me a little time to study."

She stood, stuffed her robe and her biology book into her backpack, and slung it over her shoulder. I was about to step into my jeans when she kissed me, just a quick peck, lips to lips.

"See you this afternoon," she said, and then she was gone.

12

I had planned on going to the university library and using one of the computers to work on a paper on *The Way We Live Now*, the excessively long Anthony Trollope novel I had been reading for my nineteenth century British literature class. I hadn't been able to get through the book, but I was going to write the report anyway. After the drawing class with Lydia though, I knew I wouldn't be able to focus, much less sit still. I took my modeling bag and locked it in my car before taking a long walk around the campus.

When I passed by the Life Science Complex, I knew Lydia was inside somewhere, taking that exam that had so stressed her. I hadn't wanted our art class to end, and I hated that she'd had to hurry off so soon after it had ended. How had she so quickly inserted herself into my insulated life? I had purposely isolated myself from so many people after Glenda's accident, her friends, everyone at our church. I didn't want to be responsible to anyone. Lydia had to get herself on her feet, get her finances in order, and find her own place. She needed to do that both for herself and for me. But why did the thought of not being able to look into her green eyes every day fill me with such sadness?

My walk took me away from campus, and I found myself walking around the Denton County Courthouse. I was tired and hungry, and I went into a coffee house and ordered a pastrami sandwich. I didn't drink coffee, but they had soft drinks. I checked the time on my phone as I ate. Lydia would be out of her biology test. I hoped she had aced it. She had two more classes, and then we could go home. What had been just a trickle had become a raging torrent after our class this morning. Under the same roof all night, I would be thoroughly unable to keep my hands off her. I knew she would feel the same way; *The Kiss* pose had been her plan. I had one chance to stop the raging torrent. Lydia had to know what kind of person I was. I would have to tell her things that I hadn't even thought about. I had to strip myself bare, more than just physically. What would Lydia do when I told her, if I could manage to put it into words and if I could get the words out without breaking down? I didn't know. Lydia was unpredictable, and I realized how little I knew about her. She had a key to my house. She could very easily take all my valuables and disappear. I didn't think she would, but she could.

When I finished my sandwich, I got a refill on my fountain drink and took it walking with me. Lydia would have been in her last class of the day by the time I made it back onto campus. My feet hurt from the walking, and I wrestled with the idea of going to the library and starting on that Trollope paper. I went to the campus bookstore instead, picked up the Sports Illustrated baseball season preview magazine and sat down with it. They had the Rangers picked to finish third in the division behind the Athletics and the Astros. I remembered that they had picked the Angels to win the World Series a couple of seasons and that those Angels had finished below .500 that year. So I disregarded their predictions. If baseball was anything, it was unpredictable, just like Lydia. Why did everything make me think of Lydia? I got up, put the magazine back on the rack, and walked to my car.

I sat in the driver's seat, rolled down both windows to get some air circulation, and reclined the seat back as far as it would go. The Trollope book was still in my bag, but I didn't pull it out. I closed my eyes and tried to just relax and clear my mind.

When the passenger door opened, I jerked up and realized that I must have dozed off. I looked over and was pleased to see a smiling Lydia getting into the car.

"Hey," I said, "what time is it?"

"Almost three o'clock."

"Wow."

"You looked like you were out," Lydia said. "Your mouth was open and everything. I bet you were snoring."

"I probably was. How did your test go?"

"It went good," she said as I started the car. "There wasn't anything that I didn't recognize."

"When do you find out your grade?"

"Thursday, I hope."

"Good."

I drove out of the parking lot and away from the campus. My right hand was resting on the center console as I held the steering wheel with my left. Lydia put her hand over mine.

"That class was amazing."

"Yes, it was," I agreed. "We need to talk though."

I hadn't planned on talking to her while I was driving, but I had suddenly realized that if I waited until we got home, we would be doing things other than talking.

"OK," she said nervously, taking her hand away from mine. "About what?"

"About me. I want to tell you some things that may make you not like me so much."

"I doubt that but go ahead."

I took a deep breath. I didn't know how much I would be able to get out, and I could hear the shakiness in my voice. "A couple of months before the wreck, Glenda's grandfather died. He was in a nursing home and went into renal failure. Glenda wanted to see him, to say goodbye to him, so we drove up to Kansas City. The whole family was there. The nursing home moved him to a private room, and the family stayed with him around the clock. I think I counted twenty-five people in that room at one time. And I realized that every single person in the room was either his child, his grandchild, or his great-grandchild, either by birth or by marriage. Glenda and I had been trying to have a baby for years. We'd gone to doctors and everything, and we had finally given up. When I was in that nursing home watching Glenda's grandfather dying amongst all of his descendants, I started thinking about my own death. If Glenda went before me, who would be there for me? And I realized, nobody."

"Didn't you look into adoption?" Lydia asked.

"Yeah. Glenda and I were both working. We had to because we had built up so much debt. Part of that was to pay for the fertility treatments that didn't work. Adoption was expensive, and we didn't think we would pass the social study with both of us working and our finances a wreck."

I paused to watch for traffic as I merged onto Interstate 35.

"That bothered me, thinking that I might have to die alone. After we got back from Grandpa Jack's funeral, I prayed. There was no way

I would ever have done anything to hurt Glenda physically, mentally, or emotionally. I would never, ever have left her. I couldn't stand the thought of her having to try to make it by herself. So I prayed..."

I didn't think I could say it. I had gone so long without even consciously thinking about it.

"Prayed for what?" Lydia asked.

"I prayed for something to happen. I got down on my knees and prayed aloud for a child. I didn't include Glenda. I just prayed for me, that God would make me a father. I didn't care what happened to Glenda. I didn't say it, but I thought it would be easier to have been married to someone else, someone more fertile. And just a few weeks later..."

My vision was blurring, and I wiped my eyes with the back of my hand.

"I told her I loved her multiple times every single day for all the years that we were married. And I thought I did. But apparently, I loved myself more. And I guess God decided to play some kind of cruel joke on me."

We drove in silence for several minutes. My vision cleared as I felt too ashamed to even cry about what I was confessing.

"So, was that it?" Lydia said. "What was supposed to make me not like you?"

"Yeah," I grunted.

She put her hand on top of mine again.

"That's not so bad," she said. "I don't know much about God, but I doubt that your prayer had anything to do with what happened to her."

"You doubt it?"

"Yeah. People say things they don't mean all the time. God, if he really exists, would know that. Do you know how many times I told my mom I wanted to kill her?"

"How many?"

"I don't know. A bunch. I think you're blaming yourself for something you didn't have anything to do with. I mean, if it was her time to go, it was her time to go."

"I don't know about that. I was taught that God hears and answers prayers."

"If you think God killed your wife because of your prayer-- Well, I don't know what to say to that."

"Do you believe in God?" I asked, surprised at myself for not knowing whether she did or not.

"I think so. I don't know. If he does exist, I don't think he involves himself in our individual lives much. I mean, the universe is a big place."

We were silent for a few minutes before she said, "If your prayer did have something to do with what happened, then it seems to me like you're wasting it. Four years, and you're still not re-married. You're still wearing your wedding ring for Christ's sake. Have you even gone out on a date since then? Like, a real date."

I shook my head. "I didn't think I deserved that. I thought I loved Glenda, but apparently I didn't."

"The fact that this has affected you for four years proves that you did love her. At least, that's my opinion."

"Things are so different now. I'm different."

"Do you still want kids?"

"I don't know. It seems like that ship has sailed. I'm forty years old now."

"I have never wanted kids," Lydia stated with firmness in her voice. "I want to live my life and not get tied down like my mom did so that she felt like she had to have a man supporting us. Plus, I'd make a terrible mother."

I should have told her that she would make a great mother, but I had reached the point of being exhausted by talking. I just looked at her and smiled. She smiled back and patted my hand. We were good. She wasn't going to run from me, screaming. And I felt better. Someone besides God and me now knew about my prayer. It had felt as if the secret had been squeezing the life out of me, like a disease. Getting it out was a release. And after Lydia's reaction, I felt like I had made far too much of it than it deserved.

"And for the record," Lydia said, "you are the kindest, most giving, selfless person I've ever met. And you're pretty hot too, for a forty-year-old."

"I don't know about that. But thank you."

Lydia took my hand and held it against her thigh. It wasn't the most comfortable position for me while driving the car, but I didn't want to say anything since that physical contact stirred something in me. We drove in silence, glancing at each other every few minutes, but in that silence, we were one. Some wall had broken. As I neared the house, I asked, "Should I stop at the CVS?"

"No, I've got it covered," Lydia replied with full understanding.

We entered the house through the garage. Lydia went toward her room, and I went toward mine. I took off my clothes and brushed my teeth. When I finished rinsing my mouth, I could hear water running. I walked out of the room and down the hall. Lydia was using the shower by her room, for the first time. I've never been one to catch subtle messages, but I caught this one. I went back to my own bathroom and started my own shower. After washing my hair and thoroughly scrubbing my body, I rinsed and dried off. I managed to find an old bottle of cologne in the back of my medicine cabinet and put just a tiny bit under my chin. Once my hair was perfectly brushed, I walked out of my bathroom, half expecting Lydia to be waiting for me on the bed. She wasn't there. I stopped at my dresser and looked at myself in the mirror. When I looked down, I saw my wedding ring, still there after almost four and a half years. I was about to move on, to venture forward. It was time. I grabbed the ring and slipped it off my finger, twisting to get it over the first knuckle. I dropped it into the top left drawer, where I kept my collectibles, sporting event and concert ticket stubs, autographed baseball cards, photos of my grandparents, funeral programs, and a printed ultrasound photo of the ovum that Glenda and I thought would become our baby. I closed the drawer and took a deep breath.

I ventured out into the hall, still naked. Lydia and I were professional nude models; we didn't need clothes. I stopped just before the open door to her bedroom, leaned forward, and peeked in. Lydia was lying naked on her bed, on her back, her arms over her head and her legs slightly apart. She saw me, and her eyes narrowed but seemed to glow as she exhaled. I stepped into the room and enjoyed the sight of her, of her naked body.

"I thought you'd never get here," she said.

I walked to her and knelt on the floor beside her bed. She reached for me, pulled my lips to hers, and we kissed. I caressed the side of her head, relishing the feeling of her hair gliding between my fingers as I moved my hand down to her shoulder. Breathing the smell of her shampoo, I pulled my head away, detaching from her kiss. I looked down the length of her body.

"I love looking at you," I said.

"I love it when you look at me. But right now, I want you to do more than look."

I slid my hand down her shoulder and onto her chest, moving to one side so that my palm covered and cupped one of her breasts. My thumb passed over her nipple as I continued moving my hand down the length of her torso. I watched my fingers reach her clean shaven pubic mound. I caressed downward, two of my fingers disappearing between the delicate folds of skin between her thighs. Lydia inhaled sharply and spread her legs further apart. She reached up and pulled my head down to hers, our lips locking together again. As our tongues intertwined with each other's, the pad of my middle finger slid over the hood of her clitoris. Lydia's body clenched as I touched her most sensitive spot.

I pulled away from her kiss, looking at her eyes as I moved down to the foot of the bed. I thought about her longings, her desires, whatever it was that had driven her to expose her body to art students, to flash herself to people passing in the hall, to strip down to nothing while she danced amongst strangers. I wanted to fulfill her every longing, her every desire, make her forget she had ever had those other longings. My fingertips tickled and then caressed her inner thighs as I put my mouth on her, my tongue exploring the sweet and intricate folds of skin and flesh. Then I lost myself. There was nothing except Lydia's smell, Lydia's taste, Lydia's pleasure. I used my tongue, my lips, my fingers, and Lydia responded to everything, her body tensing and relaxing, then tensing again. I moved with her, timing my moves to her response, taking her up, then up higher, back down, then higher still. Finally, there was a sudden and powerful spasm throughout her body, and she pushed on my forehead. I drew back, removing my fingers from deep within her, seeing that her eyes had seemingly rolled back into her head. She tried to say something but could not catch her breath. Now that my mouth had been on her, I didn't want it to not be on her. But she couldn't handle any more; I could see that. I wiped my mouth with the back of my hand, the hand that had been mostly inside her, feeling my own saliva mixed with her juices. I looked down and saw that the sheet under her was soaked.

"Give me a minute," she finally said between breaths.

My fingertips lightly massaged her thighs, her hips, and her belly. After a moment, her expression changed and she looked at me with her blazing green eyes. She sat up and kissed me deeply. She slipped off the bed and threw me down onto it in one smooth motion. Before I realized it, her mouth was on me, her tongue sliding and wrapping around my pulsing erection. I tried to pull her leg toward me, wanting her on top of me, straddling my head, wanting my mouth on her again, wanting to taste her, and most of all, wanting to hear and feel her orgasm again. She swatted my hand away, as if to tell me that it was my turn now and to lie back and enjoy it. So I did.

I've only had a few blow jobs in my life, from only three different women. The first two were in my early college days. The third was, of course, Glenda, although she didn't offer fellatio often and wasn't particularly skillful at it. Lydia was a different story; she brought me to the edge three different times without going over, making my feet almost cramp in each instance from the curling of my toes. When she stopped, she reached for something on her night table. I started to get up, but she pushed me back down. She ripped open the condom wrapper with her teeth and rolled it on. I had never worn a condom before, and the sensation wasn't pleasant as it was too tight on my penis. Lydia swung her leg over me, straddled me, and guided me into her. I reached up and cupped her smallish breasts and just enjoyed being inside her, being one flesh.

The sensations were muted as she rocked back and forth, up and down on me. She started on her knees, but got up on her feet, squatting over me. She pushed on my chest with her hands as she rocked up and down, riding me. I held her arms and watched her face as the orgasm hit her. She sat all the way down, impaling herself on me, and I felt all her muscles contract, squeezing me. As she came down from that, I took charge, lifting her up as I rose from the bed, flipping her around without losing the penetration. Lydia came at least twice in the missionary position, yelling and screaming loudly, telling me to fuck her harder, before she pushed me away from her. Once I was out, she flipped over on all fours.

"Fuck me from behind," she said.

I entered her, started moving slowly, and then built up speed. The motion in this position was more intense, and Lydia started pounding the side of the mattress with her fist as the waves hit her. My thrusting became faster and faster, and somewhere during that, the sensation blew open. I could feel every little pulse, every rhythm, and I felt myself building and building. I exploded in a barrage of spasms that didn't seem like they would ever stop, the feeling so intense that I didn't think I could stand much more of it. Lydia tightened on me and screamed herself, our screams mingling.

It was the most intense orgasm I could ever remember, probably because it had been building in me for four years. When my body stopped trembling, I opened my eyes. Lydia was covered in sweat, her backside still pressed against my hips. I felt myself shrinking out of her, and I withdrew. I went to grab the used condom, but all I found was a ring of rolled up, ripped latex. The condom had broken. I had felt it but hadn't recognized it for what it was.

"Oh my God," Lydia said. "If I had known it was going to be like that, I would have jumped you a long time ago."

"The condom broke," I said, lying down next to her. She scooted over to give me room.

"What?" she said.

"The condom broke," I repeated.

"Shit!"

She felt herself between her legs, raised her hand, and looked at the glob of semen on her fingers. In a flash, she jumped up and rushed to the bathroom across the hall. I lifted myself up and over the night stand far enough to throw what was left of the condom in the small trash can in the corner. Rolling back to the bed, I leaned on one elbow with my head raised, and I could see Lydia sitting on the commode, her legs open so far that it looked like she was straddling it. She bent over, opened the cabinet under the vanity, and pulled out a douche bottle. I lay back down and looked at the ceiling, thinking that I shouldn't watch such a personal, intimate act, but I could still hear the trickling splashes of water as it cascaded down into the toilet bowl.

Unbidden and unwanted memories flooded back, Glenda's post coital attempts to promote pregnancy, putting three, four, and sometimes five pillows under her butt and laying on her back, using those pillows to keep her pelvis raised. A couple of times she even went to the extreme of rolling off the bed and standing on her head in the corner next to her night table, with me standing next to her holding her feet up. She would stay in that position until the blood rush to her head caused her to almost pass out. None of these attempts to will my sperm to reach her egg ever worked.

"You shouldn't worry," I called to Lydia. "It has been my experience that getting pregnant isn't that easy."

The toilet flushed, and Lydia slid back into bed beside me.

"It doesn't hurt to take every precaution," she said.

Lydia draped an arm over my chest and a leg over my pelvis. She lifted her head to allow me to get my arm around her shoulders.

"Sorry about that," I said.

"Shit happens. I should have gotten the XL condoms for you. It should be all right. I just got off my period – when was it? I can't remember. But it hasn't been long. So we should be good."

"You should get on The Pill."

"I would if I could afford to go to the doctor."

"I thought everyone had to have health insurance now."

"I'm on my mom's plan," Lydia said, "but it's not very good. High co-pays."

"I'll take care of the co-pay."

I felt a damp stickiness on my butt and realized just how wet the bed had become.

"We should change your sheets," I said, my voice sounding dreamy and detached.

"Not now. Let's just lay here."

Exhausted and content, I dozed for a little while, my mind clear and calm for the first time in weeks, until the wet sheets started sticking to my sweaty skin.

"We should move to my bed," I mumbled.

"Are you hungry?" Lydia asked, her voice alert and awake.

"I guess so," I said, although I was still feeling quite satisfied at that moment.

"You wanna go out to eat?"

What I wanted was to lie in a dry bed with Lydia's nude body curled around me like it was now. "Do we have to put clothes on?" I said, my half dozing state making my voice sound dreamy and far away.

"Yes."

Lydia unwrapped herself from me and jumped up. I rolled off the bed and started stripping the sheets off.

"Sorry," Lydia said, helping me with the sheets. "I get-- Well--"

"It's OK. It was awesome."

I carried her bedding to the laundry room and threw it straight into the washing machine. I threw in some detergent and some fabric softener and started the machine cycle. Lydia stood in the entrance between the kitchen and laundry room, watching me. Her face was still flush, and her body still gleamed with sweat. Her hair was disheveled and hung wildly around her face. I glanced down toward her hips, noticing that her labia were still red and protruding, and I wanted her again. I could feel my arousal growing already.

I dropped the lid on the washing machine and took Lydia by the hand. I led her to my shower and started the water, as hot as we could stand it. I washed her body, kneeling down in front of her to scrub all of her. Once she was rinsed, I kneeled down in front of her again and put my mouth on her.   Since I didn't think Lydia had any more condoms, not any that she would trust anyway, I simply stood up and washed myself while she recovered from the orgasm I had just given her.

Once we were both clean and dressed, I drove us to a nearby barbecue place.   After a dinner during which I paid rapt attention to Lydia's description of the differing timelines of the original Star Trek television series and the recent movies, we stopped at Walmart and bought a fresh box of Magnum XL condoms.   We finally made it to sleep somewhere around one AM.   We avoided the room I used to share with Glenda until it was time to sleep, going at it in the shower again, against the bathroom counter, and in the game room with a couple of beach towels under Lydia's derriere.   Once we were completely spent, I brought her to my bed. After four years of sleeping by myself in the middle of the king size mattress, I moved to Glenda's side. Lydia slept in my old spot.

13

Lydia and I pulled ourselves out of bed at 6:45 on the morning of Saturday, April 6th. I made sure we had my camcorder, the signs that Lydia had made, and our driver's licenses. Anticipating a possible need for bail money. I had gone to the bank earlier in the week and withdrawn four thousand dollars. I took that cash from the bottom drawer of my dresser and stuffed the bills into my jeans pockets. The temperature outside at 7:15 AM when we walked out of the house was a comfortable sixty-five degrees, and the sky was clear. I was glad that we weren't going to be freezing for our protest.

After checking to make sure the two large beach towels were still in the back seat where I had put them on the day of my trip to the bank, I drove my Prius toward Dallas. Lydia talked about the Internet-spread theories on different Game of Thrones characters' lineages as she fidgeted in her seat. We had spent part of the previous ten days binge watching the first five seasons, in between sex and school work. We only had two seasons to watch in the next week before the eighth and final season premiered on HBO. Our conversations during this time had all revolved around science fiction and fantasy movies or TV shows, sex, school work, or other superficial, trivial things. I think we both realized that we both had painful pasts and didn't yet feel comfortable enough to talk about them.

The last time I had seen Lydia so jerky and jittery like this was on the way to the Ecstatic Dance. I listened, letting her talk to calm her nerves, and marveled that she had seemingly memorized what I had thought were some complex genealogies of fictional characters in just a few days. We both loved the Game of Thrones TV series, and Lydia had even ventured to Half Price Books and bought inexpensive paperback copies of the first five books of the series on which it was based.

We got to the Whataburger near the abortion clinic at 8:30. Lydia tried to take my hand as we walked from my car to the front door, but I shook her off. Crystal was waiting for us inside, and I didn't want her to know about my relationship with Lydia until after the project was done.

Crystal waved at us as we stepped inside, and we walked straight to her booth.

"Good morning," she said.

"Morning."

Lydia and I slid in across from Crystal.

"Did you guys ride together or something?"

"Yes," I said.

"Did you go all the way to Denton to get her?"

"I moved to Fort Worth," Lydia said. "Recently."

"Oh. OK," Crystal said.

She was in the middle of eating a breakfast sandwich that looked greasy and smelled delicious.

"Do you want something to eat?" I asked Lydia.

"No, I'm not hungry." Her leg bounced repeatedly, and I put my hand on her thigh to try to calm her.

"How about a drink?" I asked her.

"Yeah, I'll take a Diet Coke."

I went to the front and ordered two breakfast taquitos and two soft drinks. I took the two drinks and my plastic order number indicator back to the table.

"...class starts at 10:30," I heard Crystal tell Lydia, "and we are done before 12:00."

"What class?" I asked, handing Lydia her drink and sitting down beside her.

"Crystal was inviting me to her church tomorrow."

"Which church?"

"Hulen Church of Christ," Crystal replied.

"You go to church in Fort Worth?"

"My parents live close to there. You could come too. But our class is technically for young singles... Where's your wedding ring?"

"Yeah," I said. "I finally took it off."

"You're not married?" Crystal asked.

"I'm a widower."

"Oh, I'm sorry."

"It's OK," I said. "It has been four years. So I am single, see? And I'm still young. I mean, I'm a college student, right."

Lydia patted my leg under the table.

"Sure," Crystal said.

An orange-shirted Whataburger employee brought my taquitos and exchanged them for the plastic number.

"Would you like some hot sauce?" she asked.

"Yes, two."

She handed me two packets and said, "Here you go. Enjoy your breakfast."

"So, we're really doing this, huh?" Crystal asked as I unwrapped my first taquito and squeezed hot sauce into it. "You're really going to go out there naked?"

"Yep," Lydia said.

"Aren't you nervous?"

"A little. But not from being naked. I'm just worried about the police."

"When they get there," I said after swallowing my first bite, "just be nice and do what they say. Don't answer any questions about why we're here or what we're doing. It'll be fine."

I took another bite of taquito.

"Fifteen minutes, right?" Crystal said.

"Yes, fifteen minutes, and we are gone," I agreed.

"Am I driving?" Crystal asked. "What if someone gets my license plate number?"

"Do you want to drive my car?" I asked.

"Can I?"

"Have you ever driven a Prius?"

"No. Is there anything special about it?"

"You don't have to use a key," I said. "You just need to have the key fob in your pocket somewhere. You start it with a button, but if the car doesn't sense the fob, it won't start. I can show you when we get in."

"OK," Crystal said. "If you're OK with it."

"It's fine with me."

I ate quickly, and as nine o'clock approached, I felt the nervous flutters in my gut more and more. By the time I finished the first taquito, I wasn't hungry. In fact, I was sorry I had eaten at all; the flutters were making me want to throw up.

"Do either of you want that?" I asked, motioning to the second taquito.

Nobody did, so I left it on the tray.

I took a deep breath and said, "We ready?"

"Yes," Lydia said.

The three of us stood up and headed to my car. I unlocked it with the fob and handed my keys to Crystal. Lydia and I got in the back seat while Crystal got behind the wheel and started adjusting the seat and mirrors. That meant I would have to adjust them back, and it was always a pain getting them all exactly where I liked them.

Lydia and I stripped in the close quarters of the back seat, laughing every time we bumped into each other. Crystal pressed the Start button on the car, but that only turned on the radio.

"Ok, how do I start..." she said, turning to look at me and stopping when she saw that I was completely naked. "Oh!" She turned back toward the front again, her face red.

"Step on the brake while you push the button," I told her.

She did that, and the car came to life.

"That little thing there is the gear shift," I said, leaning forward and pointing.

"OK."

She put it in reverse and backed out of the parking space.

"Hold the brake and move the gear shift to D," I said when Crystal paused in the middle of the lot. "It'll pop back to that base position. You have to look at the display to see what gear you are in."

Crystal managed to get the car into D, and she drove to the parking lot of a radiology lab across the street from the abortion clinic. A news van from Channel 4 was also parked in the lot.

"How do I turn it off?" Crystal asked.

"Same way. Just step on the brake and hit the button."

She did, and the car powered off. Lydia and I stepped out, barefooted and wrapped in the beach towels, the concrete feeling rough and cold. Cars zipped by in both directions on Greenville. Russell and his family were in the median, walking back and forth just like they had been the last time I was here. A woman in a skirt suit stood at one end of the median, alongside a young guy in a t-shirt and jeans, a large, expensive-looking camera on his shoulder. The woman held a microphone in her hand.

Crystal walked around to the back of the car with us, my keys in her hand.

"Looks like somebody from the media is here," I said. "Good job."

Crystal shrugged and said, "My cousin sent them."

I opened the back hatchback and retrieved my camcorder from its bag.

"Go ahead and put those in your pocket," I said to Crystal, nodding toward my keys.

She put the keys away and watched as I showed her how to start and stop recording with the camcorder and how to switch to still photos.

"Take lots of pictures," I said. "Zoom in, but not too far. And don't try to just get PG rated pictures. Take shots of everything."

"OK," she said, taking the camcorder from me.

I pulled our two signs from the back and handed one to Lydia.

"Are you ready?" I asked.

She took a deep breath and looked across at the median. Everybody in the median, Russell, his wife and daughter, and the two media people, were all looking at us with curiosity.

"Yes," Lydia said.

"All right," I said. "Next break in traffic and we toss the towels and run across."

"OK," she said again.

Crystal stood behind us, shaking her head.

I watched the cars going by, my sign upside down and leaning against my leg, my hand holding the towel together. A group of cars passed, with a Volkswagen Beetle trailing behind. Behind the Beetle, the street was clear.

"All right," I said. "One, two, three—"

"Wait!" Lydia exclaimed.

One side of my towel had slipped out of my hand as I had been about to throw the whole thing off and into the back of the Prius, exposing my backside to Crystal. I crouched and snatched it back up, almost knocking my sign over in the process.

"What?" I snapped.

"I'm not ready," she said.

She picked her sign up from the ground where it had fallen. I hadn't noticed that she had dropped it.

"Sorry," she said.

I looked back at the street, but a large group of vehicles was bearing down on our crossing area.

"OK," I said. "Next break."

The current group of cars started to dwindle. A Honda Odyssey van was the tailing vehicle, and nothing was in sight behind it.

"What time is it Crystal?" I asked.

"9:07," she said.

"Honk the horn at 9:20," I told her.

"OK."

I realized my feet were bouncing up and down in nervous anticipation. I was almost dancing.

"Lydia?"

"I'm ready."

"One, two…" The van passed by, and I said, "Three!"

I whipped the towel off, tossed it into the back of the Prius, clutched my sign with both hands, and dashed across the street to the median. I could see Lydia next to me in my peripheral vision. The guy in the median frantically changed settings on his camera. Russell grabbed his daughter's shoulders and turned her away from us. His wife had stopped in her tracks and was staring at us with her mouth open in astonishment. Every sensation was magnified in my naked state. The cool air enveloped my whole body. The concrete of the street felt even rougher under my bare feet than in the parking lot, and I flinched as I stepped on a pebble.

Lydia and I bounded onto the grassy median, still wet from that morning's watering, and stopped. I looked at her, smiled, and winked, slightly out of breath. She winked back. We raised our signs and started walking up and down the median.

"What do you think you are doing?" Russell said indignantly.

"Making a statement for life," I said.

"How is this a statement for life?"

"Did you ever read Isaiah chapter 20?" I asked.

"I have read the entire Bible many times," he said. "You and your gal should get clothes on."

I nodded toward the lady with the microphone. She had it pointed at Russell and me, but I don't know if it could pick up our voices at that distance, about fifteen feet.

"Do you think they would be here if we were just doing what you were doing? I want to take a stand for the babies that people will listen to. Now, read Isaiah 20. The first few verses."

Russell's wife was thumbing through her Bible. She stopped and read, her mouth falling open again. Russell moved over to her and read over her shoulder. His daughter was standing behind her parents, looking at me with wide eyes. I felt like I should cover up, the way she was looking at me, but I realized she was just curious. I turned and started walking toward the other end of the median. Cars were speeding by, and we heard several horns blare at us.

I looked at Lydia to ask if she was all right, but when I saw how her face seemed to glow, I realized that I didn't need to ask. The lady with the microphone stood at the end of the median waiting for Lydia and me as her partner kept the camera trained on us.

"Hello, I'm Maggie Driscoll from Fox 4 News," she said as we walked right up to her. "Would you mind if I asked you a few questions real quick on camera?"

"No, go ahead," I replied.

"Could I get your names?"

"Sure. I'm David, and this is Lydia."

She nodded to her cameraman and waited for his cue, with his camera pointed at us, before continuing. I stood with my sign still held high in the air, trying to remember everything I had imagined saying. The cameraman held up a fist and counted, "One, two," extending a finger with each count. Three was silent.

"Ron, I'm standing on the median of Greenville Avenue outside the Women's Health Associates clinic, which is a well known abortion provider. With me are David and Lydia, who, like many others before them, are protesting legalized abortion. What makes their protest unusual is their attire, or lack thereof. David, why are you and Lydia protesting here completely naked?"

"Because the babies who are being killed in this clinic are naked and defenseless. We stripped naked to stand in solidarity with them. Our culture usually associates nakedness with shame, and the fact is, we should all be ashamed that we are allowing such things as abortion to happen in our society."

"How did you come up with the idea to protest naked like this?" Maggie asked.

"That was actually Lydia's idea," I replied, and Lydia smiled for the camera. "We both model for art classes at colleges in the area, so we're used to being nude in front of other people. We figured, why not use our comfort with nudity to make a worthwhile statement."

"Are the authorities aware of this protest? Did you apply for a permit?"

I wasn't expecting a question like this, so I had to come up with something on the fly. "The First Amendment to the United States

Constitution is our permit," I said. "We didn't apply with the city since they never would have approved. In some instances, civil disobedience is called for, and I think that the legalized murder of our fellow human beings qualifies as such an instance."

"Nudity seems like something that would be used by those who identify as pro-choice. What do you say to others on your side who object to the nudity?"

"The perception is that everyone who is pro-life is a Bible thumping Christian. By doing this, which most people in the church would object to, we are showing that that isn't true. You don't have to be Christian to be pro-life."

"So you're saying you're not a Christian?"

I paused, not knowing how to answer. I'd never stopped to consider what I had become, what I really believed, since Glenda's wreck.

"No, I'm not saying that," I finally replied.

Maggie started to ask another question, but a horn from a slow-moving Cadillac blared right next to us. Lydia had started walking, almost strutting, the other way in the median, holding her sign up high. I saw a line of cars in line to turn into the parking lot of the radiology lab where my Prius was parked and a small crowd gathered on the curb, watching us, most of them with cell phones pointed at us. I didn't want Lydia far away from me, for safety reasons, but the reporter was still trying to continue the interview. I realized that she was waiting for me to say something.

"I'm sorry?" I said.

"What will you do if the police try to arrest you?"

"Then I guess we'll get a ride downtown," I replied with a smile.

I didn't really like that Maggie wasn't asking questions about abortion itself, so I turned away and walked toward Lydia, holding my sign lower, trying to make sure it showed up on camera.

"This is Maggie Driscoll for Fox 4 News," I heard the reporter say.

The cameraman kept taking footage of Lydia and me as we walked to the end of the median and turned back toward him. I saw Crystal on the curb among the crowd, still holding my camcorder pointed at us. Four people darted across the street and joined us on the median. They looked to be teenagers, two males and two females.

"Can we get a picture with you?" one of the girls asked us.

I started to say no, but Lydia bounced forward and said, "Sure."

The two guys and one of the girls stood beside us while the other girl took a picture with her iPhone. We started to walk away along the median after she took the picture, but the girl said, "Hold on. Jimmy!"

One of the guys stepped forward and took the phone from the girl. She took Jimmy's place while he snapped another picture.

"Thank you," the other girl said, as they all gathered around Jimmy to look at the photos they had captured.

"This is amazing," Lydia said to me as we continued along the median.

I watched the four teenagers start back across Greenville. They were paying more attention to the iPhone than to the traffic and almost got hit by a pickup truck. The truck slammed on its brakes, and the squealing of tires seemed to wake the teenagers up. One of the girls put the phone in her pocket as they all finished crossing the street.

Russell was gathering his signs and box of pamphlets.

"Are you leaving?" I asked him.

"I'm not going to expose my daughter to this. To you."

"We don't plan on being here very long."

"I should say not. The police will probably haul you off soon."

"Look, just ten more minutes, and we'll be gone."

I had reached the end of the median, so I turned around and started walking back the other way, still following Lydia. Russell led his wife and daughter across the street, to the radiology lab parking lot. On the other side of the street, several people from the abortion clinic had come outside to watch us. One of them was talking on her phone while others took photos or video of us. I stopped on the street, stood facing them, and moved my sign down so that it hid my face from them. If they were trying to get pictures of me, I wanted to make sure the sign was in the shot. Lydia had continued on up the median, so I only stood still for a moment. I caught up with her just as she reached the other end, where Maggie was.

"Was this really your idea?" I heard Maggie ask, still speaking into her microphone.

"Abso-fucking-lutely," Lydia replied.

"And how does this feel?"

"What?" I chimed in.

"Being naked in public with such a large crowd," Maggie said.

"Amazing," Lydia replied before I could. "It's so liberating. I wish we could be free to be naked wherever and whenever we wanted."

I grabbed Lydia's shoulder and turned her away from Maggie before she said something that would ruin my planned legal defense.

We started toward the other end of the median just in time to see the first Dallas Police Department car arrive. Another patrol car joined it by the time we got to that end. They parked so that they blocked the two left lanes of southbound Greenville Avenue, their red and blue lights flashing. We turned and started back up the median again, away from the police cars and toward Maggie. I saw Crystal looking at us from across the street, her hands held out in a "What now?" gesture with my camcorder turned toward the ground. I just waved at her, telling her to carry on taking pictures and video.

The officers, four of them in all, three men and one woman, got out of their cars as Lydia and I started walking toward them.

"What do we do now?" Lydia whispered to me.

"Just play it cool," I said. "Remember, let me do the talking."

We got to the end near the police cars and, ignoring the officers, turned and started walking back the other way. The Fox 4 cameraman was still shooting.

"Excuse me," one of the officers said from behind us. "We need you to stop walking."

I stopped and turned, still holding my sign. Lydia turned and stood beside me. Two of the officers approached, a large black man and a short blonde woman.

"We're going to have to ask you to cover up," the female officer said. "Do you have any clothes with you that you can put on?"

"Wearing clothes kind of kills the point that we are trying to make," I said.

"I understand, but you can't make that point here."

"If you don't comply, we'll have to place you under arrest," the big guy said.

"Arrested for what?" I asked.

"Indecent exposure, for one."

"For indecent exposure, there has to be the intent to sexually gratify someone. There is no such intent here. We're trying to make a statement about the defenselessness of these babies that are being killed. The First Amendment guarantees us..."

"You cannot be naked here on the city street," the female officer said. "It's a safety hazard. You're going to cause an accident. Why don't you cover up, and we can talk about it."

After having seen the four teenagers almost get run over, I could see her point. I lowered my sign and took Lydia's hand.

"Our clothes are across the street," I said, nodding my head toward the Prius.

"All right," the blonde said. "I'm Officer Tyler. This is Officer Brown. We're going to walk you across the street. You can get dressed, and then we can talk about what we do from here."

As we started across the street, Officer Brown put his hand on my shoulder as if guiding me. I noticed that Tyler did something similar with Lydia. As we crossed, the people who had gathered applauded. I didn't know if they were applauding Lydia and me for the boldness of our protest or the cops for ending it. Crystal was ready with our beach towels when we got to the Prius. Lydia and I set our signs down and wrapped up.

"Now why shouldn't we take you in?" Brown said.

"This kind of protest is completely unacceptable," Tyler said.

"But it makes a point," I countered. "Look at everyone around. They are talking about abortion in a new light."

"No, they're talking about the crazy naked people," Brown said.

"Well," I said, "we're done now."

"Yes, I should say so," said Tyler. "Do you have your identification?"

"In the car."

"Could you get them?" Tyler said.

Lydia and I walked to the passenger side of the car. I opened the back door, handed Lydia her purse, and retrieved my wallet from the back pocket of my jeans. The two officers shadowed us. Brown even grabbed the waist band of my jeans feeling the lumps in my pockets.

"What's all this?" he asked.

"Cash, in case we needed bail money."

"So you expected to get arrested?"

"I thought it was a possibility. But like I said, there was no intent for the sexual gratification of anyone." I grabbed a sheet of paper from my back seat and read from it. "So that makes this fall under Texas Penal Code Forty-two Ten, Disorderly Conduct which is a Class C misdemeanor. Such an offense is citable. You don't have to arrest us."

I was feeling more and more like a pre-law student as I pulled my driver's license from my wallet and handed it to Officer Tyler.

"Mr. Michaels, is this your current address?" Tyler asked as she examined my identification.

"Yes. I've lived there for ten years."

Lydia had retrieved her ID and handed it to Tyler. "My address is wrong. I just moved in with him."

Tyler looked at the card and said, "You both wait here. I'll be right back."

Brown stayed with us, and the other two officers had walked over and now stood in front of my car.

"May I put these on?" I asked Brown.

He shrugged. I put my jeans on under my towel, removed the towel, and put on my t-shirt. Lydia also dressed under her towel although her breasts were exposed for a split second when she dropped the towel to get her shirt pulled down. Crystal stood beside us, a look of fear in her eyes.

"It's all right," I said.

"I've just never been in trouble," Crystal replied.

"You're not in trouble."

"Are you sure I'm not like an accomplice or something?"

"Don't worry," I said and patted her arm.

Officer Tyler was sitting in the driver's seat of her patrol car, looking at the computer monitor inside. I could see her talking to someone on her radio. Brown stood silently, just looking at us while the other two cops whispered among themselves.

"How many people called about us?" I asked Officer Brown, just to try to relieve some of the awkwardness.

"I don't know. We just got the one dispatch."

He didn't say anything else, and from the curt tone of his voice, I decided not to ask anything else. Traffic was backing up on the southbound side of Greenville since everyone had to squeeze over to the right lane to get around the police cars.

"You think we're going to jail?" Lydia asked me in a low voice.

"We're not in handcuffs yet," I replied.

Officer Tyler finally stepped out of her patrol car and walked over to us carrying a clipboard.

"I'm going to sit in the car," Crystal said.

Crystal shrunk away, and Lydia and I turned toward Tyler. Lydia took my hand.

"All right Mr. Michaels, Ms. Nelson, you are not going to be placed under arrest."

Lydia sighed, and her entire body seemed to relax. I probably did the same thing. I hadn't realized how tense we had been.

"I have issued you both citations for disorderly conduct," Officer Tyler continued. "Instructions for making arrangements with the court will be on your copy of the citation. You have 20 days to either contact or appear before the court. If you don't, a warrant will be issued for your arrest, and you will face additional charges for failure to appear. Do you both understand this?"

Lydia and I both nodded.

"Do you have a phone number where you can be reached?" Tyler asked.

I recited my number, and Tyler typed it in. She then handed me her clipboard, which was an electronic pad with a stylus attached by a small chain.

"Please read what's on the screen and sign in the space. Your signature is a promise to appear; it does not admit any guilt for the offense."

I skimmed the citation on the screen, took the stylus, and signed the blank. Tyler took it back and pressed a couple of buttons. A long strip of paper emerged from the bottom. When it finished, Tyler tore the paper off and handed it to me. She punched another button or two, typed in Lydia's phone number, and handed the pad to Lydia. Lydia signed it and got her printed copy.

"Do not try this stunt again," Officer Tyler warned. "If you do, you will be arrested and face more serious charges. Do you understand?"

"Yes ma'am," I said. Lydia nodded.

"Have a nice day."

All four of the officers got back into their patrol cars. Lydia leaned into me and put her arms around my waist.

"That was scarier than I thought it would be," she said. "I really thought we were going to go to jail when they showed up."

Crystal bounced out of the car.

"I don't believe they didn't arrest you," she said.

"Let's go before they change their minds," I said.

Lydia and I climbed into the back seat. Crystal got back into the car, started it up, and drove the short distance to Whataburger.

"I mean, seriously," Crystal said as she drove my car. "You were out there naked in front of everyone, in front of the police, and they didn't arrest you. How did that happen?"

"Disorderly conduct was really the only thing they could charge us with," I said. "And since we complied with their order to stop, they didn't have to arrest us."

"They didn't have to write us tickets either," Lydia complained. "Why couldn't they have just let us off with a warning?"

"Hey!" Crystal exclaimed suddenly to Lydia. "You moved in with

David?"

"Yeah."

"When?"

"Just the other day," Lydia replied.

"Why? I thought you two just modeled together."

"I got kicked out of my apartment. David is really helping me out."

"It was just temporary," I said. After I said it, I realized that I had used the past tense. Did I no longer think of it as temporary? Lydia must have realized what I said because she gave my hand a squeeze.

Crystal drove my car into the Whataburger parking lot and parked in the same spot we had vacated a half an hour before.

"Well, here we are," she said.

"Oh, where's my camcorder?" I asked.

Crystal had it in the passenger seat. She handed it back to me, and I powered it on and started looking through the photos and video she had taken on the camera's small display screen. There were over twenty different photos and fifteen video clips of Lydia and me walking the median, talking with Russell, speaking to the reporter, waving our signs to oncoming traffic and to the clinic workers on the far side of the street, posing with the teenagers, and talking to the police. Lydia looked at them with me, but I didn't scroll through each one.

"These look awesome," I told Crystal.

"Yeah, I can't wait to see them on the computer monitor," Lydia said.

"Thanks." Crystal turned in her seat and looked back at us. "This was a totally crazy morning."

We all laughed, and I held up our two citations.

"Yes it was," I said.

"I guess we're done then?" Crystal said.

"I guess so. We'll have to write our reports. I guess we're supposed to write them separately. I'm going to pick out the best photos from here and turn mine in via e-mail. Crystal, I'll email you all the stuff from the camera so you can include whatever you want in your report."

"Um, well, OK. Although it will be weird getting nude photos from a man."

We all chuckled.

"OK," Crystal said. "I'm going to go home. Here's your keys."

I took my keys from Crystal, and we all stepped out of my car. I walked around to the driver's side and the three of us stood looking at each other for an awkward moment. Crystal finally shrugged, gave Lydia and me hugs.

"I'll see you Monday," she said, apparently having forgotten the invitation to church she had made to Lydia. Perhaps she had reconsidered after hearing that Lydia and I were now living together in sin.

"See ya," I said. "Be careful going home."

She walked to her car, and Lydia and I got into the front seat of my Prius where I began the long process of getting my seat, mirrors, and steering wheel back where I liked them. I was still adjusting when I merged onto North Central Expressway.

14

Lydia and I watched the six o'clock news on channel four that evening with great anticipation. The story on us was about half way through the telecast, just before the weather. The footage had been edited to about a minute and a half, with a recorded voiceover by Maggie Driscoll, and the parts of our bodies deemed too inappropriate for television were pixelated. The only interview footage that aired was a two second clip of my comparing the shame of nudity to the shame of abortion. I wished that they had included the part just before, when I'd said that we were naked and defenseless to stand in solidarity with the babies being killed, but at least the footage displayed our signs for almost ten full seconds. Lydia, sitting beside me on the couch, squeezed my arm whenever she appeared in a shot.

"This is so cool!" she said when the report finished. "I've never been on TV before."

After Glenda's wreck, one of the other local stations had done an exposé on a few local trucking companies and how they had allowed their drivers to falsify logs to drive more hours per day than was allowed by law, and they had interviewed me about Glenda's death and the resulting lawsuit. I had hated seeing myself on screen then as my grief and anger were still written all over my face. But I didn't feel like bringing that up to Lydia, so I simply agreed with her, that it was cool being on TV.

The next day I left Lydia at the house and drove to Dallas to model for the Sunday open drawing lab at the Creative Arts Center. Only five artists showed up to draw, but one of them had seen me on TV the night before and told everyone else about it. All five of them kept asking me questions about the protest, Lydia, and the encounter with police even while I was in a pose. I kept my answers short during the drawing time. I never liked to talk when posing, and most colleges even have policies prohibiting models from speaking to students while on the stand. One of the appeals of modeling is that I get to spend so much time alone with just my own thoughts, and the conversation with the artists during that session took away from that, especially since the talk was about me.

When I got home that afternoon, Lydia, naked as usual, met me in the laundry room as I walked in from the garage. She grabbed my hand as she started bouncing away.

"David, come here," she said, her voice full of excitement, "you have to see this."

"What?" I said, allowing her to drag me to the study.

A Youtube page was loaded on my computer monitor. "Naked and Pro-Life?" was the title of the video.

"I pulled this up twenty minutes ago," Lydia said. "Look at the number of views." It was at just over 415,000. "Now watch." Lydia clicked the refresh button. The page reloaded, but the view count went up to 453,000.

"Twenty minutes?" I said. "Almost forty thousand views?"

"We're going viral!" Lydia said with a giggle and a clap of her hands. "Can you believe it?"

The picture on the screen was of Lydia and me on the median, naked with our genitals and her breasts obscured by a blur and our signs held high. I could see Russell and his family huddled at one end of the median. The shot was taken from the side of Greenville Avenue where I had seen several people gathered to watch. I took the mouse and clicked on the play button. The still frame came to life, with sounds of passing traffic, muffled voices of the people gathered near the person taking the video, and the motion of Lydia and me. I watched myself talk to Russell for a brief moment. The picture zoomed in to Lydia, blurring and regaining focus. I joined Lydia as we walked back across the median. The camera stayed with Lydia as she walked the median alone while Maggie Driscoll interviewed me. Altogether, the video was less than ninety seconds long.

"I don't understand why that would go viral," I said, shaking my head.

"Maybe because of this," Lydia said, moving the mouse cursor to the video description, which contained a link to what purported to be uncensored footage. Lydia clicked the link, and another Youtube video loaded. The opening frame of this video was the same as the last one, except without the blurry areas. This one had over six hundred thousand views and was almost five minutes long. Lydia clicked the play button, and we watched the footage of ourselves. My penis bounced and swung almost obscenely with every step I took. I didn't remember being aroused at the time, but in the video, I looked like I had a semi-erection going. I turned away, embarrassed, wondering how I could have done such a thing.

When I looked back at the screen, Lydia was walking along the edge of the median, holding her sign high, her small breasts jiggling with each bouncing step she took, her smile infectious as she waved at passing vehicles. Even though I saw her nude much more often than in clothes, seeing her on display in the video, in such a public setting, outdoors with people in the background watching her, her thick muscled thighs and round smooth buttocks flexing with each movement she made, sparked a longing somewhere in my core. As the video continued past the point where the censored version had stopped, I heard someone near the camera say, "Look at that ass!" I touched the small of Lydia's back, my fingers caressing one of the dimples there, and moved my hand down the curve of her buttock. Lydia backed into me, welcoming the touch, wanting more of it. She jerked her head to the side, her hair falling to her far shoulder. She kept the tilt of her head, inviting my lips to her neck. We did somehow manage to watch the entire video before giving in to our mutual urges.

Afterward, as I sat up in bed with Lydia stretched out and napping beside me, I wondered what my mother would say if she saw the video or the news report. I hadn't told her anything about Lydia in any of the almost weekly calls she had made to me, but I think she would have been thrilled that I was seeing someone, that I was finally connecting with other human beings. But I was hesitant to tell my mother anything. Lydia was so obsessive about her own nudity, exposing her body to as many people as she could, that I had to wonder how promiscuous she might have been before moving in with me. There was so much that Lydia and I didn't talk about, so much that I didn't even know how to bring up into conversation. It was that gap in our ability to talk along with the fifteen-year age difference that made me doubt the seriousness of our relationship. And if we weren't serious, I didn't see the point in telling Mom about her.

My cell phone buzzed on the table next to my bed, and I figured it was Mom somehow reading my mind and calling me. I rolled over, grabbed the phone, and glanced at the display, pausing when I saw a number I didn't recognize. The area code was 972, which was local to the Dallas area. Thinking that it might be a modeling job, I answered.

"Hello."

"Hi! May I speak to David Michaels?"

The female voice on the other end was very loud and enthusiastic.

"Speaking."

"Mr. Michaels, this is Kristin Miller from Fox 4 News. I believe you spoke with one of our reporters, Maggie Driscoll, yesterday."

"Yes."

"Who is it?" Lydia mumbled, still half asleep.

"We were wondering if you and Lydia Nelson could come in to our studios and do an on-camera interview about yesterday's protest."

I glanced over at Lydia, unsure of how to answer.

"Who is it?" Lydia repeated.

"Can you hold on for a minute," I said into the phone.

"Sure."

I held my hand over the phone and whispered to Lydia, "It's Channel 4. They want us to come in and be interviewed in the studios."

Lydia darted up into a cross-legged sitting position. "You mean, like be on TV?"

I nodded.

"Well, hell yeah."

I put the phone back to my ear and said, "Sure. When?"

"We'd love to do a live interview on tomorrow's *Good Day* morning show if you're available. If not, you could come in at another time and tape something."

Looking at Lydia while I spoke, I said, "Well, we both have classes in the morning."

"We can skip them," Lydia whispered.

"What time would we have to be there?"

"We're hoping to do a 6:45 segment. I know that's really early, but the show starts at 4:30 AM."

"6:45 AM," I repeated for Lydia's benefit. She immediately nodded her head.

"OK. What time do we need to be there?"

Lydia bounced off the bed, almost dancing around the room. The lady on the phone told me to be there at 6:00 and gave me the address.

I scrambled about the room for a pen and a piece of paper so I could write down the instructions she gave me (what door to go in, whom to ask for, what to wear and not wear, etc.). I wound up using the back of a Walmart receipt.

Lydia had stopped dancing around the room by the time I got off the phone.

"Wait, we have to talk on TV?" she said.

"That's the general idea of an interview."

I realized, of course, the problems in interviewing Lydia about our pro-life protest when she didn't really believe in the cause.

"Oh wow. What kind of things are they going to ask?"

I shrugged. "I'm sure they won't devote a lot of time to us. We'll probably only have time to talk about how we came up with the idea and what happened. Don't worry. I can do most of the talking."

"I want to say something though. I don't want to just sit there looking like an idiot."

"Tell you what, whenever they ask about doing the protest naked, you answer. I'll talk about the abortion stuff, especially since you don't agree. Deal?"

Lydia tilted her head to the left as she considered it, and said, "Ok."

I still had my concerns about what she might let slip, making the whole protest seem disingenuous, not to mention damage our case if we decided to plead Not Guilty to the disorderly conduct citations. But I swallowed those concerns for now.

"Let's figure out what we're going to wear. She said to try to wear solid colors, no stripes or patterns. And no visible logos."

"Damn. We did the protest naked; they should let us be naked for the interview," Lydia said as she stalked off to her room. I could only shake my head.

Once Lydia and I got to the studios the following morning, everything happened in a blur. As instructed, we had each worn the clothes we intended to wear on the air, but we had also brought backup clothes on hangers. The clothes we had on were approved, and the production assistants stored our extra clothes. We were shown into an office in the legal department, and someone went over the release giving the station the rights to broadcast our image. We signed those and were given copies, which production assistants took to store with our extra clothes. From legal, we were taken to the soundstage, walking behind the cameras pointed to the news anchor desk. Having watched *Good*

Day most mornings for the past few years, I recognized the two people behind the desk, Tim Ryan and Lauren Przybyl. They must have been on a commercial break, since other staff members were behind the desk with them, going over notes or touching up makeup. We were shown onto another set that looked like a lounge. I recognized it as the place where they interviewed guests during the show. Those interviews never lasted much more than five minutes.

Microphones were clipped to our collars, with the cords from each hidden under our shirts, and a little bit of makeup was applied to both of us to hide any blemishes that the cameras would pick up. When we were shown where to sit on the set, Maggie Driscoll had appeared and was taking the seat opposite us.

"David, Lydia," she said with a smile, "how are you?"

"Fine," I replied.

I had seen her on the evening news but never on the morning show, so she had to have claimed ownership of our story.

"Thank you for coming in so early," she said.

"No problem. I don't think I've ever seen you on *Good Day*."

"I've been on once or twice," Maggie answered, "when they've wanted to feature one of my stories. I don't hand my stories off to other people. So, did you have any idea that video of you would go viral?"

"No, not really."

"That's one of the things I want to talk about on the air." Before I could answer, Maggie continued. "We'll be going out live, although there is a seven second delay. But still, try to refrain from any bad language. Tim will introduce the story and throw it to me, then I will talk about what I saw and experienced on Saturday before starting with the questions. Sound good?"

I shrugged.

"Sure," Lydia said.

Maggie touched the microphone in her ear, listening to some instructions.

"Thirty seconds," she said. "So take a deep breath and relax. Or try to look relaxed anyway."

I sat back in the chair and wondered whether I should cross my legs. Lydia followed Maggie's advice and took a deep breath. She leaned on the arm of her chair closest to me, her shoulder almost touching mine. Her hand reached out and found mine where I had it resting on my thigh. She grabbed it and pulled it up onto the arm of my chair, our fingers interlocking. We glanced at each other, and I gave her a little wink.

One of the directors on set was motioning to Maggie, and I saw a red light light up on one of the cameras.

"Yes Tim," Maggie began, "it was quite an unusual scene on Greenville Avenue on Saturday morning. The usual abortion protestors were joined by a completely nude couple. Now you would think that a naked couple would be there to disrupt the protest, but this couple agrees with the pro-life position. I have here in studio with me that couple, David Michaels and Lydia Nelson. David, Lydia, welcome to *Good Day*."

"Thank you," I said. "Thank you for having us."

"The first question that comes to mind is why. Why do an abortion protest, in public, naked?"

I squeezed Lydia's hand, and I wondered what Maggie would say if I told her that doing the protest naked was the only way to get Lydia to agree to do it. But I wasn't about to mention that.

"Lots of reasons," I replied. "The biggest one would be to get attention. I don't think we would be sitting here in a TV studio if we had gone to that protest in street clothes."

"It sure has gotten a lot of attention. Video of you, both censored and uncensored, has gone viral on the Web. How do you feel about that?"

"I think it's great," Lydia said.

"You don't mind that millions of people can watch you walking naked in the middle of a busy street?"

"If we minded, we wouldn't have done it," Lydia answered.

"People make too much of a big deal about nudity," I added and started to say something about being nude models for art classes before thinking better of it and saying something that I thought sounded lame even as the words came out of my mouth. "I mean, we were all born naked, right?"

"You were not well received by the other abortion protestors," Maggie said. It was not a question.

"No, I wouldn't say that we were."

"How long did you plan this protest?"

I took a quick look at Lydia. Maggie's questions weren't going where I wanted them to go. She seemed to be more interested in just the nudity and the logistics. I wanted to get out what we—or I, since Lydia considered herself pro-choice—wanted to say with this protest.

"It wasn't that long," I replied. "A couple of weeks. I went to the site there on Greenville the week before and met that family. I guess they go and protest every week. They seemed very devout in their religious beliefs. That seems to be the standard among pro-life activists, and that was another reason for doing the protest nude. We wanted to show that you don't have to be devoutly Christian to be against abortion. It's a very human issue. If you saw the signs we were carrying, you should have noticed that we said that babies in the womb are naked and defenseless against such violence. And abortion is a horrendously violent act. By standing naked and defenseless in the city street, we were standing with those babies, trying to make people see the real issue. They can talk about choice all they want, but when that choice results in the violent death of a human being, and make no mistake, a fetus is a human being, then it just seems like they are missing what abortion is really about."

Maggie was silent for a couple of seconds. I took a breath to keep going, but she got another question in before I could start. "So you wouldn't consider yourself Christian?"

"Christian, yes. Devout, no, not really. I don't go handing Bibles out on the street corner or anything."

"No, obviously not," Maggie said, and I took some offense at that.

"That's not to say that being naked in public is incompatible with Christianity," I offered. "Most of the nude art in existence is Christian based. Take the Sistine Chapel, for instance. And I know of a good many nudists today who are also Christian." I didn't know any personally, of course, but I had seen websites about them.

"I see," Maggie mused. "Lydia, what did you think of the idea to be nude for the protest."

She smiled, and I could see a bit of red on her cheeks coming through the TV makeup. "It was my idea actually."

"Really? And why would you have come up with something like this?"

Lydia shrugged. "It was something bold that would get attention."

"And you did get attention," Maggie said, "most notably from the Dallas Police Department. What happened there, and how did you not get arrested?"

I explained the differences between indecent exposure and disorderly conduct to her in the same way I had explained it to the Dallas police officer, the way Greg Duplantis had explained it to me during our lunch at La Familia.

"Are you going to fight the citation?" Maggie asked when I finished. Lydia and I looked at each other.

"It just seems like there would be first amendment issues involved with this," Maggie continued to fill the silence, "especially since the nudity was so intrinsic to your message, that, as your sign put it, these fetuses are naked and defenseless."

"I haven't really thought about what to do about the citations," I replied.

"You do have a few days to think about it. If you do fight the charges, I wish you good luck."

"Thank you," I said.

"And thank you for coming on *Good Day*. We have the link to the censored video of David and Lydia's protest on Fox4News.com. Tim, back to you."

There was an eerie two second pause, and then everyone on the set relaxed, as if air had just been let out of a balloon. Technicians rushed to us and started unhooking the microphones from our shirts.

"That was great," Maggie said. She handed a couple of business cards to each of us. "If you do plead not guilty on those tickets, please shoot me an email. I'd like to keep following this story."

"OK," we both said, taking the cards.

Lydia and I were escorted back to our spare clothes and then out to the building lobby. I saw that we could still make it to our first class, so I had us on I-35E heading toward Denton less than fifteen minutes after the segment finished.

"That was fun," Lydia said. "I can't wait to get home and watch it."

We had set the DVR to record *Good Day* last night before going to bed.

"It was all right."

"Are you disappointed?"

I shrugged. "It just seemed like it went by so fast. I wanted to get our message out, you know. But all she wanted to talk about was the charges against us."

Lydia grunted in disapproval. Of course, she didn't care about the message since she was part of the other side. "Our video went viral, which means our signs went viral. And we got to be on TV. You should just have fun with it." She paused and looked out the window. "It doesn't seem real, you know. Like it's a dream."

"Surreal," I offered.

"No, not real, I said."

"I didn't say 'so real'; I said 'surreal', which means unreal, like a dream."

"Oh. Oh, yeah."

She reclined her seat and closed her eyes. It had been an early morning for both of us, so I drove in silence. I couldn't help but think about how different we were, the fifteen-year age difference, our views on the topic we chose for our protest project, and our differing views on things in general. She seemed so dependent on me and carefree at the same time. And now she was living in my house. What had I been thinking when I invited her? We hadn't been a couple then, but I should have realized that that would change once we were living under the same roof, especially with her proclivity for nudity. I still believed that men and women were perfectly capable of being nude around each other while also maintaining a platonic relationship. It hadn't been the nudity that brought us together. It had been that kiss pose in class. Even though that experience was so intense, the most intense experience I had ever had while modeling, it had been just a one-time thing. Lydia and I didn't have a future together. Yes, I enjoyed her company most of the time, and the sex every time, but I missed having the house to myself.

I almost chuckled out loud as the words to an old Mac Davis song, "Hard to Be Humble", came unbidden to my mind: "I never get lonesome 'cause I treasure my own company." What was wrong with me? How could I prefer being alone to being with Lydia? Because we were not compatible, that's why.

I wondered if she felt anything for me? Was our sex just casual, just a physical activity designed for mutual pleasure and nothing more? Or did she want more from me? I tried to imagine the two of us getting married one day. All I could picture was a small group of people, me waiting at the altar, and Lydia walking down the aisle as naked as the day she was born, with everyone, my mother included, gasping as she came into view. I couldn't picture Lydia in a wedding dress of any kind. She just didn't seem to me like the marrying kind. And if our relationship wasn't leading to love and marriage, what were we together for? Was I just her meal ticket right now?

There were five weeks left in the semester. I could let her stay at the house for that long. And with her running around naked all the time and draping herself all over me, I could even keep having sex with her. But after that, we would have to have a serious talk.

15

Our attitudes toward each other changed after that television interview. We still had sex three or four times a week, and Lydia stayed naked whenever we were in the house. But we didn't laugh as much. Our conversations were fewer and farther between. Lydia stayed out of the game room when I was playing Call of Duty or any other game. I don't know if she sensed my own change and reacted to it or if she was just busy with school work. She did spend a lot of time in her room either studying or writing papers.

Dr. Brady did mention seeing our spot on *Good Day* in class that Monday, the day of the *Good Day* live interview.

"In all my years of teaching this course, that's the first time that any students have made the television news. I can't wait to read your reports."

Crystal and I blushed and tried to sink in our seats as all the other students turned to look at us. Lydia smiled and sat up straighter with her chest out. When class ended, we were bombarded with questions from the other students. I looked to escape, but Lydia stood and answered them, unconcerned that she had another class across campus to get to.

Later that week, I drove Lydia to Dallas to see an attorney to represent us in the disorderly conduct charges against us. We paid the attorney fees and signed some paperwork. They gave us copies of the citations and kept the originals. Four days later, a legal assistant from the attorney's office called us and told us the charges against both of us had been dismissed. When I asked why, she told me that the original complaint had been filed by the manager at the abortion clinic. That manager had decided not to pursue those charges. Since there weren't any other official complaints, the charges were dismissed. I suspected that there was more to it than that, but I didn't ask any more questions.

The drawing classes were all going to be finished using models before May arrived, but the last two weeks of April had us doubling up for most of the sessions. Audrey had asked for Lydia and me for at least one of her classes, so we got to model together again. This time we did a reclining pose, Lydia on her back and me on my side with my arm draped over Lydia's waist. The pose was comfortable enough for the three hours, but the sweat generated from the contact of my arm with her abdomen made that part of it uncomfortable. The fact that we weren't gazing into each other's eyes made this a more normal modeling session than *The Kiss* pose we had done. Still, we were all over each other as soon as we got home from that session.

As the end of the semester neared, the more I struggled with how to handle the Lydia situation. Part of me wanted her to stay, but a bigger part of me wanted to go back to my misanthropic lifestyle. Did I just enjoy wallowing in misery? Did I feel like I was somehow being unfaithful to Glenda? Did I want to remain single all my life, and if not, did I think someone better was going to come along? I asked myself these questions repeatedly as April progressed. I would think I was ready to sit Lydia down and have the talk with her when she would do something like put her arms around me and lick my earlobe. She would lead me to her bedroom, and my resolve would dissipate like an ice cream cone in a hot Texas summer.

The last week of regular classes began on the final Monday in April. Lydia rode with me to and from the university as usual. We got our protest project reports back that day, and Lydia, Crystal, and I had received perfect scores. Lydia and I were both in a great mood during the ride home. I didn't want to bring anything up while I was driving, so I listened to Lydia talk about her day. I parked in the driveway as the garage door rolled up.

"What are you going to do this summer?" I asked her.

"What?"

Lydia got out of the car before I could repeat the question. I followed her inside through the laundry room, pushing the garage door button on the way in. She had once told me that she planned on taking classes all summer, but when the registration period arrived, she told me that she had only registered for the next fall semester.

"I mean, are you staying in town or going home to Lubbock?" I asked over the rattling noise of the garage door closing.

"I don't know," Lydia replied.

"You don't know? We got a week of classes and a week of finals and that's it."

We walked into the main living area, and Lydia started toward her room. I grabbed her hand.

"You ought to have a plan by now," I said. "If you want to stay here, we need to talk about that."

Lydia sighed and squeezed my hand. She looked into the living room and then down at the floor.

"What?" I asked.

"Here," she said and, still gripping my hand, led me into the living room. "Sit down."

I sat.

"I wasn't going to tell you this until the semester was over, but I might as well do it now."

"OK," I replied.

Was she going to break up with me? If so, that would be such a relief. I always hated being the bad guy, hurting anyone. If this were one of those mutual break ups, things couldn't have been any better. Lydia sat and stared at the blank screen of the TV for what seemed like several minutes. I was about to say something when she finally blurted it out.

"I'm pregnant."

Lydia paused for two or three seconds, and I don't think the full impact of what she had said hit me.

"I had planned on staying here and taking summer classes," she continued, "just to get finished with college sooner, you know. Before this. But I can't do that now. I'll probably go to my mom's."

I held up my hand to stop her since it looked like she was going to keep going.

"What?" I asked.

She stopped and sighed. "Yeah, I'm pregnant."

My first impulse was to ask if I was the father. Lydia and I didn't know each other that well. We hadn't been together long. But I thought she would get offended by such a question, so I used a bit more tact.

"How far along are you?"

"Seven weeks."

"Seven weeks? But we didn't start..."

"Seven weeks since my last period started. That's when you measure it from."

I should have remembered that from all the infertility consultations Glenda and I had had. So many thoughts went through my head, and I wanted to ask her so many questions that I locked up and couldn't come out with anything. I wanted to be thrilled. This, a baby, was what I had wanted for so many years, but it wasn't the same. Lydia wasn't Glenda. I barely knew Lydia. I stood up and walked across the room, stopped, and turned back around.

"You don't have to worry," she said.

"Why would I worry?"

"I mean, you don't have to do anything."

I stopped my pacing and stood in front of her, shaking my head. "What are you talking about? This is my baby. This *is* my baby right?"

"Of course. I haven't been with anyone else all semester."

"Have you figured out the due date?"

"Yeah. December 18th."

"Ok. Good. You should be able to get finished with the fall semester then."

Lydia held up her hand. "We have a lot of stuff to talk about before we ever get that far."

I started pacing again. I couldn't help it. How could one sit still after hearing news like this? "I know, I know, but it doesn't hurt to plan."

"I don't even know if I want this baby."

I stopped, wheeled around, and stared at her.

"I mean, I decided a long time ago that I never wanted to have any kids."

I thought back to the day in class when we decided to do the abortion protest. Lydia had said that she was not pro-life. She only participated in it because she could do it naked. But now that she was faced with a pregnancy that she just said she didn't want, that she had never wanted, what was going through her mind? I started to ask her the question, but I stopped. My mouth couldn't have formed the word abortion. Lydia stared at the carpet between her feet, as if she were afraid to look at me. She knew my feelings on the subject. I had told her the story about mine and Glenda's infertility struggles.

"I'll –" I started to say, but she had also started to speak.

"We have some time before we have to decide on anything."

"Yes, we do," I agreed with some reluctance.

She sat on the couch for a minute or two. I stood in the same spot, thoughts of the month after month of disappointments with Glenda. Was conceiving a baby supposed to be this easy? Lydia and I had been careful. I wore a condom every time, although that first one had broken. That was it, I realized, the day of *The Kiss* pose, the day we had made love for the first time. At least, I tried to think of it as making love. Lydia probably thought of it as just fucking. And that seemed to sum up the problems I had been having with our relationship over the past month.

"Well," Lydia said, standing up, "I'm going to cook dinner."

She walked past me toward her room. I blundered into the game room, thinking I would fire up Call of Duty, but when I got there, I felt like doing anything else besides playing a game. Glenda and I had tried for years to conceive a child, and it had never happened. Lydia and I tried not to conceive one, but it had happened on our very first time. There didn't seem to be any justice in the universe.

"I'm sorry Glenda," I whispered.

My baby was inside Lydia. That thought would not leave my mind. I had spent the last three weeks thinking about ways to end our relationship, but things had changed now. I wanted this baby. At least, I thought I did. Or had I been programmed from years of infertility struggles to want any baby, with or without Glenda? One thing I did know for certain was that I did not want the relationship with Lydia to end. Not anymore.

I walked into the kitchen to offer my assistance with dinner. She was naked, as usual, and I could see a package of frozen hamburger meat turning in the microwave. If Lydia wanted things to go on as before, I would play along. I snuck back to my room, took off my clothes, and padded back to the kitchen.

"You need some help?" I asked.

She was crushing some saltine crackers while the meat defrosted.

"You can chop that onion."

The cutting board was sitting out on the counter, a knife, an onion, and a bell pepper on top of it. I got to work on the onion. Other than cans of soup or ravioli, Lydia and I hadn't cooked together in the kitchen in the few weeks she had been living here, so I couldn't keep from thinking back to sharing the kitchen with Glenda in the early days of our marriage. She and I always wore clothes when we cooked, but we always tried to have fun with it. If my hands were clean, I would pat Glenda's bottom, almost a spank, and she would rub her whole body against mine. Life had been nice even if it had been missing something.

Lydia took the hamburger meat out of the microwave and dumped it into the mixing bowl on top of the crushed crackers. Using the cutting board, I slid the chopped onion in on top of the meat. Lydia brushed past me to the fridge and handed me a couple of eggs.

"Put these in," she said.

I cracked the eggs on the edge of the bowl and watched the yolk plop out, the slimy whites drooping out of the shells, and I couldn't stop thinking about the child inside Lydia, now much more than an egg. My bare skin brushed past Lydia as I stepped over to the trash can to dispose of the egg shells. She added ketchup, Worchester sauce, crushed garlic, parsley, and salt and pepper to the bowl. She raised her hands up to me, wiggled her fingers, and then plunged them into the bowl, turning and mixing everything together. She nodded her head to me, and I drove my hands into the gooey mess with hers. We stood with our sides touching as we finger-wrestled in the meatloaf mixture, laughing but not saying anything. Perhaps the weight of the pregnancy revelation had caused both of us to turn reflective. I couldn't believe how much my feelings toward her had changed. Hadn't I just been thinking about sitting her down and talking to her about moving out? Now, knowing that she was carrying our baby, I thought of her as some kind of sacred vessel.

Once we got the meatloaf all mixed, Lydia dumped it into a pan, patted it even, and lathered a layer of ketchup on top. She slid it into the oven, then turned and flicked her fingers toward me, flinging little pieces of raw hamburger meat onto my chest. I did the same to her, but before we could have a full-scale food flicking war, I grabbed her and planted a kiss onto her mouth. She sighed, the air she exhaled going into my mouth, and she put her arms around me, hands on my back. I didn't care that the raw egg raw hamburger mess from her fingers was getting on me. My fingers did the same to her back.

We sank to the floor, on the little rug between the sink and the stove. I didn't touch her intimate parts with my hands. I didn't want the raw egg and meat concoction to cause any kind of infection. Instead, I went at her with my mouth, grabbing the inside of her thighs but letting my hands go no further. When Lydia couldn't stand it anymore, I positioned myself above her. When she nodded, I entered her for the first time bareback. She was already pregnant after all, and I felt that we were both clear of any diseases. Was it the full contact of all our parts without barriers, or the knowledge that we had conceived a child together that made the sex more intense than it had ever been? Probably both. Whatever the case, she and I both had simultaneous orgasms, neither of us doing so quietly.

After I had dumped the kitchen rug into the washing machine, Lydia and I showered together, washing off the food mess, sweat, and other bodily fluids. We didn't say much to each other. It was as if we didn't know how to speak without bringing up the baby, and neither of us wanted to bring it up.

By the time we got back to the kitchen, the meatloaf was done. I heated up a microwaveable bag of broccoli, just so we would have a vegetable with the main course, and we sat down to eat.

"I'm going to go to my mom's after finals," Lydia finally said after we had eaten most of the meal in silence.

"You said you were just thinking about doing that."

"Yeah, well, I decided."

I couldn't help but wonder if it had been our lovemaking in the kitchen that had helped her decide. I don't see how she could have thought it was less than any of the other times, so perhaps it had been the intensity that had scared her.

One of the things about my marriage to Glenda was that we rarely argued. I was never one for being aggressive and yelling, especially with loved ones. A couple of incidents from my childhood taught me that once a thing was said, it couldn't be unsaid. So, I was always careful about what I would say to Glenda in the heat of the moment. With strangers, those things didn't matter so much, but with a loved one, I knew I always had to choose my words wisely. That unwillingness to assert myself showed itself now with Lydia, more evidence that my feelings for her had taken a swift change.

I wanted her to stay with me all summer, of course. Now that she was pregnant with our child, we needed time to bond, to get to know each other on a more intimate level.

"And your mom is in Lubbock?" I asked.

Lydia nodded.

"How long are you going to stay?"

Lydia shrugged. "If I'm not taking classes, I might as well stay the whole summer."

I sat across the table from her looking into her eyes, those beautiful green eyes, wondering what was going through her mind. Lydia returned my gaze without flinching, almost defiant. Something in my core shivered. The only thing I felt was fear, for the baby and for Lydia and me. It seemed that everything about our relationship was sitting on top of a house of cards, and just a light breeze could make it fall apart.

I wanted to ask her outright about an abortion. Was that one of the options she was considering? Would she ever do such a thing? But fear kept me silent.

"OK," I finally said.

I took my last bite of meatloaf, although I wasn't hungry anymore. I wiped my mouth with my napkin, got up from the table, and moved the rest of the meatloaf from the pan to a plastic leftover dish. Lydia continued to sit, picking at her food as I rinsed the dishes and put them in the dishwasher.

"Does your mom know you're coming?" I asked when I finished.

Lydia nodded as I sat back down across from her.

"What did she say about the baby?"

"I haven't told her yet. I'm waiting to do that in person."

We sat quietly for just a moment. Lydia stopped picking at her food and took a real bite.

"Well, if she wants to meet the father of her grandchild, let me know. I'll drive out to Lubbock to meet her."

Lydia gave me a blank look like that was the last thing she expected her mother to want. I wanted to plead with Lydia to stay here through the summer. If she wanted to see her mother, we could see her together. We could take my car which was much more reliable on a long trip than hers. But I kept quiet. Instead, I got up and headed toward the game room and a round of Call of Duty with anonymous strangers.

16

After I finished my last final exam of the spring semester, I arrived home to an empty house. Lydia had taken all her things, what little she had, and left. There was a note from her on the kitchen counter explaining that her mother was expecting her today and that she didn't want to have to do any driving after dark. "I'll call when I get there," she said in closing and then signed her name, just "Lydia", not "Love, Lydia".

I had spent the week since Lydia's revelation about the pregnancy feeling as if I were going through penance. Glenda could never have a baby, but she and I had been on the same team. I had always thought of us as one unit, and I am sure that she thought the same. We bore the disappointment together month after month. It was only when I selfishly asked God to somehow give me, not us, a child did that team break apart. And now someone I barely knew was carrying the child that I had so desperately wanted all those years, a girl who had stated that she had never wanted a baby and who thought abortions were just A-OK.

The uncertainty was the worst part, not knowing what Lydia was thinking or what she might do while she was gone. I wanted Lydia here. I wanted to go through every step of the pregnancy together like a regular couple. But we weren't a couple. I had been ready to throw Lydia out before I knew about the baby. And now that I did know about the baby, Lydia wanted out. The thoughts just kept rolling around in my head, and since the semester was over, I didn't have any studying to do to take my mind off the situation.

Stripping my clothes off when I got home had become a habit

thanks to Lydia. I took my cell phone with me into the game room and started Call of Duty: Black Ops. I spent the next five hours playing match after match, blowing people away and getting blown away. It was dark when I decided to quit. I was looking at the stats screen of the match just completed, listening to voices from faces I would never see, names I would never know, and an overwhelming feeling of loneliness enveloped me. I had spent four years alone in this house. Solitude was something I had wanted, but I had also felt I had deserved it. Something had changed, and I didn't want solitude anymore.

Lydia still hadn't called. I exited the Black Ops program on the PlayStation and grabbed my cell phone from the coffee table, hitting Lydia's number and listening to see if she would answer.

"Hello," she said after enough rings to make me think the call would go to her voicemail.

"Hey," I replied, trying to keep the surprise that she had answered my call out of my voice. "I was just checking to make sure you got there safe."

"Oh yeah. Mom and I are talking, but I made it here fine."

"Good. So you told her about the baby?"

"Yeah."

"How did she take it?"

She paused, then said, "Listen, I can't really talk now. How about I call you tomorrow?"

Lydia was brushing me off.

"Sure," I said. "I'm glad you got there OK."

"Thanks. Talk to you later."

She disconnected, and I sat staring at my phone for several minutes. I finally pulled up Facebook and went to Lydia's profile, just to see her photo. Seeing her beautiful green eyes staring up at me from my phone screen just made me miss her more, so I shut it off. I got up, dressed in a t-shirt, shorts, and tennis shoes, and went for a long walk through and around the neighborhood.

Sleep was elusive that night. I lay awake while forcing myself to keep my eyes closed as thoughts of Lydia kept circulating in my mind. Had I done something wrong? Would she still be here if I had reacted differently to the pregnancy? Had she sensed that I was thinking about ending the relationship before she told me about the baby? I mulled these questions and more as I tried to think of anything I could have done to keep her here. And the questions wouldn't go away no matter how much I wanted my brain to shut down and just go to sleep. Every few minutes I checked the time on my phone on my night table hooked to the charging cable. When I saw 4:30 displayed on the screen, I knew I must have slept at least a little since it had read 2:20 at my previous check. I got up to pee and lay back down. I stayed there for another hour, but I knew that I was done sleeping. The worst part was that I had nothing to do. School was over, and modeling jobs in May, when the semester had just ended, were hard to come by.

I showered and dressed and took another walk around the neighborhood in the dark. By the time I circled back to the house, it was light enough to see. An idea occurred to me, and I rushed into the house to find the papers we had gotten from the lawyers. When I found them, I thumbed through to the copy of Lydia's citation. On it was her address, her permanent address, the one that had been on her driver's license. It was in Lubbock, TX. I entered the address into the maps app on my phone. It showed a drive time of four hours and forty-five minutes.

I knew it was crazy even as I was getting in the car, but I had nothing better to do with the day. Lydia needed to know how I felt, I told myself. I mean, I hadn't ever told her I loved her. I hadn't known I had loved her until she had left. But now that I knew that I did, she needed to know it, and telling her over the phone didn't seem like the right thing to do.

The quickest route to Lubbock had me driving north on US Highway 287, the same road I took to Mom's house in Wichita Falls. I stopped for fuel and a Mountain Dew in Decatur, and the maps app had me turn west on US Highway 380 not long after I left the gas station. The open country and long highway made me think of my last road trip, coming back from my sister's in Colorado. I remembered the pregnant woman I had met in the bar on New Year's Eve. It took me a couple of minutes to remember her name. Rachel, it had been. Her boyfriend had wanted her to have an abortion, but, like me, she equated abortion with murder. Hadn't she told me that the guy had threatened violence if she tried to go after him for child support? Her situation was like mine, a child we wanted but that was not wanted by the other parent. Except that that wasn't fair to Lydia. Lydia didn't know what she wanted, only that she had decided a long time ago that she never wanted kids. I wondered where Rachel was now, and whether the asshole of a boyfriend had left her alone. Her baby would be at least three months old by now.

That the life of an individual human being could be extinguished based on the whim of that human being's mother, at least before a certain point was reached, was unfathomable to me. The law and Lydia's indecision were putting my child's life in jeopardy. I fervently believed that my child was alive right then. It had a heartbeat and its own DNA. And I loved that child with all my heart. How could killing it now be legal under our system?

I had to put these thoughts aside, I told myself. Thinking that Lydia might do this was not fair to her. She had to have been as blindsided by this pregnancy as I was, probably more so. I had to quit thinking about the baby and just think about Lydia. She was why I was driving all this way, not the baby. Of course, I knew I had to admit that the baby changed things between us. All the stuff I had been thinking of before I knew about the baby, mine and Lydia's age difference, her dependence on me for the past couple of months, the passion of our lovemaking, and the lack of any kind of verbal confession of our feelings all passed through my mind. None of that mattered anymore.

I made it into Lubbock just before noon, and I turned onto Lydia's street just as my car's digital clock flipped to 12:00. I rolled past the address, half of a shabby looking duplex on the end of a block with an unkempt yard and an overflowing City of Lubbock garbage dumpster on the side near an alley that ran behind the house. Lydia's white Corsica was in the driveway behind a red ten-year-old Ford Festiva. I drove down another block, took a right and then three lefts and drove back on that street from the other direction. I stopped my car two houses down, and parked.

As I started to get out of my Prius, this impromptu trip and showing up on Lydia's mother's doorstep unannounced, suddenly seemed like a bad idea. Lydia had told me she needed time to sort out her feelings, and I was trying to deny her that because I was afraid of what she might do to the baby. I sat back down behind the wheel of my car and did a Google search on my phone for abortion clinics near my current location. There were hotlines and counseling services, but the closest place that did actual surgical abortions was way back in Fort Worth. I sighed, thankful that the state of Texas had so many restrictions on abortion providers. If Lydia did do the unthinkable, it wouldn't be a snap decision. She would have to put some planning behind it. There were other places way out in El Paso, but that was a harder drive than going back to Fort Worth. She wouldn't try that, especially not in her old Corsica.

I had just driven almost five hours, and I was looking at another five-hour drive to get home. If I left now, it was all for nothing. But what would I say if I walked up to Lydia's mom's house and knocked on the door? How would I not seem like a stalker? Was that what I was doing? Was I stalking Lydia?

As I was pondering this last question, a woman with brown and gray shoulder length hair walked out the front door of the side of the duplex where Lydia's car was parked. She wore a turquoise house dress with flower patterns and carried a plastic trash bag stuffed full and tied closed. Her face was worn with heavy wrinkles, especially around her mouth, almost as if she had spent too much of her life frowning, but the shape of her nose and eyes bore a striking resemblance to Lydia. This had to be her mother. I couldn't tell much about her build since her house dress was so loose and billowed around her as she walked to the dumpster, tossed the trash bag in, and headed back to her house. She took short, deliberate steps, like a much older person. Lydia was in her mid-twenties, so her mother ought to be around fifty. This woman looked to be past seventy. Lydia had told me that her mother had had a difficult life with long hours at menial jobs and several failed relationships. I didn't know the detailed history, of course, and I was again struck by how little I knew about Lydia's background.

The woman stopped at her front door and looked up the street straight at me. I quickly looked down and pretended to punch buttons on my phone. When I took a quick peek back up, the woman was walking back into her side of the duplex, shutting the door behind her. I decided not to wait around to deal with an upset Lydia and started the car. I drove past the duplex and back toward the freeway.

Before I could get up to highway speed though, my vision clouded, and the tears rolled down my cheeks. I was sad and frustrated and lonely and lost. An ache started in my chest and tried to come up through my throat. I was letting Lydia go, which meant that I was letting the baby go. I couldn't protect it short of kidnapping and holding Lydia hostage, and I couldn't do that. The realization of that letting go was stirring up all kinds of emotions, and I had to pull over on the side of the road and just break down and cry. I cried for Lydia and this new baby. I cried for Glenda and the children we could never have. I cried for myself and the last four years I had wasted by shutting myself off from everyone.

I didn't remember the last time I cried. When Glenda had been killed, I had gone into a state of shock. But I never cried, and I remembered feeling angry with myself for not being able to. What was wrong with me? Did I not have any emotional depth? Or was I just a selfish bastard who deserved to lose everything and therefore felt like crying would have betrayed that? Those were all questions I had asked myself. But I never found the answers, and eventually the questions became forgotten. Everything came out now as I sobbed in my car. I must have sounded horrible, crying like a small child with a gravelly voice.

When I had finally cried myself out, I found an old napkin in the glove compartment and wiped my face and blew my nose. I took several deep breaths as I looked at myself in the mirror on the back of my sun visor. After I had my emotions under control and my face looking not as red as it had been, I flipped the visor up and merged back onto the highway.

The drive back to Fort Worth seemed to take twice as long as that morning drive to Lubbock. I was tired and disheartened, and I just wanted to be back home. While I tried to resign myself that I was giving up on Lydia, I had my phone sitting in the cup holder, its screen toward me so that I could see it light up if anyone tried to call. As the miles rolled by and as the phone remained dark and silent, I would hit a button on it and take a quick peek at the screen to make sure there were no missed calls.

I stopped for gas and a quick convenience store lunch in a small town called Guthrie and made it back to my house at ten after five. My eyes were tired, and my right leg was sore after ten straight hours of driving. The Prius was equipped with cruise control, but I had always refused to give up control to such an automated process. My phone did not ring once during the long drive which made me think about how few calls I had received over the past few years. If not for modeling jobs at various schools in the area, I probably wouldn't even need a phone.

I walked into a dead house, my iPhone in my hand, and sat down on the sofa in my game room. The dark TV hung on the wall, the game controllers on the coffee table in front of me. Playing games had been my existence since Glenda had died, but I no longer felt the call to play. I set my phone on the cushion beside me. I wanted to call Lydia, needed to call Lydia, although I had spent the last five hours trying to convince myself that I had given her up. She had left me, left this house, and I couldn't go chasing after her, especially if she was going to do what I thought she was contemplating. But I still wanted her. After Glenda, I never thought I would want anyone again, and yet, here I was.

I grabbed my phone and scrolled through my short list of contacts until I came to Lydia's name. My thumb hovered over the call button as I thought about her note. She would call me when she arrived at her mother's, it had said. But she hadn't. I had given her ample time to do so before I had given in and called her. I couldn't give in again, I told myself. Lydia was going to have to call me. I thumbed back to the phone's home screen and set it back on the sofa cushion and grabbed the PlayStation controller and waited for the unit to boot.

Rather than get myself locked into a Call of Duty team death match and risk missing a call from Lydia, I navigated to Netflix and started an episode of Parks and Recreation. I almost jumped off the couch when my phone rang about ten minutes into the episode. Finally, I thought, but my heart sank when I looked at the screen and saw that the caller was my mother. Taking a deep breath to try to hide the disappointment from my voice, I paused the show and answered the call.

"Hey Mom."

"Hi David. How are you? Are you all finished with school?"

Once I answered that I was fine and that I was finished for the semester, Mom proceeded to narrate the latest escape attempt of Bridget, one of her dogs. I wasn't sure which dog since I had never been able to keep them straight, but I listened to Mom's inane story, saying "Mmm-hmm," and "Yeah," at the appropriate places. At what seemed like three hours into Mom's tale but was probably only about ten minutes, my phone vibrated in my hand. I pulled it far enough away from my head, Mom still talking, to see the screen. Lydia was calling.

"Mom," I said, interrupting her, "I have to go. I'm sorry. Lydia is calling."

"What? Who's Lydia?"

It was only then that I realized that I had never mentioned Lydia to my mother, not one word even though she had been living with me for a couple of months and was now carrying my child.

"She's a friend," I said.

"A girlfriend?"

"I'll call you right back," I said and switched over to Lydia's call. "Lydia?"

"Hey David," she said in a rough voice that sounded like she might have a sore throat. "How are you?"

At first, I didn't know how to answer. If I sounded too upbeat, Lydia might think I didn't miss her, but if I sounded down and depressed, she might think she had too much power over me and that I was weak. I flashed back to that brief period when I thought I was going to end the relationship. Did I have a problem with her, or did I have a problem with how I thought she saw me?

"I'm hanging in there," I replied in what I hoped was a neutral tone. "How about you? How are you doing?"

"I'm OK."

"Good," I said, and then there was an awkward, almost painful, silence.

"So you told your mom about the baby?" I finally asked.

"Yeah."

"How did she take it?"

"Not too great. She went into a long lecture about what she had to go through when she had me."

This was followed by another long silence. I wanted to ask her if her mother had given her any advice about what she should do, but I was too afraid of what the answer might be to ask the question.

"I miss you," I said for lack of anything better to say. "I mean, I miss having you here, seeing you every day."

"I know. I'm sorry." She paused for a moment. "I just wanted to call and let you know I was OK."

"I'm glad you did."

Neither of us wanted to broach the subject that we really wanted to talk about, so we both once again remained silent.

"Well, I guess I had better go help Mom with dinner," Lydia finally said.

"OK. Thanks for calling. I love you."

As soon as I said it, I cringed. I had driven all the way to Lubbock with the intention of telling her this very thing in person and then couldn't go through with it. Now I had said it to her for the very first time over the phone, something I did not want to do. But it had just slipped out when all I had really wanted to say was that she was welcome back here.

Still, I hoped she might say something like she loved me too, but "Talk to you later," was all she said before disconnecting. I sighed and resisted the urge to throw my phone across the room.

17

I picked up a couple of modeling gigs over the next week, one for the Friday night artist group in Dallas and the other for a small art school, something called an atelier that focused on classical realism. The atelier place was just starting their summer term, and they booked me for five weeks at three sessions per week, Tuesday, Wednesday, and Thursday afternoons.

Lydia and I did talk two other times during the week, but we never mentioned my big love statement. That topic seemed to be as off limits as Lydia's decision about what to do about the pregnancy. Our conversations consisted of making sure the other person was all right (whatever that meant), my telling Lydia that I missed her, and Lydia saying that she would see me later. I didn't explicitly say that I wanted Lydia to move back in. Saying "I miss you," implied that, I thought. But she never mentioned when or if she might be coming back.

About two hours after I told Lydia I loved her, my mother called me back. I had, of course, forgotten to call her like I said I would. I explained that Lydia was a fellow student at UNT and that we had gone on a couple of dates. I never mentioned that she had moved in for awhile or that she was pregnant. If things didn't work out, I didn't want Mom to know or worry about anything. She had spent enough time worrying about me after Glenda's death.

The atelier was a few blocks south of downtown Fort Worth in a brick building that looked like an old warehouse. The walls inside were painted white, but there was no ceiling blocking the view of the rafters, air conditioning ducts, and electrical lines and boxes. On those walls hung figure and portrait drawings and paintings of such intricate and exquisite detail they made the drawings I had seen in most of my past modeling gigs look cartoonish or amateurish. There was one big open space surrounded by smaller rooms that were used as offices or small studios. Part of the open space was separated with long black curtains, and it was in this curtained space that the models posed and the artists did their work.

The man who called and hired me was the director of the school. He met me just outside his office and introduced himself. His name was also David which I hoped wouldn't be confusing during the session. I didn't want to turn my head in a pose just because I thought someone was talking to me when they were addressing him. There were nine students all standing at easels arranged in a semi-circle around the model stand which was against the far wall. I changed out of my clothes and into my robe in the building's only restroom, putting my street clothes into my bag. When I came out, David already had an idea of the pose I was to take, a standing one with my back to the students, one arm up and holding a pole. This meant, of course, that I would be staring at a wall, which was covered from the twelve-foot-high ceiling to the floor with a gray cloth drape. I did turn my head just a bit while we were setting the pose so that I could see the corner of the studio and, in my peripheral vision, the last student in the semi-circle, a woman who looked to be in her mid-fifties with light blonde hair.

Once David got the lights set and proclaimed the pose started, I could hear the scratching of pencils on paper. I took a deep breath and fixed my gaze on a vertical seam in the drape. There wasn't much else to look at. I then promised myself that I was not going to think about Lydia while in the pose. I thought, instead, about Glenda. In all the thousands of phone conversations she and I had shared over the years, I ended almost all of them by saying "I love you." That habit must have manifested itself while talking to Lydia the other day. It would have been nice if she had acknowledged it in some way. I might not have felt so mortified about saying it then. Of course, I wouldn't have wanted her to say "I love you" back to me if she didn't really mean it. If that had happened, how could I have known if she did mean it and wasn't just saying it as a reflex? As it was, I imagined that she did love me but didn't want to say it over the phone or be perceived to have said it just because I had.

But I wasn't going to think about Lydia, I reminded myself. I had to think about something else, like how to get back into this pose after a break. The biggest problem, I thought, was the diagonal angle of the pole. We could (and would, I was sure) mark where the end of the pole rested on the floor of the model stand and where my hand gripped the pole, but it was going to be difficult replicating the exact angle and, thus, the position of my arm. How were we going to do that? Lydia had only been modeling for six months; I wondered if she had ever given thought to problems like this when trying to get back into a long pose after a break. I wondered if Lydia would be interested in doing a long pose like this. The artwork I had seen on the walls was very realistic. People would be able to tell any drawings of her done here were actually her. She would probably like that. I wondered if I should give Lydia's number to David before remembering that she was in Lubbock now.

I was thinking about Lydia again. How did that happen? When I drove away from her mother's house in Lubbock, I had told myself that I was giving her up. And then I had gone and told her I loved her over the phone. Another tough thing about that little faux pas was that I didn't get to see her reaction. If I had told her in person, I could have at least seen her facial expression.

That was it; I had to stop thinking about her. I would have to resort to counting to pass the time. After all the modeling I had done, I didn't even have to think about how many seconds were in five minutes (three hundred), seven minutes (four hundred twenty), fifteen minutes (nine hundred), or practically any other number. As I started counting, trying to find the beat that would come close to one second per number counted, I wondered how long the pose had been going. For that matter, how long would I be in the pose before a break? The standard was twenty minutes, although I had gone longer for seated or reclining poses. This was a standing pose though, so David would probably stick to twenty minutes. But we didn't talk much about it beforehand. If the pose got too strenuous, I could always say something.

I was in the five hundreds when I heard a alarm from someone's phone.

"Hold on just a second, David," David said. "Let's mark you."

I looked down and saw him applying strips of blue masking tape around my feet. He marked the bottom on the pole before standing up and marking my hand position on the pole. As he did this, I wondered how long I had been in the pose. I didn't feel tired. Although the counting was dreadfully boring, it had kept my mind off Lydia. I thought about the angle of the pole again as I continued staring at the wall, and I had a sudden idea.

"Can you mark the shadow on the wall?" I asked.

David looked up and stepped down off the platform and back to get a view of the whole pose.

"To get the angle of the pole right," I said.

"You know, that's a great idea."

He jumped back up on the platform and put a long strip of tape on one edge of the pole's shadow. I would just have to remember which edge. Once all the marks were applied, I was able to relax, put the robe on, and take a break. I had only been in the pose for fifteen minutes, which seemed like such a short time, but after only five minutes, the alarm on David's phone signaled the end of the break. The rest of the class proceeded in the same manner, fifteen minutes in the pose with five minute breaks between. I started each fifteen minute segment just like the first, unable to keep my thoughts away from Lydia until I started counting. And even then, she would sometimes interrupt my counts. While I had thought the fifteen minute segments extraordinarily brief at the beginning of the class, I struggled to make it through that last fifteen minute session. My calf was cramping, and my shoulder hurt from holding the pole for most of three hours.

The next two days' classes at the atelier were almost identical to that first one, and again I had trouble keeping Lydia off my mind while in the pose. If I hadn't had art classes scheduled each remaining day of the week, I might have considered another drive to Lubbock, although I don't know what I would have done once I got there. Still, when I woke up early on Friday morning, I was tempted to drive to Lubbock anyway. The modeling gig I had didn't start until seven PM, and figuring the driving time to Lubbock and back, I thought I could spend a few minutes talking to Lydia. It took me about thirty seconds to realize that was a stupid idea. And that Friday night artist group met in a high traffic area in the middle of north Dallas, so I didn't even know for sure how long it would take to drive there from my own house, much less Lubbock.

Rather than spend my Friday sitting around my house playing Call of Duty: Black Ops, I drove to Dallas, found a theater near the gallery where the artist group met, and watched two movies, the latest Marvel superhero movie and a new Stephen King book adaptation. When I left the theater, I had a little over an hour until the art session started. I drove straight there and waited in my car for someone to unlock the door of the gallery, listening to a classic rock radio station. A middle aged man parked next to me and got out with a stretched white canvas, wooden folded easel and a canvas bag. I recognized him from the session I had modeled for this group two months before. Led Zeppelin's "Stairway to Heaven" had just started playing, so I stayed in the car to listen and watched him walk up to the gallery entrance, set his supplies down, and unlock the door. Three other artists arrived during the next three or four songs, all of them forty or older. I didn't remember seeing any of them the time before. I wondered if they were professional artists or just people who missed their art classes from college.

At 6:45, I got out of the car and, with my modeling bag containing my bath robe, pillow, and beach towel, walked into the art studio/gallery. The first guy who arrived was still setting up his portable easel, but he stopped and walked over to me when I came in.

"David?" he said.

I nodded, noting the small space, the portrait and landscape paintings on the walls, and the small modeling platform against one of the long walls.

"I'm Ray. You were here in March."

"Yes, I was," I said as we shook hands.

"There should be about 8 people drawing tonight. It's one long pose just like before, and you can do it nude or costumed. You didn't bring a costume, did you?"

"No, I'm afraid not."

"Street clothes are OK, but we love costumes. There was a guy here about three weeks ago who posed as a pirate. We have a break every 20 to 25 minutes, whatever you're comfortable with. There's the restroom in the back where you can change. But you know that."

"OK," I said. "Thanks."

I set my bag on the model stand and removed the pillow and beach towel. Leaving them on the platform while Ray began arranging the lights, I took the bag, which contained just my robe now, to the restroom. I didn't have to think much about what I would wear or not wear on the model stand. Two times at UNT, instructors had asked me to pose fully clothed, and both times felt unnatural. When I looked at the drawings at the end of class, they didn't look like me. The way they drew the clothes, the generic shapes, they might as well have drawn the clothes on a mannequin. When I see drawings done of me nude, I see me. Sometimes the students get the proportions wrong, and sometimes the face doesn't look much like mine, but some aspect of the shape of my body in those drawings is always distinctive, always me. And there was nothing special in modeling clothed. Almost anyone could have done it. Very few of us would or could model nude, so I felt like those two classes missed an opportunity with me as their model.

When the session officially got started, there were ten artists crowded into the small studio. My legs were weary and my shoulders sore after that standing pose of the last three days, so I sat on a stool for this group. I twisted my upper body at the waist with my right arm across my chest to make the pose, I hoped, more dynamic. The majority of my weight was on my left side, so although I had my small pillow and my beach towel between me and the stool, my left foot would be numb before each break. I would have to get off the stool on my right leg and sit on the platform with the left leg as horizontal as possible so that the blood would gradually return to the foot. If it rushed back all at once, I would feel a sensation like thousands of needles piercing the bottom of my foot. The art session went all the way to ten o'clock, no ten minute buffer between classes like at the colleges and universities, and by the time that last 25 minute segment ended, I couldn't even move my toes if I had wanted to. It took a few minutes to get the blood flowing again.

Lydia occupied my thoughts throughout the three hour pose, and I resolved that I would just have to let things take their course. It would take all my willpower, especially since I had more free time than most people, but I would not go to Lubbock under any circumstances, nor would I call her more than twice a week. If Lydia wanted to talk to me more often than that, she could call me.

But once I got in my car and on the freeway toward home, the first thing I wanted to do was call her. I glanced at my cell phone in my car's cup holder, sitting there upside down with the charging cable plugged into the bottom port. I could just pick it up, unlock the screen, and dial her number with two clicks. But it was 10:20 at night, and I had just promised myself that I would only call her twice a week. This could be one of those two times, I told myself, not counting the other three times I had already called her this week. And why did I want to call her anyway? We never talked about anything much when we did talk. I wanted to beg her to come back, to keep the baby, but we always skirted around those subjects. Still, it was always nice to hear her voice.

It was past eleven when I finally turned onto my street, and I was thinking that I should have stopped back in Dallas and gotten a Mountain Dew to help me stay awake. I perked up when I noticed what looked to be the shape of a car in my driveway. Surely, it had to be the neighbor's driveway, I thought, but as I got closer, I became sure that the car was in mine. I was almost there when I could see through the darkness that the car was a white Corsica. Lydia had come back!

I switched off my lights before turning into the driveway and parking next to her car. The Prius's dome light didn't illuminate much, but I still looked at myself in the rear view mirror, combing my hair with my fingers. My weariness from four straight days of modeling in long poses was forgotten. Taking a deep breath, I hit the button on the garage door opener on the visor which, if Lydia hadn't been watching for me, would announce my arrival. The door rattled up, and the light from inside flooded out into the driveway, and still, I sat in my car. The impending meeting with Lydia would be a crossroads affecting both of us for the rest of our lives. I knew that, so I wanted to prepare myself, to give the moment its proper gravity, although I had no idea what Lydia had decided. That fear of the unknown was the biggest factor in keeping me in my car, but I knew I couldn't stay there much longer. I took a deep breath and stepped out.

The house was dark when I walked in. I hit the button to close the garage door and turned on the light in the laundry room. It was after eleven, and Lydia had driven here from Lubbock. Maybe she was asleep. If she was really tired, I didn't want to wake her up just to tell her I was glad she was home, so I pulled up the flashlight app on my phone, turned off the laundry room light, and made my way to the master bedroom. Lydia was in my bed, either asleep or acting like it. I took off my clothes, dropping them on the floor by the side of the bed, and slipped under the covers next to her. Lydia sighed and moved toward me until I was spooning her in front of me. I put my arm around her waist and kissed the top of her head, and it almost felt like she had never left.

18

Sunlight filtered through the blinds and into the bedroom when I awoke. Lydia was still beside me under the covers, her head against my shoulder. She was on top of my left arm, and my hand had gone numb. Her eyes were open, staring up at the ceiling. I tried to pull my arm out from under her, and she moved to let me.

"Sorry," she said.

"I'm an art model; I'm used to things going to sleep," I said as I shook out my hand and wiggled my fingers.

She smiled and snuggled against me. I put my arm under her neck where Lydia wouldn't have any weight on it and my hand on her shoulder. Under the covers, her naked body was warm against mine.

"You came back," I said.

"Yeah."

"I missed you."

"Missed you too."

We lay together in silence for a few moments. I wanted to ask her what she had decided about the baby, but fear held me back.

"How's your mom?" I finally asked.

"You mean how did she take it when I told her about the baby?"

"Well, yeah."

Lydia sighed and moved down in the bed to put her head on my chest. I waited for her to say something, but it took her a few minutes.

"She told me about my father," Lydia finally said. "All the time I was growing up, every time I asked about him, she never would say anything. 'Oh, he never knew anything,' she always said. She would never even tell me his name. Until this week…"

Lydia's voice trailed off. I stroked her hair with my fingers as we lay there in silence for a few minutes.

"Ted Moore," she finally said. "That was his name. He wanted Mom to get an abortion. Insisted on it, she said. Of course, she thought she was in love, so she was going to do what he wanted."

Lydia's story sounded familiar, and it took me a moment to remember why: the woman from Amarillo I had met on New Year's Eve, the one with the abusive boyfriend.

"He took her to a clinic," Lydia continued, "and when she got there, she realized she couldn't do it. They had a big fight right there in front of everyone. And I mean a fight, not an argument. This guy, my biological father, threw an ash tray at Mom and cut a gash on her head. She still has the scar, something I always remember her having. Anyway, they had to call the police, and Mom had to have stitches in her head."

Lydia stopped talking for a moment. I started to ask about what happened to her father, whether he was arrested there in the clinic, but I didn't. Better to let her tell it in her own time.

"I keep thinking about what would have happened if he'd gotten his way, if Mom hadn't been stronger. My father wanted to have me killed. That was me they were fighting over. That was me, not some clump of cells."

I pulled her closer to me, hugging her as well as I could with her head still on my chest.

"Makes it personal, doesn't it?" I said, remembering our pro-life protest and how she wasn't in agreement with Crystal and me.

"Yeah, I guess." She paused a moment, then continued. "I mean, Mom had told me before that she had thought about abortion when she got pregnant with me. But I never knew the whole story, how close she had come to it."

I stroked her hair, feeling its silkiness between my fingers.

"So I grew up without a father. Mom did the best she could, but it was a struggle. I never had the cool toys, never bought the school pictures or the yearbooks. I didn't even notice at the time. When you're a kid and being poor is all you know, then you don't know any different. Mom had boyfriends, of course. Some were nice. Some weren't. One was— he was worse than anyone. But Mom stood up for me again. When she found out, that is."

Lydia looked up at me with a gaze of such intensity that I wanted to turn away from her. But I made myself return that gaze.

"Mom told me that if I had a man who was willing to stay and be a father to my baby that I should run, not walk, back to him."

I thought of the shabby looking woman in the house dress carrying her trash out during my brief trip to Lubbock, the wrinkled frown that she seemed to wear on her face. I had imagined her to be someone who had been abused by men and would thus advise her daughter to steer clear of me. My brief first impression turned out to be far different from the way Lydia made her sound.

"I'm glad you're back," I said.

"I'm scared."

"Of what?"

"Being a bad mom."

"You're going to be a great mom," I told her. When she didn't immediately reply, I added, "And you won't have to do it alone like your mom did."

"You're really OK with this? Having a baby?"

"Oh my God, yes," I said, trying and failing to not sound so enthusiastic.

"You're not going to leave or send me away?"

"Not planning to."

I thought about her non-response to my slip on the phone, when I had said "I love you" to her.

"My concern is how you feel about me," I said. "I've grown very attached to you, and I don't think you took my feelings into account when you ran off to your mother's."

I waited for some kind of objection or rebuttal, but Lydia stayed silent. I didn't want to just leave it like that, so I kept on going, not knowing whether I was making sense or digging myself into a deeper and deeper hole.

"My fear is that I'm just convenient. We share common interests, like nude modeling, and I have a nice house and not many bills. But I have this vision of you bolting when someone younger or more interesting comes along."

"And you believe that?"

"No, I don't believe it. At least I don't think I do. But it's a fear I have. I mean, I don't know. We've never talked about the future. But with the baby coming along, we *have* to talk about the future now."

"Yeah, we do," she said and paused for a moment. "Did you mean what you said the other night? Or did you just say it out of habit because that's how you always ended phone calls with your wife?"

The import of this conversation hit me, and I decided that we needed to sit up where we could see each other. I pushed the covers down and sat up. Lydia sat up too, and we wound up sitting cross legged on the bed fully exposed and facing each other.

"I did mean it," I said, "but I didn't mean to say it right then. I wanted the first time I told you I loved you to be in person, not over the phone. And then when you didn't say anything, I got scared."

"So say it again."

"Huh?"

"Say it again."

"I love you?"

"You make it sound like a question."

"It was a question," I said. "Is that what you wanted me to say again?"

"Yeah. Duh."

"OK. I love you."

"Are you sure?" She had a smile on her face, playing with me.

"Yes, I'm sure. I love you."

"I love you too."

"Well, good!"

There wasn't much else to say after that. I felt a warm surge in my heart as we leaned toward each other and engaged in a kiss that became long and passionate and led to long, slow lovemaking. It was, I thought to myself at one point, the first time we had ever done it on this bed and in this room. It felt similar to our lovemaking in the kitchen after she had told me she was pregnant, a kind of milestone in our relationship, although that kitchen session was marked with so much uncertainty that it was almost combative. We were much more in sync on my bed, each trying to please the other. Afterward, we lay in post-coital bliss on wet sheets, wrapped up in each other's bodies.

"I have a confession to make," Lydia said after a few minutes.

I hadn't realized that I had been drifting off to sleep until her words stirred me into a full wakefulness. "What's that?"

"You remember our first date?"

Had we ever had a real date? "What? When we met at the Drafthouse in Denton?"

"Yeah."

"I remember."

"Well, I wasn't exactly honest with you."

I had to think back, but I did remember why we met there. "The note?"

"Yeah."

"What about it?"

"It wasn't exactly left for me."

"You mean, you wrote it?"

"Yeah."

We were silent for a moment.

"You don't sound too surprised," Lydia said.

"No. The idea that someone typed that up, and since it was typed it would have had to have been done ahead of time, and then left it for you in your book seemed kind of unbelievable."

"But you met me there anyway."

"Sure. Why not?"

"I might have been a crazy psychopath."

"You might still be a crazy psychopath."

She pushed away from me and playfully punched my arm. We both chuckled, and I grabbed her and pulled her back to me. Her skin felt soft and warm.

"So why did you do that with the note?" I asked.

"I don't know. I didn't think you'd go out with me if I just asked. You were hot, and you seemed to have your shit together. And I thought you were married."

"Ah. Well. For the record, I wouldn't have agreed to meet you there if I had still been married."

Lydia thought about that for a moment and then said, "I know."

She put her head back on my chest and we continued lying in bed. I thought about my life since Glenda's wreck and how easy it would be to consider the last four years of lackadaisically going to school while isolating myself from everyone I had known before Glenda's passing wasted time. But if I had done anything differently, not gone back to school, not started modeling again, not taken that political science class, I would never have met Lydia. Without her, I would not be here excited and scared about what lay ahead. It was with some degree of wonder that I realized for the first time in a long time that I was in a good place in life.

"It's Saturday," Lydia said after what might have been five minutes or fifty minutes.

"It is."

"What are we going to do today?"

"How about this?" I said.

"This is nice. But it's so pretty outside. You don't want to stay cooped up in the house all day do you?"

"I guess not. What did you have in mind?"

"I don't know. Something. Maybe something outside."

We could have stayed at the house and made use of the swimming pool, but I still hadn't taken the cover off or treated the water in any way. There was always Six Flags, but I hadn't been there in over ten years. It seemed like a place for families or teenagers. Of course, Lydia wasn't a teenager anymore either. If Lydia wanted to do something outside, we could go to the zoo. Fort Worth has a great zoo. But a sunny Saturday in May would probably bring a huge crowd. Besides that, I didn't know if Lydia would enjoy the zoo. I wondered what she would enjoy. I thought about the things we had done together, modeling, the ecstatic dance thing, the nude protest, and tried to think of something that Lydia would love. The idea of a nudist resort was an obvious one.

"I have an idea," I said, grabbing my phone from the night stand next to me.

Lydia leaned toward me, trying to see my screen as I pulled Google up in a web browser.

"Go shower," I told her, turning my phone away. "I don't want you to see in case it doesn't work out."

"Hmpf. Fine."

She got out of bed and disappeared into the bathroom. I searched for nudist resorts in the area and was surprised to see that there were two of them just off Highway 287 past Decatur. I drove right by both of them every time I went to Mom's. I listened for Lydia to start the shower before I called one of the places. A lady with a slight accent I didn't recognize answered. I told her that my girlfriend and I were interested in visiting the resort that day, and she took down my information. They ran a quick background check on visitors, she said, but that if everything checked out, we could come out that day. I wondered what kind of background check they could run that quickly, but I didn't ask about it. They probably just checked us against the sex offender registry which, in Texas, anyone could see online. When I told her that Lydia and I had never been to a nudist resort, she said we needed to bring towels to sit on and whatever else we thought we might need during the day. They were having a burger and hot dog cook out for lunch and a potluck dinner that evening. The lunch was seven dollars a person, but we were welcome to the potluck without paying extra. The lady sounded friendly and seemed excited that we would be first-time nudists. I didn't mention that Lydia and I were both nude models.

Everything was arranged with the resort by the time Lydia got out of the shower. I even had a temporary code to get through the gate and into the office. She stood at the mirror, still nude, and blow dried her hair while I showered.

"So where are we going?" she asked when she shut off the hairdryer.

Part of me wanted to let the destination be a surprise once she got there. But I also thought that liking to be naked herself did not automatically mean she wanted to be naked with a bunch of other naked strangers.

"I thought we'd spend the day at a nudist resort," I said from my spot in the shower.

"What!"

The trouble with telling her in the shower was that I couldn't see her reaction through the blurry glass.

"Is that OK?" I asked.

"Hell yeah, it's fan-fucking-tastic. I've always wanted to go to one."

"I figured you'd like it, at least to try it out. We don't have to stay all day if we don't like it," I added.

"Sure, of course not. Have you ever been to one?"

"No."

"So you only thought of it because you thought I would like it?"

"Yeah."

Lydia opened the shower door, leaned in, and kissed me. "Thank you. You're so thoughtful." She pulled away, her hair wet again.

"I try," I said, turning the water off and grabbing my towel.

"I assume they have a pool."

"Two of them," I said, remembering the photo on the website.

"Cool. I won't bother re-drying my hair."

Lydia smiled the entire morning as we dressed and loaded a couple of beach towels and an empty cooler into my car. She had seemed so broody when we met, never showing much emotion, but now so much had changed. We were embarking on what I hoped would be a long term relationship and having a child together. I didn't know if her newfound sunny disposition was the result of the relationship, the baby, going to the nudist resort, or my choosing our destination just for her, and I decided that for now, it didn't really matter.

We stopped at what I always called the Haslet Walmart off Highway

287 although it was technically still in the sprawling city limits of Fort Worth. We bought sunscreen, bottled water, beer for me, Diet Coke for Lydia, and two bags of ice. We loaded the drinks and ice into the cooler in the back of my Prius in the Walmart parking lot and continued on our way toward the resort. We found it without any trouble thanks to the map app on my phone. We stopped at the office, an old single wide mobile home, as instructed. The lady I had talked to on the phone was the only person inside, wearing a pair of gym shorts and nothing else, her skin dark and even as she seemed to be of Polynesian descent.. She made copies of our driver's licenses and took our ground fees. Lydia and I both undressed at the car, sprayed a coat of sunscreen on each other, grabbed our towels, and waited by the golf cart for the tour.

"And this is your first time at a nudist resort?" the lady asked as she locked the trailer's sliding glass door.

"It is," I confirmed. "But we are both nude models."

"Really? For art classes?"

"Yes."

"Oh, one of our regular visitors does that. Has been doing it for years."

We spread our towels out on the seat, and the three of us crowded together on the golf cart. We ambled along the dirt road, looking at mobile homes where people lived and a sculpture that served as a meeting place and a symbol of the resort, and stopped at the pool area.

"Water volleyball is the big pastime here, so we had to build a second pool a few years ago," our guide said.

The two pools were perpendicular to each other in the same concrete space with wooden decks wrapping around them. A net was stretched across the center of one of the pools. At the end of one of the pool areas was a small building with an open shower area and separate men's and women's restrooms. A walkway led from the pool area to a brick building which housed the clubhouse, kitchen, library, and game room. Across the dirt road from the pool and clubhouse area were several parking spaces and a fenced in area with tennis and volleyball courts. As it was over ninety degrees already, the tennis and volleyball courts were empty, but we could see quite a few people in or near the pools.

After parking the golf cart, our guide showed us into the clubhouse first. A middle aged lady with frizzy hair, wearing nothing but flip-flops and sporting a dark even tan, was in the kitchen unwrapping hot dogs and putting them in a large foil tray, but the rest of the building was empty. There was a stage at the end of the dining area, and on that stage was a big screen television.

"This is where we have our potluck dinners. After dinner, we move these tables and have karaoke on Friday nights and dances on Saturday nights, usually."

Next to the dining hall was the game room with pool and ping-pong tables. On one wall of the game room was a large book shelf, a "Take a book, leave a book" sign taped to one of the shelves at eye-level. From the game room we went through a solarium built onto the side of the building and out onto the pool deck. The dozen or so people, all of them nude, took immediate notice when we walked through the gate. There were at least two signs posted listing the rules for the area, the first of which was that no clothing of any kind was allowed in the pools. Our guide introduced us by name to each group of people in lounge chairs. Those in the pool or in the showers were left for us to meet later. Everyone we saw seemed to be my age or older, a couple of them much older, and I thought Lydia might be put off by being the youngest person there. But when I glanced at her face, she seemed to be enjoying every second of being nude in the sunshine.

Once the tour was done, we climbed back into the golf cart and rode back to the office near the front gate. I drove us in the Prius back to the pool area, parking by the tennis court, and Lydia and I took our cooler to the pool deck. When we stopped and tried to decide on a spot, one of the groups that we had been introduced to invited us to sit with them. They re-introduced themselves as Lydia and I each got a drink from our cooler. We sat and talked on several subjects while watching a fit bald man in his seventies exercise with a couple of dumbbells across the pool. At one point, someone in another group got up and rang a bell near the side of the pool with the net. The bell ringing was followed by several calls of "Volleyball!" Most of the people in earshot began climbing into the water.

"Come on and play," a large woman, one of the friendliest and most talkative in our little group, said to Lydia and me. "It's a lot of fun. And we're not that serious. You don't have to be good."

I turned to Lydia to see if she wanted to play, but she was already getting out of her chair.

"I guess we're playing," I said to the woman.

Getting into the pool without a suit on was always invigorating. The last time I had been in a pool outside of my own back yard, the air in my swim trunks kept causing them to balloon up. It had taken me several minutes to get all the air pushed out. Being in the water without those trunks felt so much more natural.

Eleven people got into the pool, but rather than make someone leave to even the teams, several people called to a short lady sitting by herself and wouldn't leave her alone until she agreed to play. Lydia and I wound up next to each other on the same team, and we rotated our position with each change in serving team. According to their rules, only the serving team could score. If the serving team let the ball hit the water on their side or hit it out of the pool, the other team got to take over serving. Our team won handily, 21-10, so we switched sides of the pool and played again. The second game was a bit closer, but we still won 21-15. That apparently ended the best of three series, so everyone got out and resumed what they had been doing, sunbathing, socializing, drinking beer or sodas. Getting out of the pool was even more of a revelation than getting in was. I didn't have a heavy wet suit hanging off of me. The sun dried my body quickly when a suit would have remained wet long after.

We ate our lunch of hot dogs and chips out by the pool, talking with our fellow nudists. It didn't take long to stop thinking of them as "naked people" and just think of them as people. I also started to forget that I wasn't wearing anything either. One of the older guys recognized us from our viral video in front of the abortion clinic and asked Lydia several questions about it. She answered to the whole group, talking about the class project and about how we had decided to do it naked both for the attention and to demonstrate the helplessness of the aborted babies. I smiled when she said babies instead of fetuses. Lydia never mentioned her views on abortion and choice, and I wondered if they had changed after her visit with her mother. We hadn't had a chance to really talk about them yet.

We stayed at the pool all afternoon, playing in two more volleyball matches. After over four years in isolation, it was good to socialize with people. Oddly enough, being with the people at the nudist resort reminded me of the church group Glenda and I had belonged to. There were differences of course, the most notable being that everyone here was naked. I also didn't have to censor myself like I had always done when around our church friends. Once you got past the fact that something had brought each person here to something as unusual as nudism, they all seemed rather normal.

Lydia seemed to be having a great time. She got up and took a dip in the non-volleyball pool a couple of times and even found a raft to float on for awhile. Late in the afternoon, I took Lydia on a walk on the nature trail.

"So what do you think of this?" I asked her once we were out of sight of the pool area.

"It's awesome! I wish we could live here."

"You want to get a membership then?"

"Sure."

We walked, hand in hand, along a trail that wound through deeply shaded woods until we came out near some of the mobile home lots. I could see the office straight ahead. I had had the foresight to carry my keys and wallet, not wanting to leave them at the pool area. We walked over to the office and filled out the membership papers. They agreed to apply our grounds fees for the day to an annual membership, and we paid the difference with my credit card.

Rather than walk back through the woods, we stayed on the main drive on the way back to the clubhouse, stopping at the sculpture we had seen on our tour. Lydia and I took turns taking pictures of ourselves under the sculpture. When we got back, we told our new friends that we had become members, and they all responded with hoorays and words of welcome. After my self-imposed isolation, it was good to belong to a group again, although I couldn't help but feeling a bit unworthy of being in polite company, even if that polite company was naked as jaybirds.

19

Being out of school and not having regular jobs, Lydia and I returned to the nudist resort on Monday only to find the place nearly deserted. That was fine with us as we had both pools almost all to ourselves. It was cooler than it had been on Saturday, so we even ventured into the hot tub which was tucked away behind the pool decks. I didn't think Lydia should be in the hot water while she was pregnant, so we didn't stay in very long. I had a tent in the garage, and Lydia had wanted to camp out at the resort. But I had that art class on Tuesdays through Thursdays to model for, so we went home at the end of the day.

We went back to the resort the following Saturday, brought the tent, and camped out into Sunday. We didn't have anything to bring to the Saturday potluck since we didn't have any facilities with which to cook, but when we tried to skip the dinner, several of the other members persuaded us to attend and eat anyway. I had never felt more welcomed by any other group of people, and I think Lydia felt the same way.

When my five week pose at the atelier ended, they hired Lydia to model for them based on my recommendation. They had her do a four week pose in spite of her warnings that her pregnancy was going to change her body from session to session. I found myself wishing I could be in the class drawing her, but I took some modeling gigs for summer classes at two other universities.

Lydia and I spent every Saturday that summer at the resort in spite of my mother's pleas for us to come visit her in Wichita Falls. I'd had to tell her about Lydia and that she was living in the house with me, but I had withheld telling her about the baby. After the experience with Glenda's blighted ovum miscarriage, I wanted to be sure that this pregnancy was much further along before I told Mom or anyone else.

Lydia and I finally made the drive up to Mom's house one Sunday in August after she had invited us for a spaghetti dinner. Lydia's baby bump was showing by then, but she wore a loose blouse that billowed out around her middle.

"What do I do if she asks me if I'm pregnant?" Lydia asked me in the car on the way there.

"She won't."

"How do you know?"

"Because she would never do anything to a guest that might be construed as an insult," I said. "Asking a woman if she is pregnant right after meeting her would be like telling her she's fat if she turns out to not be pregnant. Mom would never take that risk."

Lydia pulled her shirt down so that it was tight over her belly and looked down at herself. "And what if she asks you when I'm not around?"

"That I don't know."

"Are you going to lie to your mother?"

"No," I said.

"I think you should just tell her. I mean, why the hell are we going up there if we're not going to share that bit of news?"

"I don't want to overwhelm her. Let's let her meet you first, get to know you."

"When the baby comes, she's going to do the math and realize how far along I was at this first meeting. Don't you think she's going to be pissed that you didn't tell her today?"

"I don't know," I admitted. "Maybe. Probably."

Even though I had told Mom on the phone that Lydia was a lot younger than I was, a look of dismay crossed her face as she saw Lydia for the first time when she came out to the car to meet us. That expression lasted only for a second, but she said, "Oh my goodness, she looks so young," to me as I got out of the car.

I ignored her comment, hoping that Lydia hadn't heard it, and said, "Mom, this is Lydia. Lydia, Mom."

"Rita," she said, offering her hand.

"Nice to meet you," Lydia said when she shook it. "You look so young too. And for the record, I am almost twenty-six."

Mom looked over to me as I tried not to cringe. "Well, that's not so bad. Davey is only forty."

Lydia laughed. "Davey?"

"He'll always be my little Davey. Well, let's not stand out here; let's go in and introduce you to Davey's step-father."

Robert met us at the door, and he seemed anxious to meet Lydia.

"You look like you're getting around better," I said to him after the introductions were done.

"Yeah, I've been going to physical therapy," he said.

"Finally," Mom added. "Come on in and sit down. I'll have dinner ready in a few minutes."

Lydia followed me into the living room and sat as close to me on the sofa as she could without sitting in my lap. Mom disappeared into the kitchen, and Robert sat in his recliner.

"So you met David at the college?" he asked Lydia.

"Yes, that's right."

"What are you studying there?"

"Political science."

"Oh, that's right. Same as David."

We sat there in an awkward silence for several moments before launching into small talk about when the semester started up, how bad the Cowboys were playing this preseason, and how preseason games don't matter and are not an indication of how a team would do in the regular season. I thought about suggesting to Lydia that she help Mom in the kitchen, but she had such a strong grip on my hand that I didn't. When Mom finally called us into the dining room, we were more than ready to eat and get back on the road toward home.

Mom had already dished up the spaghetti on each of the four plates, along with a slice of garlic bread. Robert said grace, and we all dug in.

"So how did you two meet?" Mom finally asked.

I paused to swallow a bite. "We had a class together last semester," I said as Lydia smirked. I squeezed her hand to try to get her to be more discreet. I didn't want to tell Mom about the nude modeling where we had actually met, and I didn't want Lydia prompting more questions from Mom.

"Are you planning on going to law school too?" Mom asked Lydia.

"I'm not sure yet. I just want to get the Bachelors degree and see what opportunities come. Besides, I don't think we could both be in law school together."

"Why not?"

Lydia stopped and looked at me. "Well, um, I don't know. It just seems like one of us ought to be working."

"That sounds reasonable."

I took another bite of spaghetti and started to breath a sigh of relief that Lydia hadn't spilled the beans about the pregnancy when Mom looked straight at Lydia and said, "You've changed a bit since you were on TV."

I almost gagged as I swallowed the bite in my mouth.

"You saw me on TV?" Lydia said.

"Yes. Both of you. Although I don't know why my son couldn't have bothered to tell his mother that he was going to be interviewed on television."

"Well," I said with a stammer, "I didn't think you could get Dallas stations up here."

"We can get anything with the Internet. Or maybe you just didn't want me to watch it."

Of course I hadn't wanted her to watch it. I had always envisioned that Mom thought of me as her little boy and that I didn't do things that she wouldn't do. "I didn't think you would understand," I said. "I mean, it was for a class project, and it became this big thing."

I did not under any circumstances want to discuss with my mother why I had been cavorting naked in the median of a busy Dallas street.

"It was kind of my idea," Lydia said as I was trying to decide how to deflect the conversation elsewhere.

"We thought it would get attention," I added.

"Well, it certainly did that. You didn't worry about something like that following you around? What if someone turns you down for a job because they see indecent exposure?"

I took a deep breath, ready to go into my spiel about how simple nudity isn't indecent, especially when it's used for a political purpose. But I stopped. "No," I said. "I didn't think about that."

"Well, you should have." Mom paused and took a drink of her iced tea. "But for the record, I am proud of you for standing up for the babies."

"Thank you," I said.

After a moment, Mom turned to Robert with raised eyebrows.

He cleared his throat. "You said this was for a class project?"

"That's right," I replied.

"Did you get an A for the project?"

"We did."

Robert nodded and looked back at Mom. She huffed as if dismissing him.

"We figure that it was worth it if it made people think about the issue in a different way," I said. "We definitely were not typical pro-life protestors."

"You can say that again," Mom said.

I felt like a wayward teenager getting interrogated by a parent.

"I'm sorry I didn't tell you about the interview ahead of time," I tried to explain. "It just happened so fast, and the reason why they wanted to talk to us — I didn't know how to bring it up."

"I thought it would be fun," Lydia said. "I model for art classes, so it seemed natural."

The shocked expression on Mom's face made me almost want to laugh. "And you model naked?"

"Nude, yes."

Mom looked back at me. "And you're OK with this?"

I took a deep breath and decided that I just needed to be honest with her. "Yeah. We actually met in an art class."

"Davey? I didn't know you were taking art."

"I wasn't. I was modeling for the class too."

I think Mom was stunned into speechlessness. I saw her mouth move, but it took a few seconds for her to get anything out. "You mean the two of you modeled together naked in front of a whole class of people?"

I nodded.

"And that was how you first met?"

"Yes," I said.

"Well." She sat straight up in her chair and looked from me to Lydia.

"I actually modeled for art classes when I was in college the first time, way back when. I took it up again when I went back to school."

"You never told me."

"I didn't know how. I mean, how does one bring it up in casual conversation?"

Mom shrugged. "My son is a nude model."

"It's not as glamorous as it sounds," I said.

She took a drink of her tea, looked down at her plate, and took a bite. "How much do you get paid for that?"

"Twenty an hour at most places," I replied.

Mom looked surprised. "That's not bad. Where do you apply?"

I probably laughed too loudly at that, and Mom looked a bit hurt. "I'm sorry. I didn't expect that."

Mom waved it off. "It's OK. I'm joking, of course. But if I had gone to college, I might have done the same thing myself."

"What?" I said in disbelief. I'd always had an image of my now fifty-nine-year-old mother as an upstanding, almost pious, Christian lady, always ignoring, of course, the fact that she had married my father only five and a half months before my birth or that she and my father had split up when I was six and my sister Tammy only three.

"I'm not saying I would have," she said, "but I might have considered it."

Robert was staring at Mom with his mouth open. I wanted to laugh, partly at Robert's reaction and partly because I felt such a relief that the secret of my modeling job was finally out to my mother. But I managed to hold the laughter in.

"You said most places pay twenty an hour. You model at other places then? Other than UNT, I mean."

"Oh yeah," I replied.

"Well, I was wondering what you did with your time. I always hated the idea of you holing up in that house all by yourself."

"I could never model enough hours to make a living doing that," I said. "But it has been enough lately to pay the utilities, put gas in my car and groceries on the table."

"Good," Mom said. "I wondered how that settlement you got could still be lasting with all the tuition you were paying."

"Most of that is in a high yield savings account, so most of my tuition is coming from the interest."

"That's a good thing, considering..." Lydia said.

Oh crap, I thought.

"Considering what?" Mom asked.

I took a deep breath and let it out with a sigh. I looked at Lydia and then back at my mother. "Mom, we're having a baby."

There was a long silence at the table as Mom's eyes seemed to grow distant and glaze over. They filled with water, and a tear slowly rolled down one cheek.

"Oh Davey," she finally managed to say. "It was what you always wanted."

"Yeah." My eyes welled up too.

Mom stood up and walked around the table toward me. "Come here."

I stood up, and Mom and I held each other in an embrace. Robert got up from the table, and Lydia soon followed. I tried to hold back the tears, but I had trouble swallowing. I hadn't expected this rush of emotion at seeing Mom's reaction. And my emotion wasn't at just Mom's reaction either, but at the thought of finally becoming a father.

"I'm assuming, of course, that this is a happy thing," Mom finally said.

I hadn't known it when she said it, but she had been looking at Lydia.

"It is," Lydia replied.

Mom patted me on the back as we broke the embrace.

"Good," she said. She held her arms out to Lydia, and Lydia reluctantly allowed herself to be hugged.

"Congratulations," Robert said to me.

For a moment, I thought he was going to hug me, but he merely grabbed my shoulder while shaking my hand.

"Thanks," I said.

We all sat back down to eat. It didn't take Mom very long to ask the question that I knew was coming.

"Any wedding plans?"

I shook my head, glancing over at Lydia. "We haven't talked about it. We don't want to rush into anything, you know."

The thought of marriage had crossed my mind, of course. Although we were going to be parents together, Lydia and I were still just now getting to know each other. We had some common proclivities, like being comfortable in just our own skin, but we came from different backgrounds. I grew up going to church, and in spite of my absence of the past four years, I still considered myself a Christian. Lydia had told me that, not counting weddings or funerals, she had only been to three church services in her life. Two had been Easter services when she was a girl and had been made to dress up in stiff and uncomfortable clothes and had been generally miserable for the duration. We were at home and naked at the time of that conversation, so I made the joke that Lydia found almost all clothes to be uncomfortable. We had only ever talked about spiritual matters once, when I confessed that I blamed myself for Glenda's death for that prayer I had made. I had asked Lydia what she believed about God and the universe, and she cited what she had learned in her high school science classes, that all life had evolved from single-celled organisms over many millions of years.

"But where did those single-celled organisms come from?" I had asked.

Lydia had shrugged. "I don't know."

"Don't you believe in any kind of spirituality? That we are more than just our bodies, that we take some other form after we die?"

Lydia shook her head. "I don't know that either."

"It's not about knowing. It's about believing."

"I guess I don't know what I believe then," she admitted. "What about you? What do you believe?"

"I believe that God created the universe. It didn't just come from nothing. I believe that however we came about, God created us, all of us, and that He gave us free will. And because of that free will, we rebelled from God, and that because of the law that God handed down, we have to die for that rebellion. But God provided his son Jesus as a sacrifice to take our place and give us a way back to him."

"That sounds kind of preachy."

"I'm sure a preacher could have said it a lot better than I just did."

"And what is it that makes you believe that?" Lydia asked.

I thought a moment. "Because that story originated at the earliest beginnings of our history and has survived all this time. It's not some new thing that someone just made up not long ago, like Scientology."

Lydia laughed and shook her head. We'd had previous conversations about how crazy Scientology was, and we had wondered how celebrities like Tom Cruise and John Travolta, who seemed otherwise fairly intelligent, could have fallen for it.

"And I refuse to believe the alternative," I had continued, "that when we die that's it, we no longer exist."

"Would that be so bad? It would be like going to sleep and not waking up."

"But we would miss out on so much. Imagine seeing and learning all the secrets of the universe that we could never know while we're on earth, all because we are with the Creator of that universe."

"Is that what it will be like? Seeing all the secrets of space."

"I don't know," I said. "But it'll be exciting to find out. I've always thought that if the atheists are right and the Christians wrong, then, yeah, it'll be sad, but we'll all be gone and won't know anything anyway. But if the Christians are right, then the atheists are really in trouble."

Lydia had shrugged at that bit of logic, and I got the impression that she wasn't ready to change her beliefs no matter what I said. And now, sitting in my mom's dining room trying to figure out what to tell Mom about the possibility of marriage, I realized that the longer Lydia and I stayed together, the more one would pull the other toward the opposite set of beliefs. After Glenda's death and my self-imposed exile from all things God or church related, I didn't think I was strong enough to pull her my way. Was I ready to push everything I had grown up believing aside and embrace her agnosticism or whatever it was?

20

According to the obstetrician we had found for Lydia's prenatal care, the baby was due on Christmas Day, not on the 18th as Lydia had originally calculated. Since the possibility of an early arrival could not be counted out, Lydia registered for only three classes, nine semester hours, for the fall semester. About a week before those fall classes were to start, I took Lydia to the doctor for her big ultrasound appointment. We had decided early on that we wanted to know the sex of the baby.

"Are you sure you want to know," the doctor asked after she had swiped the ultrasound paddle over Lydia's gel-covered belly several times.

I was able to detect a spinal column and a beating heart in the garbled mess on the screen, but not much else.

"Yes," Lydia replied.

The doctor hit a button, and the image on the monitor froze. She grabbed a pointer and drew a little shape over the static on the screen and wrote the letters BOY above that.

"Oh wow," Lydia said.

The doctor hit another button, and the screenshot printed on a small slip of paper. She handed it to me, and I could see the shape she had drawn which, now that I was looking at it, resembled a scrotum and penis.

"A boy?" I said.

"Yes, it's a boy."

Lydia and I had told each other that we didn't have a preference for either a boy or a girl, but after growing up with a younger sister and no brothers, I had secretly wanted a boy.

"He looks healthy and on track," the doctor said.

I couldn't contain my sense of joy and relief. Leaning toward Lydia, who was lying on the table, we touched foreheads, and I gave her a soft whisper of a kiss on her mouth.

"You're happy with a boy?" she said.

"Yes."

"Good."

"Are you?"

She nodded. "Yeah, I am. I was afraid I'd have a girl and she'd be just like me."

We both chuckled as the doctor started shutting down the ultrasound equipment.

The day after that ultrasound appointment, we woke up early and drove to Lubbock. Lydia wanted me to meet her mother, and she wanted to tell her the baby's gender in person. The night before, we had watched Youtube videos of gender reveal parties for creative ideas about how to tell her, but most of what we watched seemed too cheesy for us. They were also geared toward big parties, not telling people one on one. Lydia and I both agreed that we didn't have enough friends between us to have a party. So she had just decided to tell her outright.

I was both nervous and excited to meet Lydia's mother. She was, after all, the woman who had sent Lydia back to me in spite of the rough first impression I'd had of her taking out her trash during my previous trip to Lubbock. Because of the distance and because Lydia wanted some time to visit, this would be a two day trip. If things didn't go well after our arrival, spending the night there might become problematic. Lydia assured me that wouldn't happen, that her mother was very understanding and tolerant. When I reminded Lydia of the negative things she had said about her mother right after we met, she brushed me off.

"We'd had an argument on the phone the day before that," she said.

This did not make me any less nervous about meeting her.

When I started typing Lydia's mother's address in my phone before leaving my driveway, it showed up as a previous destination in my maps app. I was glad that Lydia was looking for music on her own phone and wasn't looking at my screen. I left the charging cord plugged into my phone and allowed the app to navigate for the duration of the trip. Lydia played a bunch of songs that I don't think I had ever heard before. She sang along to a lot of them when we weren't making small talk. I couldn't stop thinking about Lydia's mother as I drove, how old she had looked. I remembered that, for an instant, she had looked at me as I sat behind the wheel of my car parked on her street. Surely she wouldn't remember me from that, especially after three months. But the thought still worried me.

"What's your mom's name?" I asked not long after we left the house.

"Elizabeth, but she goes by Betsy."

"Betsy," I said just to get a feel for it on her tongue. "Should I call her that? Or should I call her Ms. Nelson?"

"I think Betsy will be fine. She's pretty laid back in her old age."

"How old is she?"

"Sixty-two, I think," Lydia said, looking up and seeming to count in her head. "Yeah, sixty-two."

"And you're only twenty-six," I said, musing.

"Yeah, she had me late. That may be why she didn't go through with aborting me. I think she probably realized she might not get another chance at having a kid."

"Well, I'm glad she did," I said, patting Lydia's thigh.

We arrived in Lubbock at one in the afternoon, skipping lunch since Lydia said her mom would have food ready for us. Lydia said I could park on the street in front of the duplex. I shut off the motor and remained seated until Lydia got out of the car and stood waiting for me.

"Are you coming?"

I got out of the car and walked around to stand beside Lydia. She took my hand as we walked up to the front door. Instead of knocking or ringing a doorbell, Lydia just opened the door and walked into a medium sized living room.

"Mom," she called.

I stood behind her, still on the small square of concrete that passed as a front porch. Lydia's mother emerged from a back room, dressed in jeans and a multi-colored blouse. Her hair was tied in a bun, and she wore makeup that made her look much younger than she had the first time I had seen her. She smiled when she saw her daughter and embraced her in a short hug. Lydia's mother stepped back and took another look at her.

"You're really showing now," she said with a laugh, her voice raspy and rough.

"Shut up," Lydia said playfully. She turned around and saw me still on the stoop. "Come on in, silly."

She held her hand out to me, and I walked three paces inside and grabbed it.

"Mom, this is David. David, Mom."

I had to awkwardly let go of Lydia's hand right after taking it to offer to shake with her mom.

"It is a pleasure to meet you," she said as we shook. "You can call me Betsy."

I smiled at that and felt relief that the stern face I had seen in May had been replaced with this smiling, happy one. After pointing out the restroom and allowing Lydia and me to use it after our long drive, she ushered us into the kitchen and fed us a lunch of tuna salad sandwiches. We had not finished eating when Lydia said, "We had our ultrasound yesterday."

"And?"

"It's a boy."

The two of them shrieked like schoolgirls and hugged. I couldn't help but smile watching them.

Once they sat back down, Betsy said to me, "I bet you're glad it's a boy."

I shrugged. "I just want it to be a healthy baby."

"And the doctor says he is," Lydia added.

After lunch, we sat in the living room talking about school. Lydia told Betsy about her schedule for the upcoming semester and how she had to get a waiver for this semester to take fewer than twelve hours and still receive her grant money for the tuition. Betsy talked about Lydia's uncle and cousins, and I sat silent, listening to the names. I had never had any connection with these people, but now they would be my child's relatives, thus making them mine. Though I tried not to, I thought of Glenda's parents and her aunts and uncles. She and I had been married, but without her and without any children of our own, what connection did I have to them now? I hadn't talked to Glenda's parents in several months. How could I tell them about Lydia and about the baby? I felt a surge of guilt. Glenda was gone, her time on this earth done, and here I was with another woman, someone who had been a mere girl during most of my marriage to Glenda. How could I deserve this happiness?

"David!" Lydia said in a sharp voice.

"I'm sorry," I replied. "What?"

"I said you should go get our bags from the car."

"Oh yeah," I said, glad that I hadn't missed a more important question.

I got up and let myself out into the midday August heat and grabbed our bag out of the back of the Prius. Betsy was standing alone at the front door when I came back in.

"Here," she said, "I'll show you to Lydia's old room."

I followed her, noticing the closed door to the bathroom as we walked by. Lydia's room was small, but there was what appeared to be a queen size bed with beige sheets. There was no comforter, but as warm as it was inside even with the duplex's air conditioning running non-stop since we arrived, we wouldn't need one. A small stuffed unicorn sat on the pillow, and a poster of Lady Gaga, wearing nothing but a white t-shirt and squeezing her legs together to keep her crotch covered by the bottom of the stretched out shirt, was on the wall. Lady Gaga's blond hair was combed back, her hands on her head and her lips as red as blood. Her mouth was open wide, and the tip of her tongue touched the edge of her upper arm. The faint outline of her nipples could be seen through the white shirt. The word "Supreme" was printed in a small red rectangle across the middle of the shirt. It seemed like the sort of thing Lydia would pose for, except without the shirt.

"Here you go. Since you live together, no sense in making you stay in separate rooms."

"Thank you."

I walked in and sat our bag down on the foot of the bed.

"You know, Lydia's scared," Betsy said in a quiet voice.

"It's her first baby, so I imagine she is."

"No, she's afraid of you. Of losing you. You not sticking around."

"She shouldn't be," I said.

"Her history with men isn't very good. That's my fault. I never did find a good step-father for her. Do you love her?"

"Yes."

"Why?"

I took a deep breath, wishing that Lydia hadn't selected now to disappear into the bathroom.

"Because I choose to," I said.

"You choose to?"

"Yes. I don't believe love is a feeling. It's a choice and a commitment to that choice. That's all. Lydia and I share a lot of things in common. We have our differences too, but those don't matter all that much. I love her because I have decided to love her. She is going to be the mother of my child, and I hope that she will be the only woman ever able to make that claim."

Betsy smiled at me. "That doesn't sound very romantic."

"Life isn't a fairy tale."

She nodded. "OK."

We heard a commode flush.

"Why didn't you knock on the door in May?" Betsy asked.

"What?" I wondered how much shock was showing on my face.

"Yeah, I saw you. I wouldn't have recognized you except for that TV interview Lydia sent me."

"That was a rough day," I said after a careful pause. "I wanted to make sure she was OK, but I also wanted to give her her space. You know?"

"I see. I think you made the right decision."

"I hope so. I sometimes feel like I'm walking on eggshells."

"Sometimes women make their men feel that way on purpose. But don't listen to me. I've never had a relationship that didn't end in a train wreck. But then again, most of the men I've dated.... Well, never mind."

The door to the bathroom had opened, probably prompting Betsy to stop in mid-sentence.

"Mom," Lydia called from the living room.

"We're back here in your room," Betsy said.

"Interesting poster," I said to Lydia when she joined us in her room.

"Oh, I love Lady Gaga."

Betsy just shook her head and said, "Madonna wannabe."

"And Madonna was a Marilyn Monroe wannabe," I added.

"Only in the 'Material Girl' video," Betsy said.

We spent the rest of the afternoon visiting. Betsy produced a photo album, and Lydia and I looked at pictures from her childhood. When we came to a photo of her as an infant, lying naked on her belly, I said, "You got an early start on your nude modeling career."

Lydia elbowed me in the ribs, and I realized that I had no idea whether Betsy knew of her daughter's job at college or not. Lydia flipped over to another page in the album and asked her mother about a picture of her and another girl in swimsuits. The conversation turned to where they had been living at the time some of the pictures had been taken. I enjoyed seeing Lydia at various stages of her life, especially now that she had become such an important part of mine.

Betsy took us out to eat that evening at the Twisted Root Burger Company. The burger I had was one of the best I had ever tasted. Throughout the rest of the visit, from sitting around Betsy's living room to eating at the restaurant and the drive to and from, I managed to avoid being alone with Lydia's mother long enough to have another conversation. I liked her, but I was afraid of any awkward questions. I knew that I did not want to talk about my previous marriage or any of my life up to meeting Lydia.

Lydia and I slept naked like we always do, although we didn't engage in any sexual activity. It surprised me how good her warm body felt against mine under the sheet given how warm it was in her room. I would have been up for a little fun, but since we were in Lydia's mother's house, I waited for her to make the first move. She never did.

"So what do you think of Mom?" Lydia asked me as we lay in bed under a ceiling fan that seemed to be working in overdrive.

"She's nice," I said. "She seems pretty laid back."

"Yeah."

Lydia's breathing soon slowed, and I could tell that she was asleep. The forest smell of her shampoo filled my nostrils as I leaned in to kiss the top of her head. After meeting her mother and seeing all those pictures of her, I felt closer to Lydia now more than ever. It seemed strange that a year ago, I had never even met her. I thanked my lucky stars that I knew her now as I surrendered myself to sleep.

21

I only needed to take nine hours in the fall semester to complete the requirements for my Bachelors degree, and Lydia was only taking nine hours to minimize any potential make up work she might have to do in the event the baby came early. As a result, we had a lot more time to model. After doing a four week pose for the atelier in the summer, Lydia began modeling other places besides UNT. Because she was female, she was almost automatically more in demand than I was. Being pregnant also got her a few extra gigs as many artists love the opportunity to draw an expectant mother. Once word got around the independent artist groups that a pregnant model was available, Lydia began getting calls from all over the Metroplex: Dallas, Mesquite, Frisco, McKinney, Fort Worth, Arlington, and other suburbs that I didn't know even had life drawing sessions. She attended classes in Denton two days a week and modeled around that schedule. Lydia even modeled a few evenings and a few times for the Sunday painting session at the Dallas Creative Arts Center.

"You need to slow down," I told her one night in October after she had come home late after modeling for the Dallas Friday night artist group I had posed for the night she returned from Lubbock. Lydia looked exhausted, with slumped shoulders and dark circles under her eyes. Modeling can be physically strenuous under any circumstances, but even more so for someone pregnant.

"Yeah, I know, but I have trouble saying no when they ask," Lydia said.

I nodded since I had the same problem. Modeling could never be a full time job, with lots of slow periods between semesters. I tended to take any modeling job that was offered to me. I had even skipped three or four classes for modeling jobs over the past year.

"You just look worn out," I told her.

"I feel OK though." She had just arrived home and was still dressed and sitting on the end of the couch. She gazed with a blank expression at the frozen image of a white-haired Emilia Clarke on the TV. I had been watching a Game of Thrones episode and had paused it when I heard her come in.

"You sure?" I said.

Lydia nodded almost imperceptibly and stood up to go back to our bedroom. I watched her shuffle back before turning off the TV and following her. When I got into the room, she had her shirt over her head, her arms tangled in the sleeves. I helped her get undressed and into bed. She was asleep before I got finished using the bathroom. I turned out the light and crawled into bed with her. I wrapped my arm around her and put my hand on her belly. The baby seemed to kick back. Lydia didn't even stir. Usually, Lydia couldn't sleep unless the baby was still, so I knew her exhaustion level was well past that of a normal day. I pushed on her belly and felt the baby kick back at me again. Lydia stirred, but didn't awaken. I rubbed her belly as if to say good night to our son and turned over to go to sleep.

The following day was Saturday, and we spent it at the nudist resort. The water in the pool was too cold to swim in even though it was a nice enough day to be naked outside. We sat around visiting with people that we now called friends. We left right after the potluck dinner, and when we got home, Lydia ran herself a warm bath. I sat in the living room playing Call of Duty, but Lydia called me into the bathroom before my first match had ended.

"Just a minute!" I called back.

"Hurry!" she yelled.

"Sorry everyone," I said to myself as I abandoned the match and left my teammates, wherever they were in the world, shorthanded.

Lydia was lying in the bathtub, the water so high that I could hear the water seeping into the overflow drain in spite of the washcloth that she had stuffed into it to prolong the time the tub stayed full. There were no bubbles, so I could see her entire body. Her hair was tied into a bun on her head and beads of sweat or bath water sat between her lip and nose. Her breasts had grown with the pregnancy enough that they appeared to be floating above the rest of her body.

"Do you see it?" she asked.

"See what?"

"Watch." She pointed to her belly.

Lydia shifted in the water ever so slightly, and I saw the baby move under her skin, seeming to swim from one side of her to the other.

"Oh wow!" I said.

"I know, right."

I dropped to my knees and put my hand on her belly. The baby rolled toward me and then away.

"What is he doing?" I said. I could hear the glee in my voice.

"I don't know." Lydia's grin seemed to take up her entire face. "Isn't it cool though?"

"Yeah." I couldn't say much else. I was awestruck. Our baby was moving on his own. I moved my hand over Lydia's belly, and the baby moved away and then toward me. It was like playing tag with a much older child, and it really hit me that we were going to be parents to an individual that would be separate from us. And it was up to us to teach him everything. "Oh my God," I said. "He's a little person."

"Yes, he is. I think he's going to be a swimmer. Maybe in the Olympics even."

"He could turn out to be anything," I said. "He hasn't come to any forks in the road. His road is just starting."

"Yeah." The smile faded from Lydia's face, and I wondered if the weight of the responsibility was hitting her now too.

My knees started to hurt from all of my weight on them, so I sat down on the bathroom rug, my arm still draped over the side of the tub and my hand on Lydia's belly.

"I hope we don't fuck him up," she said, and I saw that she was about to burst into tears.

I got back on my knees and drew her into a hug, glad that I didn't have any clothes on to get wet.

"We are going to do the best we can," I said. "That's all we can do. That and love him as much as a kid has ever been loved."

"I just never pictured myself a mom. What if I—"

"You will be an excellent mother. I'm sure of it. You are capable of so much love. I see it every day."

She kissed me and almost pulled me into the bath with her. I helped her up and out of the tub and started to pat her dry with the towel. I started with her neck, kissing her neck after I had dried it.

"Mmmm," she said, tilting her head to give me better access.

I dried her shoulders, her back, her breasts, kissing each part once it was dry. Kneeling, I patted dry her belly, legs, and pubic area, still pausing to kiss each part. Being on my knees felt like I was worshipping her, and perhaps I was. This girl who pursued me, even wrote a fake note to lure me on a date, had caught me. After Glenda, after I shut down and shut myself off from the world, I never thought I would experience this depth of feeling, this longing devotion, this love, again. Lydia ran her fingers through my hair as I kissed her thighs.

"Let's get married," I said as my kisses moved toward a more sensitive spot.

It was something that just came, like when I told her I loved her on the phone when she was away at her mother's, and it took me a moment to realize what I had said. I used to joke with Glenda, telling her that we should get married even after we had been married several years. Like saying "I love you" during that phone call, did this come out of my mouth just from an old habit? Of course, Lydia and I had been together for several months, but I had never said anything like it before. She pushed my head back to look in my eyes.

"What?" she said, her face grave and serious.

I remembered her telling me when we first met that she didn't plan on ever getting married. She probably didn't plan on ever having a child either, but our baby was on his way. I could see the skin on her belly bulge as the baby kicked her. Lydia put her hand on the spot, still looking at me. I started to say something about the baby liking the idea, but I didn't. The moment seemed too serious for such a light speculation. I realized I was on my knees in front of her as she stood over me, the classic pose of a marriage proposal. Such a formal proposal seemed like the right thing to do.

"Lydia Nelson, will you marry me?"

Her face softened, and I could see the tears welling up in her eyes. She tried to say something, seemed to get choked up, and nodded. I dropped the towel on the floor and stood.

"Is that a yes?"

"Yes," she managed to say.

I took her in my arms and kissed her long and deep. As we kissed, I realized with some chagrin that I didn't have a ring. I hadn't even looked at rings. Lydia broke the kiss off and looked at me again. The tears were still streaming down her face. I wiped them away with my thumbs.

"Don't cry," I said.

"I'm not. It's just— I can't believe it."

"It makes sense."

"I know. I didn't think I would want it as much as I do now that you've asked. I never thought anyone would want to marry crazy, fucked-up me."

"I don't have a ring to give you."

She shook her head. "That's OK. My fingers are swollen anyway. Everything is swollen."

I rubbed my hand on her belly.

"Let's wait until after the baby comes," she said. "I don't want my wedding dress to be a maternity dress."

"I didn't think we'd rush out and get married today."

Lydia returned my smile. I took her hand and walked her back to the bed.

About a month later, Lydia and I were scheduled to model for Audrey's figure drawing class at UNT. I couldn't help but notice that the date was only one day off from the anniversary of our very first meeting. This class would be in the same room, in the same time slot, and with the same instructor as that first meeting. I was excited to be included in drawings with a pregnant Lydia. The drawings would be like family portraits.

We drove up to Denton together in my Prius and continued the discussion we had been having about Thanksgiving. We both wanted to spend it together, but we also both wanted to go to our respective mother's houses.

"Mom doesn't have a boyfriend right now," Lydia said, "and I hate the thought of her eating Thanksgiving dinner all alone."

I didn't have as compelling an argument for going to my mother's, so I knew I would eventually capitulate and go with Lydia to Lubbock. I just dreaded having to call my mother to tell her that I wasn't coming to see her on Thanksgiving. I thought about telling her that she should be used to my absence after those years right after Glenda's death, but she would probably just tell me that that was why I needed to be there, to make up for those years.

Audrey had us do a few two minute gesture poses to get the class warmed up. Lydia was, of course, pretty far along, and her belly had grown quite large. We kept the gesture poses a bit less athletic than I was used to doing, but I didn't want Lydia to strain herself. For the long pose, we sat Lydia on the bench, and I sat on a pillow on the floor, holding her calf and looking at her belly. I thought about leaning in and putting my mouth on her, as if kissing our baby, but I thought the strain on my neck and shoulders from the lean would be too much in a two and a half hour pose. At each break, I walked around the room snapping photos of as many drawings as I could with my phone. There were three that were really good, a lot of details and great likenesses of both Lydia and me, by experienced students I recognized from the past four semesters. When Audrey called an end to the pose, ten minutes before the class was scheduled to end, she had the students all turn their easels toward the middle of the room for a mini-critique. Lydia and I covered up but remained on the platform looking and listening to the comments. I had to use the zoom on my phone's camera, but I got photos of each drawing.

When I did finally tell Mom that we would be spending Thanksgiving in Lubbock with Lydia's mom, I agreed that we would stop by her house in Wichita Falls on our way home that Saturday. Thanksgiving weekend was fun but exhausting, and as usual, I ate too much. I was glad to get home that Sunday afternoon. My modeling gigs dropped to near zero after that, but Lydia was still in demand from independent art groups. It seemed like the bigger she got, the more the artists wanted to draw her.

The semester was ending, and we were both entering final exams with A's and B's in all our classes. I was taking Lydia to the doctor once a week, and both she and the baby appeared to be healthy and on course for a normal delivery. After all the failures I'd experienced with Glenda, getting pregnant and having a baby with Lydia seemed to be easy, almost too easy. I was surfing the Internet on a Tuesday night, the day after Lydia's first exam, looking for a Christmas gift for her when my cell phone rang. Lydia was modeling for the open drawing session at the Fort Worth Community Arts Center. That session didn't end until 8:30, almost an hour away. I wasn't surprised when I saw Lydia's name on my phone. She sometimes called me during her breaks.

"Hey."

"Something's wrong," she said right away, and I heard the worry and pain in her voice. "Oh fuck, something's major wrong."

I sat up straight in my chair. "What is it?"

"I'm bleeding. Like, a lot. More than a period. And it fucking hurts."

I was up, running to our room to get clothes and a coat on. This can't be happening, I told myself. She has to be exaggerating. Please God, let her be exaggerating.

"Can you drive?" I asked.

"I don't think so. David, I'm scared."

I was scared too. "OK. Maybe you should call an ambulance then."

"Somebody here already did."

There was noise in the background, someone telling Lydia they were on the way.

"You're close to Harris downtown," I said, meaning the hospital. "Tell the ambulance driver to take you there, and I'll meet you."

"I'm sorry," Lydia said.

"There's nothing to be sorry about. We don't know what this is yet. Just hang in there, OK."

Lydia was crying on the phone as I finished getting dressed. I threw a coat on and found the keys to Lydia's Corisca on the nail in the laundry room. Whenever she went out alone, I always had her drive the Prius since it was newer and more reliable. A cold wind was blowing as I locked the door and ran out to her car.

"I'm about to be driving," I told her, "so I'm going to put you on speaker."

Lydia was talking but not to me. It sounded like the paramedics had arrived. The Corisca's engine cranked weakly, and for a second, I didn't think it was going to start.

"Thank God," I said as it roared to life.

I could hear the static of walkie-talkies.

"David," Lydia said.

"Yeah baby, I'm here."

I sped through the neighborhood and peeled out onto the entrance ramp to Highway 287.

"They're loading me on a stretcher right now. I'm going to the hospital." The fear was evident in her voice.

"OK. That's a good thing. They'll get you checked out."

My vision blurred, and I wiped tears from my eyes now. The helplessness seemed overwhelming. This couldn't be happening.

"I have to hang up now, they say."

"OK. I'll see you soon. I love you."

I hoped that meant they were wheeling her out and loading her into the ambulance as I hurried to the hospital. My dinner threatened to make a repeat appearance as I had to slam on my breaks on Interstate 35W. Why did I come this way? I normally avoided 35 because of the constant construction and traffic problems. I thought about calling my mom and telling her what was going on, but I didn't think I could talk to her without breaking into a sobbing fit. As I sat in traffic, inching along in starts and stops and cussing at the drivers in front of me as a diversion, I thought about Lydia's weak voice. "Something's major wrong," she had said. I could only hope that she was wrong in that assessment.

22

The waiting area at the emergency room was packed when I walked up to the registration desk. A weary looking lady looked at me and said, "Can I help you?"

"Yes, my fiancé should have been brought here by ambulance."

I gave the name and date of birth, which I was glad I was able to remember, and she looked Lydia up on her computer.

"It looks like they just took her up to labor and delivery," she said and gave me the directions for getting there.

I rode the elevator up in a daze. This wasn't happening, I told myself. This was a nightmare, and I would soon wake up next to Lydia. Everything would be fine. I followed the signs to a nurse's station and asked the woman there for Lydia Nelson.

"Are you friend or family?"

"I'm her boyfriend—fiancé. And the father of the baby."

She gave me what looked like a pitying look and told me the room number. As I walked down the corridor toward that room, I had a sudden urge to run away, to ignore everything that was happening. For the first time in years, I recalled bringing Glenda to this same hospital to get her procedure after the blighted ovum diagnosis. I remembered the emptiness I felt and how Glenda and I couldn't even talk for days afterward. This had the potential of being so much worse.

The door was closed when I got there. After giving a knock on the door, I opened it a crack and poked my head in. A woman in blue scrubs was standing at the foot of the bed talking.

"Hello?" the woman said, looking my way.

"Hi." I walked into the room and saw Lydia on the bed. Her eyes were puffy and bloodshot. There was a belt around her belly with a monitor on it. I could hear the reassuring sound of a fast beating heart from the speaker.

"Are you the father?"

I nodded as I walked in and put my hand on Lydia's cheek. She turned her head and kissed my palm.

"I'm Dr. Robbins. I'm in practice with Dr. Williams. She's doing a delivery at Alliance right now, so I'm handling Lydia's case."

"Is she going to be OK?" I asked.

"I hope so. I was just explaining to her that she's had what's called a placental abruption, a condition where the placenta detaches early."

"What about the baby?" I asked.

"The baby's fine for now, but this condition can endanger the lives of both the mother and the baby. Since we're at 37 weeks, I'm recommending an emergency cesarean section."

"OK. When?"

"Right now. They are getting an OR ready even as we speak."

I looked at Lydia, and I could see the fear in her eyes.

"It'll be OK," I said, caressing her cheek and bending down to kiss her forehead.

She trembled, and my heart melted. That feeling of helplessness just intensified. Two nurses walked in dressed in scrubs with hair caps on their heads and covers over their shoes.

"Everything's just about ready doctor," one of them said.

She patted Lydia's foot. "All right, I've got to go scrub up."

The other nurse had a set of scrubs still in the package. "Are you the father?"

I nodded, and she handed me the package.

"You'll have to put these on if you want to come into the OR."

Since it was an emergency surgery, I had expected to have to sit in a waiting room. I was surprised that I would be allowed in, but at least I would know what was going on.

"If you want to change in the restroom, go ahead. We have to get Lydia prepped anyway."

"Do I put them on over my clothes?" I asked.

"No. Just keep your underwear on."

Not wanting to tell them that I had skipped the underwear, I merely nodded and disappeared into the restroom after giving Lydia a quick kiss. There was precious little counter space next to the sink, but I managed to fold my clothes up into a ball small enough to fit there. My hands trembled as I put the scrubs on and fit the cap over my head so that it covered all my hair. The nurses were just leaving the room as I came out.

"We'll give you two a moment," one of them said.

Pulling a chair close to Lydia's hospital bed, I sat down next to her and started stroking her hair.

"Why did this happen?" she asked.

"I don't know," I replied, and I wondered if she had taken a strenuous pose at the art center that had caused or contributed to it.

"They are going to cut me open."

"I know. I'm sorry. We did talk about the possibility of a c-section though."

We were silent for a few seconds before Lydia said, "David?"

"Yeah."

"Can you say a prayer?"

I was surprised but not shocked. I remembered an old saying that there were no atheists in foxholes or something to that effect.

"OK." I bowed my head, clasped Lydia's hand, and gave it my best church prayer try. "Dear Lord, thank you for bringing Lydia into my life. I lift her up to you, that you will put your hand over her and protect her and bring healing to her and the baby. I pray for the doctors and medical staff, that you will be with them, granting them the vision to see if anything goes wrong and the wisdom to do the right things to correct it. We ask these things in Jesus' name. Amen."

"Amen," Lydia echoed, squeezing my hand.

I kissed her and told her I loved her just as the nurses came back into the room.

One of them greeted Lydia and started unlocking the wheels on Lydia's bed while the other one addressed me. "OK, Dad, you'll need to wait here in the room, and someone will come get you when everything is ready. OK?"

I stood up and moved the chair away from the bed. "OK."

As they wheeled Lydia out, she never took her gaze from mine until she crossed the room's threshold. The door partially closed, and I was alone. I paced from one end of the room to another, thinking about Lydia's asking me to pray. Had I ever prayed since Glenda died? I didn't think I had unless it was to accuse God of trickery in taking Glenda from me right after the wreck. I had felt awkward, searching to find the words just like I would have done back in my church days when called upon to pray out loud. I stopped pacing and plopped myself down in the chair, feeling drained and overwhelmed.

"Dear sweet Jesus," I said. "I'm so sorry for blaming you. I don't know why Glenda was taken, but I have to trust that it was part of your plan. I have failed to trust you. I have failed in so many ways and strayed away from you, away from loved ones. And now you have placed this cup in front of me. You know my heart, that I love Lydia and want your guidance out of this crisis. Please heal her, make her whole again. I pray for our baby too, that you will deliver him from harm. But I know that you have a plan and that you will help me to trust that plan. Please forgive me for straying away."

Tears streamed down my face as I continued to pray, to turn over everything to God. "I am helpless in this. I can't do this. I can't bear the weight. So I give it to you. Please be with Lydia, give her peace and calm. Give us both peace and calm."

I rambled on, wiping the tears off my face with the back of my hand, and that feeling of desperation seemed to ease. My breathing slowed, and I closed my eyes, trying to accept what had happened and steel myself for whatever may come. After a few moments, I stood up and resumed pacing, looking out into the corridor for signs of anyone coming to get me.

I was beginning to think they had forgotten, and I was contemplating going out to the nurse's desk to ask where the OR was when a nurse, not one of the two who had taken Lydia back, finally arrived for me.

"David? We're all ready for you."

Taking a deep breath, I followed her through several corridors and into what appeared to be a cul-de-sac. She handed me a surgical mask and then raised her own mask over her nose and mouth. Once I had my mask on, she led me through double doors into a sterile operating room. Lydia was on the table, almost unrecognizable under all the drapery and monitors.

"Dad, stand there by your wife's head," the doctor ordered.

My wife. I didn't feel like correcting her. Lydia had her eyes closed, and I kissed her cheek through my mask.

"I'm here," I said.

"Finally." Her voice was mumbled and distant.

"I know, tell me about it."

"OK, I'm going to start the incision," the doctor said.

I watched Lydia's face as the doctor went to work. She winced, and

I grabbed her hand.

"Do you feel anything? Does it hurt?"

"Just pressure. It's hard to breathe."

I raised my head up to look over the curtain hanging down over the middle of Lydia's body. The doctor's hands were inside Lydia, and from her heavy breathing, she appeared to be struggling to get to the baby.

"Ugh," Lydia said, trying to get a breath in.

"OK," the doctor panted.

I watched as she pulled my son from Lydia's womb. The baby's skin was gray, almost white, where it wasn't covered with blood, with thin wet hair on his head. His eyes seemed to be clenched shut. The doctor held him up and patted his bottom until he took in a breath and let it out in a loud wail.

"Oh my God," Lydia said.

"Here he is." The doctor handed the baby to a nurse before snipping and clamping the umbilical cord.

My knees weakened, and I almost collapsed. The nurse brought the baby to the head of the bed so Lydia could see. The baby's gray skin was slowly turning pink. Lydia gasped when she saw him, and more tears streamed down her cheeks.

"Hey little guy," she said.

"We've got to check him out Mom," the nurse said.

Lydia nodded.

"Dad, you can come over here if you'd like."

I watched the nurse take the baby over to a station across the room, but I remained near Lydia. They used a bulb syringe to clear his mouth and nose which turned his cries into angry screams. Lydia grabbed my hand and squeezed.

"Is he OK?"

"I think so." I took a step and stopped, torn between going to see my son and staying by Lydia. She let go of my hand.

"Go," she said.

I took a look over the curtain and saw the doctor remove a red gelatinous looking mass from Lydia and set it in a metal dish, glad that the surgical mask hid the expression on my face.

"Is Lydia OK?" I asked the doctor, hoping she could hear my muffled voice.

"Yes, she's fine. Everything looks great. The scary part is over."

I let out my breath and almost cried out loud. A person never understands how much stress affects him until that stress is suddenly relieved.

"Thank Jesus," I whispered, still trying to hold back a blubbering crying fit.

Some kind of gel had been put on the baby's eyelids when I got to him. He was laid on a scale, the nurse letting go of him long enough to get a reading and freeze the display.

"Six pounds, seven ounces," that nurse called to the other. She stepped aside with her hand still on the baby and asked me if I wanted a picture of the scale.

"I left my phone in the room," I said.

"Ah, Ok."

She stretched the baby out and measured him at 18 and a half inches and recited that to the nurse who was recording everything.

"Just a little peanut," that nurse said.

"How is he?" I asked the first nurse.

"He's great." She looked past me at her cohort and said, "Initial Apgar was seven. It's up to eight now."

"That's good, right?" I said.

"It is."

The nurse put a tiny disposable diaper on him and wrapped him up in a blanket. I glanced over at Lydia and saw that the doctor had finished and removed the curtain over her. The bed from her hospital room had been pushed against the wall, but someone had wheeled it next to the operating table and the whole team was moving Lydia back onto it. She groaned in pain. I wanted to help someone, and I felt useless just standing there between my baby and my fiancé.

Once Lydia was back in her bed, the nurse put the baby on the bed between Lydia's right arm and her chest.

"Let's get you back to your room."

One of the other nurses motioned for me to follow her, and she led me out of the operating room. Lydia's bed followed us. When we got back to the room, the nurses hooked Lydia's IV up to the machine and made sure everything else was plugged in. The baby was quiet now, content to be near his mother. I ducked into the bathroom and unfolded my clothes to dig my phone out of my pants pockets. I used it to take several pictures of the baby.

"What's his name?" a nurse asked.

Lydia and I had, of course, discussed names, and we had narrowed our choice down to three possibilities. I looked at Lydia to see if she had any input, but she was asleep.

"I'm not sure yet," I replied. "We thought we had a couple more weeks, at least."

"Ah." She watched me snap a couple more photos and then asked, "You want to hold him?"

"Yes," I replied at once, setting the iPhone down on Lydia's table.

"OK, come here little guy." She picked the baby up and laid him in my arms.

A rush of emotions rushed over me as I held my firstborn child for the first time, joy at seeing his little face, a gushing forth of love that felt like it came straight from my chest and out through my pores, fear of what a responsibility I had to this little boy. I tried to swallow as tears welled in my eyes, but something seemed to be blocking my throat.

"You want a picture?"

I nodded, unable to speak, and motioned toward my phone with my head. She picked it up and snapped another few photos. When I smiled for the pictures, a tear escaped my eye and rolled down my cheek. The nurse turned the phone screen toward me to show me the picture.

"Thank you," I managed to say, taking the phone from her with my free hand.

"No problem. Let me dim the lights. He might open his eyes then."

When she turned off the florescents, the baby did open his eyes in spite of the gel still on his eyelids.

"Hey there," I said. "I'm your dad. You remember my voice?"

He looked at me and started moving his mouth back and forth.

"Just a few minutes old and already starting to talk, huh?" I said with a laugh.

I looked up and found that all the nurses had vacated the room. It was just Lydia, the baby, and me here now. Sitting in the rocking chair in the room, I realized that my phone was still in my hand, so I sent a quick text to Mom, "Everyone is fine now. Had a complication. Baby born tonight via emergency c-section," and attached the photo of me holding the baby. My phone rang less than a minute later, and I explained the whole story to Mom. She promised to come to the hospital first thing in the morning.

Once I got her off the phone, I rummaged around in Lydia's stuff, found her phone, and called her mother. I didn't know if Lydia had called her mom on the way to the hospital or not, and I wasn't about to wake her up to ask her.

"Betsy," I said when she answered, "this is David."

"Oh hi. I wasn't expecting to hear your voice. How are you? Why are you calling on Lydia's phone?"

"Have you heard from her in the last three hours or so?"

"No, I haven't talked to her since yesterday."

"Oh. Well. First thing, everyone is just fine. There was an issue with the pregnancy. And, well, the baby's here. They did an emergency c-section just a little while ago."

"Oh my God! Is Lydia all right?"

"They said she is going to be fine. She's sleeping now right beside me."

"And how about the baby?"

"He is perfectly healthy. In fact, I'm holding him. I'll send you a photo of him as soon as I get off this call."

Betsy was silent for a long moment, and I thought we might have been disconnected for a second. "My grandson."

"Yes ma'am, he is."

"Well, I have to see him. I'll be there tomorrow."

"Sure thing. You can meet my mom. She'll be here too."

Betsy paused for another moment before speaking again. "I'm glad Lydia found you."

I looked down at my sleeping baby and my sleeping fiancé and thought about the time she asked if I had ever had an erection while modeling, how she came back to the models' changing room for her book after I thought I had missed her, how she appeared in my class that January, how she faked a harassing note just to get to spend time with me, how she came to me for help when she lost her apartment, and how she suggested a sensual pose when we modeled together again. I don't know what I ever did to become the object of her affections or pursuit, but I was past the point of questioning it. "I'm glad she found me too."

23

I slept that first night after my son was born on a cot in the hospital room, but I didn't get much rest with the nurses coming in to check on Lydia and the baby. They took him away a couple of times but brought him back after an hour or two in each instance. The baby started wailing at about three in the morning, waking Lydia. I gave the baby to her, and she tried to nurse him. He didn't really take to her left breast, but she had better luck with the right one.

"So which is it going to be?" I asked as the baby fed.

"Which what?"

"Which name?"

"I thought you were leaning toward Asher."

"I was. I didn't think you were though."

She gazed down at the child as he sucked with gusto. "Asher. Hey Asher."

He seemed to stop for a second as if in answer to the name.

"Asher David Michaels," I said.

"I think that's a winner."

Asher sighed and went back to sucking on his mother's nipple.

Lydia's mother arrived before eight o'clock. I was holding Asher in the rocking chair when she walked into the room. Between breast feeding and nurse checks, I held him as often as I could. He was the most beautiful baby I had ever seen, and I never tired of looking at him.

"Mom!" Lydia exclaimed, and I thought she might cry.

"I just couldn't sleep," she said, "so I got up and started driving."

She gave Lydia a hug and a quick peck on the cheek and then looked at me. I had stood up from the rocking chair.

"Hi Betsy. This is your grandson, Asher."

"Asher?"

"Asher David Michaels," I said, reluctantly handing him over to her.

"Oh my goodness, look at him. He's so cute."

We visited for awhile. My mother and step-father showed up about an hour later, and Asher got passed around until a nurse came to take him away for a few tests and for his official hospital baby photo. We would, of course, be buying several copies of said photo.

None of our out of town visitors had hotel rooms, so I offered to let them all stay at our house. It was only later that I realized I had said "our house" instead of "my house", and the thought made me feel warm and happy. Mom and Robert left the day we got Lydia and Asher home from the hospital. Lydia was still really sore from the c-section, so Betsy stayed another week to help with the baby.

Our first night home, Asher woke up at two-fifteen in the morning. He was sleeping in a bassinet in the master bedroom. Lydia had been having trouble breast feeding, so we had resorted to supplementing his diet with formula. I walked into the kitchen to make a bottle when in walked Betsy. I was, of course, not wearing a stitch of clothing. When I saw her walk in, her eyes widened and she turned completely around so that her back was to me.

"I'm sorry," we both said in unison.

"I'm just used to not wearing anything around the house," I explained. "And I forgot anyone else was here."

"Oh, it's all right," she said. "I heard the baby crying and thought I could help."

"I appreciate that."

I had the bottle ready, but I would have to walk through the spot on which Betsy stood to get back to our room. Betsy turned her head and took another look at me just standing there with a bottle in my hand.

"We got it though. I love getting to feed him."

"I didn't embarrass you?"

"No, not at all. We're family now, right?"

"Yes, I guess so."

We stood there for a moment before she seemed to snap to her senses.

"Well, I'll just go back to bed then," she said.

"All right. Good night."

"Good night."

"What are you laughing at?" Lydia asked me when I walked back into our room.

"Your mom. She stumbled upon me naked in the kitchen."

Lydia smirked before we both broke out into a muffled laughter. I took Asher and gave him the bottle. He quieted in an instant.

Lydia and I both missed two of our final exams. I was allowed to make up both of mine. One of Lydia's professors waived her final exam requirement and gave her a B for the course. The other professor emailed her and told her that she could take a C without the exam or make up the test to try to get the A that she had seemed headed for. Lydia opted to take the C. Caring for Asher was more important than a calculus test, she said, and I agreed with her. I skipped the commencement ceremony, and the university mailed my Bachelors degree diploma to me.

Now that the undergraduate degree was out of the way, I sat down and took a hard look at my finances and expenses. I had been chipping away at the principal of the wrongful death settlement my entire time in college, but I knew that my bills were about to explode. I knew the principal wouldn't last throughout law school while raising a baby. I was already forty-one years old, and I anticipated that I would be forty-five by the time I finished any kind of law degree program. What kind of career as an attorney would I have when I wasn't starting until age 45? So I started sending resumes out. It took five weeks, but I got a job as a technical support specialist at an oil and gas company in downtown Fort Worth. Lydia decided to take off the spring semester both as a student and a model and devote all her time to Asher. I was more than happy to take the baby from her in the evenings when I got home and give her some time to herself, for a warm bubble bath or a trip to the store or whatever she wanted to do.

During my first week at the new job, when Lydia and I were sitting down to dinner while Asher was napping, I said, "I think we should go to church. I want to raise Asher up in the church."

I was expecting some kind of resistance or argument from Lydia, but she just said, "OK."

"OK?"

"Yeah. I was going to suggest the same thing. I just hadn't brought it up yet. I mean, Asher's still just a baby."

"I thought you weren't sure there was a God."

She shrugged. "I changed my mind."

"You changed your mind?"

"OK, maybe you changed my mind."

I reached across the table and took her hand. "I love you," I said.

"I love you too."

Lydia and I got married in a ceremony at our house on the eleventh of June. We had a small crowd of family and friends. Crystal, our partner on the protest project, was there, as was Audrey, the art teacher in the class where we met. Unbeknownst to everyone except the minister we hired, we had actually been married a week before at the nudist resort. Lydia and I had been naked when we met, naked when we first kissed in that long pose, and naked when I proposed to her, so we figured that it would be fitting to be naked when we married. Many of the resort members had become very dear friends, and the ceremony there became a major event at the resort with several of them springing for a lavishly catered reception in the clubhouse. We also didn't figure that our families would go along with the nudist resort wedding, and we didn't want to tell them that we had a wedding without them. So we just had two ceremonies.

After visiting what seemed like a score of churches, we joined a Baptist church shortly after Asher's first birthday. I still modeled for evening classes and whenever else I could fit it around my full time job. The health insurance benefits alone made keeping the information technology position a necessity. Lydia found a daycare and went back to school the fall semester after Asher was born. She resumed modeling and got so many hours a week at it that I was a little envious. But we have a happy life, much happier than I could have ever envisioned for myself before I met Lydia. I wouldn't trade it for anything.